CASTLE

CASTLE

a novel

J. Robert Lennon

Graywolf Press
SAINT PAUL, MINNESOTA

Publication of this volume is made possible in part by a grant provided by
the Minnesota State Arts Board, through an appropriation by the Minnesota
State Legislature; a grant from Wells Fargo Foundation Minnesota; and a grant
from the National Endowment for the Arts, which believes that a great nation
deserves great art. Significant support has also been provided by the Bush
Foundation; Target; the McKnight Foundation; and other generous
contributions from foundations, corporations, and individuals. To these
organizations and individuals we offer our heartfelt thanks.

Published by Graywolf Press
2402 University Avenue, Suite 203
Saint Paul, Minnesota 55114
All rights reserved.

www.graywolfpress.org

Published in the United States of America

ISBN 978-1-55597-522-7

2 4 6 8 9 7 5 3 1
First Graywolf Printing, 2009

Library of Congress Control Number: 2008935603

Cover design: Kyle G. Hunter

Cover art: istockphoto.com

CASTLE

ONE

In the late winter of 2006, I returned to my home town and bought 612 acres of land on the far western edge of the county. The land was forested, undeveloped, and surrounded by hills and farms; no one had lived on it for years. According to my information, it had been bought by the state from a variety of owners during the 1970s, with the intention of turning it into a recreational wilderness. But the state ran out of money and the project never got off the ground. The land, and the farmhouse that stood on it, were forgotten.

My interest in the land was greeted with suspicion by the real estate agent who had been contracted to sell it. A stocky, moon-faced, startlingly short woman in her thirties, she pursed her lips and gazed at me through tired pretty eyes across a cheap aluminum desk. Her name was Jennifer.

"Will you take me to see it?" I asked her.

"I can take you around it, anyway," she told me. "No roads go through. At least not any I know about. I can show you the house, though."

"That would be fine."

"It's a fixer-upper," she warned.

"I'm very handy."

She regarded me with a wary look, as though she doubted my seriousness. We couldn't go out until after lunch, she said, when "the other girl" came in. It was ten in the morning.

"I'll take a stroll around town and see the sights," I said.

"That'll kill maybe five minutes," was her snorted reply. I responded with a smile and stepped out the door.

Gerrysburg, New York, population 2,310 and falling. That's what the internet had told me. When I lived here, as a child, the town had been growing—4,000 people at least, many of whom worked at one of the two busy factories that stood between here and the nearby city of Milan. One of the plants was owned by General Electric, which moved production to Asia in the eighties. The other was run by a manufacturer of silverware and other cooking implements that went out of business before I even left. There was, at that time, a great deal of talk about keeping families and businesses in Gerrysburg and attracting tourists. But now it was clear that all efforts had failed. The town was in a state of decay.

I stood on the front stoop of the real estate office, facing the town park, a grassy square roofed with skeletal sycamore trees and crisscrossed by footpaths. A central plaza served as a commemoration of our county's warriors: a bronze statue of a Second World War soldier, aiming his rifle, lay prone in front of a granite slab bearing the chiseled names of the dead. Three benches faced the memorial, empty now save for an abandoned fast food bag which a large black crow listlessly pecked.

The park was the only thing in the downtown area that was as I remembered. The rest had changed for the worse. Gerrysburg was laid out on a grid of perfect right angles, with the park in the center. I strolled along the cracked and weedy sidewalks, and surveyed the damage. It wasn't just the businesses I remembered that were gone now—in some cases it was the buildings that had housed them, as well. The movie theater and diner that used to reside on opposite corners of the park had been razed and replaced by parking lots, which now stood empty of cars, save for a single rusted pickup truck, its tailgate bearing a faded "Support Our Troops" magnetic ribbon. The dental clinic was still here, but appeared closed down, and had fallen into disrepair. Two of the three banks were gone, one intact but abandoned, one supplanted by a vacant lot. The former sandwich shop had been transformed into a pet store that now boarded up, and the laundromat was closed.

A few businesses were open, though none appeared to be thriving: a convenience store that advertised a large selection of pornographic magazines, a doctor's office, and an ice cream parlor. As I passed the ice cream parlor, a man walked out sipping a cup of coffee. He ignored me as he passed, but he was the only other pedestrian I'd seen so far. I decided to go in.

The moment I crossed the threshold, I knew that I had been in this ice cream parlor before. The walls were white now, replacing the wood paneling I remembered, and the dark booths had given way to tables and chairs. But the freezer, with its curved glass surface, was in the right place, and beside it stood a heavyset girl of around twenty wearing a white apron. She smiled as I approached the counter.

"Here for coffee?" she said.

"I was thinking ice cream," I replied. "If that's all right."

It was late March, and still cold outside. But the girl said, "It's always all right with me." I ordered a double scoop of rum raisin in a sugar cone and surveyed the place as the girl prepared it.

Jeremy's. That was the name printed in reverse on the front window. It didn't sound familiar. From the pressed-tin ceiling hung four fans, none of them turning. It seemed to me that I could remember them, spinning lazily on a summer's day. I felt a disturbing vertigo and touched the counter for support.

"Those don't work," the clerk said, handing me my cone. "We could sure use them in the summer, though!"

I paid her and sat down with my ice cream. It was delicious, but I soon grew cold and had to buy a cup of coffee to warm myself back up. While I sat sipping it, a man emerged from a back room and began to talk to the clerk. I thought I recognized him, but couldn't place him. He was younger than I—perhaps forty—and had a long face that terminated in a sharp chin. His hair was brown and gray, receding in the front, but in need of a cut at the back. He seemed agitated.

He walked out the front door, tossing his dirty apron on a chair. I heard the clerk sigh. After a moment, she picked it up and hung it on a coat rack.

"Is that man your boss?" I asked.

"Yes," she said, but seemed reluctant to say any more.

A few minutes later he returned, holding a paper envelope from the last remaining bank. I couldn't resist. "Excuse me," I said.

He stopped, surprised. When he spoke, his voice was deep, dry, and impatient. "Yes?"

"I'm wondering—is this the same ice cream parlor that was here in the sixties?"

"Yes," he said simply. His manner remained curt, but now he had grown curious.

"Did it have a different name then?"

"It was called Pernice's. After my father, Donald Pernice. Are you from around here?"

I remembered now—as a boy, this man had used to come in with his mother for a free treat. I recalled my high school days, passing the time here, saying hello to the pretty lady and her young son. "Yes," I said. "My name is Eric Loesch."

Perhaps it was simply that the man was distracted, or that I had interrupted a thought in progress. But when I spoke, his face seemed to tighten, and his eyes glazed over just a little, as if he'd been transported to another place. After a moment, he blinked, and said, "Jeremy Pernice."

"I remember you in here with your mother, when you were a boy."

He gaped at me for a moment. "Is that so?"

"She was a beautiful lady. Is she living?"

"My mother? No."

"I'm sorry."

He seemed to have nothing more to say, so I thanked him for the ice cream and coffee. He nodded in acknowledgment, but lingered a moment, his body half-turned to go, staring at me quizzically. I recognized in his manner the faint anxiety and uncertainty of a man thrown off his bearings, and I wondered if he would voice his puzzlement. Instead, he remained silent and still.

"You remember me, perhaps?" I asked him.

"No," he said quickly. "No. Just thinking of my mother."

"Again," I said, "I'm sorry."

His only response was a nod, and he disappeared through the kitchen door.

I fell asleep in the park and woke up cold. The wind had picked up, blowing from the west-northwest at more than twenty knots, and clouds were moving across the face of the sun. I smelled, faintly, the odor of woodsmoke, and the rot from some nearby dumpster. The ice cream seemed to have curdled in my stomach, and I felt somewhat nauseated. I wished I hadn't eaten it.

I heard a rustling to my left, and turned to find the crow I'd seen earlier, perched on the opposite armrest. It stared at me with its dumb black eyes, holding a crust of hamburger roll in its beak. Its feathers were worn and patchy, and it had been banded, a stamped metal ring fastened around one of its spindly legs. "Shoo," I said, but instead of flying off, it cocked its head and seemed to regard me with curiosity and imperiousness. It made a quick motion with its beak, releasing the bread and grabbing it again before it fell, a trick to strengthen its grip. It really was a huge bird—a raven, you might call it, in fact.

As I stared at it, a figure approached, and the bird took off, as if in slow motion, with a deep, startling flutter, like the sound of a bedsheet in the wind. It was the real estate agent, Jennifer, filling the space in my field of vision that the raven had occupied. She stopped a few feet from the bench, her hands on her hips, her feet spread apart, and said sternly, "I'm ready."

The land was located in the Town of Henford, at the northwestern corner of the county. On the drive there, the real estate agent turned to me and asked me a question. She was sitting in the passenger seat, dwarfed by my enormous SUV, her thick pale knees pressed together below the hem of a coarse green skirt. Her hands were stubby and rested on her lap, the left laid flat over the right.

She said, "So, what brings you back to Gerrysburg?"

I had, in fact, been anticipating this question, and had spent the bulk of the drive so far attempting to formulate a reasonable answer. After a moment, I told her that I was trying to get back to my roots.

"Your parents. They still around here?"

"In a sense. They're buried here," I said. "They died when I was still a young man."

"Oh."

"Their names were Cybele and Brian Loesch," I said. "They lived on Jefferson Street, where I grew up."

She frowned. "Where's that again?"

"The west end of town," I said. "I understand it's where they put the new sports field for the high school."

She paused before replying, "Oh, right. They never finished that. The high school got consolidated with Milan High." She looked up at me. "I remember it when I was a kid. Them knocking the houses down."

I nodded. "It was after my time."

"I guess so."

The village quickly gave way to farmland, much of it abandoned and overgrown with scrub. If the area's misfortune were to continue for another fifty years, it would all be forest again, as it had doubtless been before it was settled by Europeans. The road weaved and lurched, following the hills, and I grimaced as my ill-considered morning snack shifted in my stomach.

Luckily it was not far to the plot of land. Jennifer held a survey map, which she turned this way and that, studying it, then peering out the window. "Okay," she said, as we passed a road marked MINERVA. "I think this is it, maybe? Starting on the left?"

Even from my vantage point on the driver's side, it was obvious that the plot of land began, in fact, on the right. Jennifer was holding the map upside down. I told her so, and she corrected her grip with a small grunt of acknowledgment. Clearly she was not the type to accept others' authority with ease.

The road took on a more steady, if slight, grade now; the car began to climb. The land was heavily wooded, and unremarkable in every way. Yet the sight of it filled me with excitement and foreboding. I felt powerfully the rightness of the decision I had made to return here, and I gripped the steering wheel harder.

We rose gradually on the undulating pavement, and eventually came to a crossroads, the corner of LYSSA and PHOEBUS. There was a clearing here, and a white house, large and clapboarded, with drooping eaves. Saplings grew all around it, right up against the foundation. Beyond it the road sloped away, and in the far distance, outside the influence of the thick gray cloudbank that covered us, I could make out the glimmer of a lake. I drew to a stop on the shoulder.

"That's the house," Jennifer said. "Like I said, it needs work. On the other side of the street is Fordham County, and that's Wanona Lake way down there."

"It's a beautiful view," I said.

"Yeah, I guess it is," she replied, without enthusiasm.

We turned right and continued our journey around the property. From fallow spots along Phoebus Road it was possible, in places, to see over the trees and into the interior of the plot: gentle green swells of forest draining toward the village. Though the odometer indicated that we had covered very little distance, the journey seemed to be taking quite some time; I gave the car a bit more gas. Eventually we reached a road called Nemesis and turned right onto it.

"The roads have unusual names," I said.

She spoke with rote weariness. "The men who divided up the county named the roads after Greek gods," she said. "They had this idea it was supposed to be some enlightened, you know, what do you call it."

"Utopia?"

"Right."

"I didn't know that."

She shrugged. "Well, it didn't pan out, anyway."

A little while later the road ran over a culvert; a corrugated pipe jutted out on either side, admitting a small creek. "Okay," Jennifer said, "this corner isn't part of the property. The creek cuts it off." A few moments later we came to Minerva Road and turned right yet again. We crossed over the creek a second time, and soon we were back to Phoebus. We retraced our route, returned to the upper corner of the land, and parked on the shoulder to take a closer look at the house.

The windows were cracked and dirty, and on the door hung a NO TRESPASSING sign. The yard bore evidence of once having been entirely covered with coarse gravel, through which rangy weeds now grew. We stepped onto a rickety wooden stoop, and Jennifer fumbled through a ring of keys. In a moment, the door opened with a creak, and we stepped inside.

I was pleasantly surprised at how nicely the interior had been preserved. The walls were filthy, but the lath was intact, and the wide floorboards were tight and true, if scratched. Bare wires trailed out of ragged holes in the ceiling. Jennifer led me in silence from room to room. We walked slowly, gently, as if in an effort not to disturb someone or something that lived here—but of course there was nothing. The house was empty and forgotten.

The stairs creaked as we climbed to the second floor. There were not many rooms, but they were large and high-ceilinged, and the master bedroom was fully twenty feet square, with a bank of tall windows that, if cleaned and reglazed, would doubtless appear quite beautiful. The view north and east was spectacular.

"That would be the whole property, there," Jennifer said, pointing. The land sloped gently away from us, and the village of Gerrysburg was visible in the distance through the dusty windows. But what drew the eye was a feature in the very center of the woods: a large gray outcropping of bare rock that jutted out from the carpet of trees. I made a quick judgment of the distance and determined that it had to be at least a hundred and twenty feet tall, if not more.

The sight of the rock moved and disturbed me. Its incongruousness here, the way it interrupted the gentle curve of the land, seemed like some kind of challenge or rebuke. It appeared much the way I imagined a great whale might, breaking the surface of a calm sea to draw a mighty breath; and like a whale, its imposing nature enticed the viewer to conquer and claim it. I stroked my chin, to indicate to Jennifer that I was deep in thought. "Tell me about that rock," I said.

"I suppose a glacier left it," she replied, her voice echoing flatly in the empty room. Her arms were crossed and she hugged herself in the damp cold.

"It's possible to reach it through the woods, I'd imagine."

She let out a snort of laughter. "If you buy the place, you can do whatever you want," she said. "I'm sure you could get there, it can't be more than half a mile."

I nodded, as though considering. But I had seen enough. I turned to Jennifer. Her eyes widened, and the corner of her mouth twitched. I said, "I'll take it."

She scowled, blinking. "What, this place?"

"Yes," I laughed. "I'll take it. The price seems reasonable to me."

"You're kidding."

"No, I'm not. It's exactly what I've been looking for."

She stared at me, silently, seriously, judging. "Believe you me," she said. "I would be totally happy to sell you it. But I just have to know if you have any idea what you're doing."

"There's no need to worry about me," I said with a smile.

She seemed to soften, her features relaxing, her arms falling to her sides. She sighed. "Well, okay, whatever then. You can still change your mind. Come on back to the office and let's get started."

"Wonderful," I said, and for a moment, I felt as though I should shake the agent's hand, or engage her in a friendly embrace, something to commemorate the occasion. And perhaps sensing this, she quickly moved into the hallway ahead of me, and down the stairs to the door.

I would spend most of the next month working on the property. At first I was frustrated, when it became clear that it would be at least a week until I actually owned the house and land: lawyers would have to be consulted, meetings arranged. I left it all to Jennifer, however, and set to work anyway. Who could complain? My first act was to call the power company to have them turn the electricity on. But the power lines, having long ago fallen into disuse, would prove to be damaged, and it would take some time to repair them. No matter: I drove into Milan, where there was a large chain hardware store, and bought a generator. I also bought lumber, sawhorses, a circular saw, a sander, screws and nails, a hammer, and a rechargeable drill. Almost at random, I chose several colors of interior and exterior paint, and sufficient cleaning supplies to last me a year. At a gas station, I filled the tank of my SUV, and two five-gallon cans as well. I checked into a motel, paid two weeks in advance, and drove to the house to begin work.

It would please me to be able to say that I felt, upon my return to the house, a reprise of the confidence and enthusiasm that had braced me the previous day, when I announced to Jennifer that I wished to buy it. In fact, the sight of the place filled me, at first blush, with weariness and dread. Of course, up until this moment, the house was all potential—its glorious restoration existed only in my imagination. To view it now merely brought to mind the toil and frustration I might endure while renovating it. But there was something more contributing to my sense of unease: the house *appeared* different. The flaking paint revealed itself to actually be peeling, as though from an underlying dampness and rot—an impression strengthened by the moldy odor emanating from the house's interior. The roof seemed sunken somewhat, perhaps the product of weak, decaying beams. And, most disconcertingly, the house's trim lines now gave the faint impression of crookedness. I walked slowly around the place, stepping carefully over some broken cinder blocks and fallen branches, assessing the angles. Was it listing to the north? Or leaning to the west? Its lopsidedness seemed to change character depending upon my vantage point. In the end, breathing clouds into the cold air, I ran to my SUV, pulled a spirit level from my toolbox, and took some measurements. To my mingled relief and dismay, and in spite of my clear impressions, the house stood true. With a shrug, then, I set to work, determined to put all bad feelings behind me.

My first task was to prop up the sagging porch and repair the front stoop. This took me all of the first afternoon and evening. I am a highly organized and energetic person and I am accustomed to getting things accomplished quickly and thoroughly—but I must have fallen out of practice, because I made several mistakes, including an incorrect measurement and an uneven cut. Nevertheless, by nightfall I had completed my work on the porch and stoop, and was able to walk into the darkened house as if it were already my home.

That night, in my motel room in Milan, I watched television until I fell asleep. I woke up at three o'clock with every muscle in my body tensed, full of anxiety about the work ahead of me, and about the inevitable delays and obstructions that would hinder me from completing it. I had learned, however, to calm my mind and body using various relaxation techniques, and within the hour I had gotten back to sleep. I woke for good at six, showered and dressed, and returned to work on the house.

All that second day I made repairs to the roof. I had the hardware store deliver a telescoping ladder, several boxes of hot-dipped galvanized nails, and a few bales of asphalt shingle squares. I was lucky: the present roof was thin and only one layer deep, and I was able to lay my new shingles right on top. It was possible to spike the ladder into the ground at a gentle enough angle so that I could push several squares in front of me at a time, and thus make great progress without assistance. By noon I had covered half of one side, plus a gable. I also discovered that my initial impression of the roof—that it was sunken in places—was in fact erroneous. The roof was flat, and the underlying support beams strong.

The sun was bright that day, and the air moist, and I drank a bottle of water while gazing out at the monumental stone in the middle of the woods. As I watched, a hawk, a distant speck, glided across the land and alighted on the leading edge of the rock, as if to survey his domain. I felt a kinship with the bird, and was filled with a sense of renewed pleasure and purpose.

By the middle of the fourth day, I had completed the shingles and added flashing to the chimney and vent pipes. Then I started in on the clapboards. The years of dirt and peeling paint came off easily with the sander, and I was able to complete the painting prep work by the following morning. Indeed, I was beginning to feel as though the work was going my way, that I had at last taken control of the house. It was at this point that I clumsily knocked over a can of red paint that I had bought for the window and door trim; somehow the lid came loose—an irresponsible paint-mixing clerk at the hardware store was to blame, no doubt—and the paint spilled across the newly rebuilt porch and down the front steps. I began to clean it up, but soon realized that there was no point in wasting my cleaning supplies on an essentially impossible job. I decided to just leave it as it was, until I could decide on a color for the porch. However, the spilled paint left the strong, if irrational, impression that the house was drooling blood through its open mouth, like a road-killed animal. In the end, I simply painted the entire porch red.

On the afternoon of the fifth day, Jennifer stopped by to tell me that the sale would proceed on Monday, just three days away. She had failed to find me at the motel, and a sixth sense had told her I would be here. She emerged, in fact, from her car with a sly smirk, as though she harbored some kind of secret; but then she looked around the tool-strewn yard, and her expression was supplanted by one of astonishment. She gave me the good news, then asked, "Did you . . . put on a new roof?"

"And I repaired the porch. And painted it."

She frowned as she said, "But Eric . . . you don't *own* it yet."

I laughed. "In my line of work," I said, "you do what has to be done, and you do it as soon as you can."

"What line of work is that?" she wanted to know.

"Infrastructure and information," I answered.

She gazed at me quizzically, as if this weren't the answer she'd been expecting. "Okay . . . ," she said. "And you got in how?"

"Weak lock," I replied. "And tell me something. You might have phoned me. Why come all the way out here just to give me this news?"

Jennifer opened, then closed, her mouth, and blushed deeply. "Slow day," was her answer, and then she left me to my work.

By Monday, I had painted the house, and I reported to the closing meeting with my body and clothes flecked with dots of pale yellow—my choice for the clapboards. There was no room at the real estate agency, so the meeting was held in the quiet study area of the public library. There sat Jennifer, at a small study table, across from another real estate agent and an attorney, both representing the state office responsible for public lands. I was the only participant not wearing a suit, a fact that filled me with a special pride. I signed where I was told to sign, and handed out checks, drawn on the account I had opened just the other day at the only bank in Gerrysburg. When it was over, I shook hands with everyone, accepted the thick folder of papers that certified my ownership of the land, and walked to my car, breathing in the crisp spring air. For the first time since I arrived, dark clouds were massing on the horizon, and the breeze carried the metallic tang of an impending storm.

As I prepared to climb in and leave, I heard a voice: Jennifer's. She had jogged up behind me, her high heels clicking and scraping against the sidewalk. I turned and regarded her broad smiling face, free of any of the doubt or mistrust it had harbored just a week before.

"So!" she said, trying to catch her breath.

"Yes?"

The real estate agent shrugged. "Oh, nothing—it's just that it's been a real interesting week. Everyone's curious, you know. That's a big plot of land."

I took a glance at my watch. "It certainly is," I said.

A brief silence opened up between us. "Okay, well," she stammered. "I guess . . . you know, good luck doing whatever it is you came back to do. And, you know, thanks."

"For what?" I asked her, choosing to ignore her prying non-question.

She shrugged again, this time cocking her head flirtatiously to one side. "For one thing, I get a nice commission from this. You made my month!"

I felt the edges of my mouth begin to curl. "Well, I'm glad I could fill your pocketbook," I said.

She straightened, frowning. "Well, that's not the only reason I—" She stopped, and bit her lip.

"You were saying?"

"Nothing," she said.

I waved her away with one hand, and used the other to open the door of my car. "I think I understand," I said. "And I'm flattered. But I'd prefer it if we kept things between us on a professional level."

She appeared shocked. "You what?"

"Jennifer," I said. "I know we've had some pleasant moments together. But I'm just not interested in any kind of—"

Her little hands curled into fists now, and her forehead creased. "Hey, look here, mister! What kind of girl do you think I am?"

I climbed up into my seat. "Forget it, sorry. I shouldn't have said anything."

"No, you shouldn't have!" She was truly angry now, her face crumpled into a mass of pink flesh. "You really should have just left it alone!"

With a grim smile, I shut the door and started the engine. Jennifer took a step back, her mouth open in astonished disgust. She was shaking her head in mock disbelief as I pulled away. I was given, in that awkward moment, to wonder what had happened in this town to cause its inhabitants to behave so peculiarly around me. Given Jeremy Pernice's coldness, and Jennifer's absurd antics, I felt as though some strange malaise had gripped Gerrysburg in my absence, rendering all its denizens nervous and impolite.

Back on the road, I calmed my racing heart with thoughts of the work ahead. There was much to be done at what had at last become my house, and soon, Jennifer the real estate agent had ceased, once and for all, to trouble my mind.

TWO

That Monday, when I arrived back at the house after closing, I found that the power had been turned on. I walked through the empty rooms, pressing the wall switches, and to my surprise found that half the ancient light bulbs still lit. I tested each of the outlets by plugging in a high-intensity halogen clip lamp I had bought, and most of them worked, as well. It occurred to me that the remaining outlets might also be operational, that perhaps the problem was a blown fuse, and so I strolled around the place, looking for the cellar door.

I found it in the kitchen, next to a chipped, nineteen-fifties vintage refrigerator that appeared to be broken. The door was strange, half-painted from the top down, as if someone had been interrupted during a renovation. It had a ten-inch-square hole cut into one lower corner, as if to allow the passage of a cat, and sat crookedly in the frame. It opened with a scrape and creak to reveal a primitive wooden staircase leading down into a blackness that stank of mold. The light switch just inside the door had no effect, and I wondered if perhaps it was such a good idea to tramp down these rickety old steps in the dark, and fool around with an electrical system that might well present a grave danger to my personal safety. After a moment's thought, I shut the door, or at any rate tried to—now that I had loosed it from its frame, it would no longer fully close. Worse, gravity caused it to fall open when I released the knob. Such a danger was unacceptable: it was all too easy to imagine myself stumbling on the threshold, falling down the stairs, and lying helplessly on the cold floor. I might end up sprawled there, immobilized by broken bones, as rats and insects crawled across my curdling flesh. I could starve to death there, and never be found . . .

No, that would not do. My solution was to go outside, find a rock, and use it to hold the door shut: inelegant, of course, but good enough for now.

I had picked up a copy of the Milan phone book from my hotel, and now used it to make an appointment with an electrician. I would need all the outlets to be grounded, and the wiring to be inspected and upgraded if necessary. The electrician said that he could make it on Thursday morning, which was perfectly acceptable.

My phone, I should add, was quite new—I had bought it before I left for Gerrysburg more than two weeks before. It was a cell phone, of course, and I now added the electrician to my personal directory, where he joined the hardware store and power company. Jennifer, the real estate agent, was still listed as well, so I selected her name and number and deleted them.

It was getting a bit late in the day, but the electric power would give me the opportunity to work at night. I drove down to Milan and rented a drum sander, then returned to the hardware store and gathered up several packages of sandpaper to fit the sander, in several different grits. I picked up enough finishing wax to coat every floor in the house, and more paint, this time for the interior walls. I also lifted several gallons of water into my cart, and some cleaning supplies, before wheeling over to the bank of cash registers. Most were unmanned, and atop each stood a container of small American flags, the kind that could be mounted on the doorframe of your car. I approached the single register staffed by a checkout clerk.

The clerk recognized me from my previous trip. He was a tall, thin man, perhaps retired, or maybe a refugee from a previous failed career, and was quite inquisitive. I am not unfriendly, so I responded as politely as I could without rewarding his nosiness.

"Looks like you've got a major project going!" the man said, dragging my cans of paint across the bar code scanner.

"That's right."

"Bought a house, did you?"

"Yes."

He nodded. "Well, good for you. New in town?"

"No," I said, as brusquely as possible.

"We could use some newcomers, though, wouldn't you say?"

"That's no concern of mine."

This quieted him, however briefly. When I had paid, he offered to help me carry my purchases to my car.

"I'll be fine on my own, thanks."

"Oh, don't be stubborn, let me give you a hand. Pretty awkward, doing all that by yourself."

Finally, I met his gaze with as much directness and authority as I could muster. "What is awkward," I told him, "is the need to deflect your attention away from my private business. I do not need any help conveying these things to my car."

If the clerk was taken aback, he certainly didn't indicate it with his expression, which was one of mild puzzlement and acceptance, with perhaps a touch of arrogance. He shrugged, held out his empty hands, and said, "Okay, okay. Suit yourself, soldier."

I had been about to leave, and had wrapped both my hands around the handle of my heavily laden cart. But the clerk's method of address pulled me up short. I turned to him now and, bracing myself against the counter, leaned forward.

"I beg your pardon," I said, quietly and clearly. "But what did you just say to me?"

The man stood his ground. "I said, 'Suit yourself.'"

"You called me 'soldier.'"

He crossed his arms over his chest and breathed in through his long, thin nose. "You look like a military man to me."

"And I suppose you believe you can tell, do you?"

He nodded slowly. "That's right. I was a captain in the First Infantry in Vietnam. Gia Dinh Province. Battalion Intelligence. I did two tours. So, yes, I believe I know a soldier when I see one. *Soldier.*" And he leaned forward until his nose nearly touched mine.

I realized at this point that it was not in my best interest to pursue this matter with the hardware store clerk. While he had no right to make assumptions about me based upon his "instincts," I nevertheless had no wish to denigrate the man's military service. Nor would it have been prudent of me to alienate the employees of a store that I would doubtless continue to depend upon for the supplies I needed. And, of course, the longer I stood here arguing with the man, the less time I had to accomplish the task at hand, ie., the renovation of my house. So I pulled back, cleared my throat, and disengaged from the encounter.

"Pardon me," I said again, this time in a conciliatory tone. "There was no need for me to become hostile. I appreciate your offer of help, but I prefer to be alone."

"Fine," the man said, his expression unchanging.

"I'm sure we'll see one another again," I added.

"I'll look forward to it."

I offered him a final nod of acknowledgment, then took hold of my cart and pushed it toward the sliding glass exit doors. Just as I was about to leave the building, I hazarded a glance over my shoulder. The clerk was still watching me.

After a day and a half of aggressive cleaning and sanding, I made an interesting discovery. Part of the transfer of ownership of the property involved the creation of a title abstract, a copy of which the bank had given me at the time of closing. The abstract was held in a legal-sized manila envelope, and consisted of a quarter-inch-thick sheaf of papers, stapled at the corner. For some days I had left it sitting in the back seat of my car, as I concentrated upon the renovations. But that afternoon, weariness overcame me: I had overextended myself in my eagerness to complete my labors. I decided to take a break. A light rain was falling, and the air was pleasingly cool, so I took a seat on the newly repaired front stoop of the house, drank from a bottle of water, and paged through the abstract.

As it happened, the document was fascinating. The legal firm that handled the transfer of ownership had researched the history of the property, and compiled facsimiles of every document it discovered into this compact, convenient package. It was arranged with the oldest information at the back, so that is where I began reading.

The bottom document was dated October 12, 1933, and consisted of a typewritten history of the property up to that point. Evidently, most of the county had been ceded to the colonial government in 1762 by the Kakeneoke Indian tribe. We can assume that this arrangement was less than fair to the Indians, but its details were not provided in the abstract. The land was not settled immediately, but was used extensively by hunters and trappers up to, and during, the American Revolution. At this time, it was divided into large plots and given to veterans of the war as part of their compensation for military service. My plot was a portion of a much larger plot that had been assigned to a man named Ezekiel Cordwell.

No information was provided about this man, other than that he had "served honorably" in the Revolutionary War, that he did indeed come to occupy the land, and that he died in 1815. At this time, ownership of the land was transferred to his son, Daniel, and then to another son, Peter, in 1821.

Apparently no records existed for the years between 1821 and 1904, but it is clear that, at some point during that time, the land was owned by a man named M. Jefferson, for it was he who sold it in 1904. This Jefferson was a farmer and a freed slave, but the documents gave no indication whether or not he actually farmed the land. In any event, by this time the land had been further subdivided, and the plot that M. Jefferson sold had very nearly the same boundaries of that which I had bought—with one important exception that I will reveal in a moment.

The land was bought by another farmer, Gerald Jones, and some years later—we can surmise during the Great Depression—it fell into disuse. Given the density of the forest at the time of my purchase, it is safe to assume that no farming took place on the land after Jones abandoned his efforts.

At this point the abstract took a peculiar, somewhat mysterious turn. The next document revealed that ownership of the land was transferred in 1959—but this document differed from the others in one important way. The name of the person who bought it was carefully blacked out with what appeared to be a thick marker. I held the papers closer to my face and tilted them against the weak gray light of the afternoon, figuring that I could make out the words underneath the ink. But I could not. My copy of this page of the title was obviously a photocopy of the one that had been blacked out—or perhaps even a copy of a copy. I quickly flipped through the remaining pages, and found one additional blackout, on the document describing the purchase of the land by the state of New York. The rest of the land's history I have already mentioned: the state's intention to transform it into a public wilderness area, their failure to do so, and finally my own purchase of it.

I got out my phone and called the law office that had prepared the abstract—their number was printed on each page—to inquire why the previous owner's name was blacked out, and who had done the censoring. The woman I spoke with declined to give me any additional information. I was irritated, of course. But I understood that further complaint was not, at this moment, to my advantage.

The curious issue of the blacked-out name, however, was soon over-shadowed by the interesting discovery that I have mentioned. One of the new documents near the top of the abstract was a detailed survey map of the property. I say "detailed" primarily because of its impressively specific measurements; these included exact lines of longitude and latitude, and the angle and length of each property line. But the fact was, there was very little detail to be recorded. The house and the lot it stood upon were evident on the southwest corner; the creek that demarcated the northeast corner was also clear. And the rocky crag was shown slightly east of center, precisely where I'd have expected it to be.

What surprised me was that, pressed up against the western face of the rock, there was a small lopsided quadrilateral that I did not appear to own. This section of land was less than an acre in area, and was filled in on the survey map with a series of diagonal parallel lines. I searched the accompanying text for some explanation, and eventually found, buried in the packed paragraphs of legalese, a single mention: "Beginning at a point marked by an existing iron pin at . . ."—and here a series of coordinates were given—"and running thence west 80 degrees a distance of 257 feet, 6 inches to an existing iron pin, and running thence south 05 degrees a distance of 194 feet, 3 inches to . . ."—and here the remainder of the co-ordinates and distances were given, and the description concluded by saying, "SUBJECT TO the restrictions contained in the deed recorded in the Henford County Clerk's Office, and the grantor herein certifying that said restrictions have been complied with, the above-described premises are NOT included in the terms of this SURVEY."

Now, I am not a lawyer, nor do I understand fully the laws that regulate the real estate market. But this seemed to me a clear indication that a small area of land to the west of the rock did not belong to me. Needless to say, I immediately called the law office once again, and from an assistant there received confirmation that this was in fact the case. That bit of land was not mine.

"To whom, then," I asked, "does it now belong?"

The woman's voice grew distant, as if she were leaning away from the phone to consult her papers. "Err . . . ," she said, "I will probably have to get back to you on that."

I persisted. "There is nothing in your records that can answer my question?"

"I'm sure there is, Mr. Loesch. But it will take some time to find it."

"And tell me this," I went on. "If there's a bit of land there that someone else owns, it's logical to assume that there should be a right of way to it, correct?"

"Ahh . . . yes, I suppose so."

"But it would appear there is no right of way."

"Hmm," the woman said. "Yes. It does look that way."

"And so this must be some kind of mistake, correct?"

She sighed. "I would think so, yes. But as you said, it's quite clear there on the survey map. And in the text on Schedule A. So it can't be entirely mistaken."

I laughed. "Big mistakes do get made, though."

"I suppose they do, sometimes," she replied. "I'll have to consult one of the attorneys."

"You'll get back to me about this, then?"

"I certainly will."

Having done all I could to resolve that small mystery, I resumed work on the interior of the house. The process of cleaning each room and sanding its floor gave me ample opportunity to take stock of the place, and really see what it was I had bought.

I have likely given the impression that the house was entirely empty. This was not, in fact, the case. While steps had obviously been taken by the previous owners to clear out their property, some of their possessions had remained, and I dragged many of them out into the yard, for eventual conveyance to the dump. I would come to a room, remove its contents, clean it to the best of my ability, and get to work with the sander. Thus, a good deal of the former owners' things passed through my hands.

The front room, into which a visitor arrived upon stepping through the door, was high-ceilinged, and about twenty-five feet square. High, narrow windows covered two sides, with uninspiring views of Lyssa and Phoebus Roads. When I arrived, torn and moth-eaten curtains hung over these windows, and bits of cardboard or plywood covered some broken panes. Two of the windows had been boarded over entirely. A single chair, of a simple wooden design, leaned against an interior wall, as two of its legs were missing. There was a calendar on that same wall from 1964. It was the tear-off kind, mounted on stiff cardboard bearing the name of a metal fabrication business, and the month of June was on top. There was exactly one thing written on it, in a shaky, left-angled hand: RACHEL DOCTOR 2PM, on Monday the eighth. On the other interior wall hung a penciled drawing of a house—or, rather, a kind of castle, made of stone and turreted, with crenellated parapets, cannon ports, and a broad keep with round-arched windows. The drawing, though clearly the work of a child, was very good, the individual stones carefully traced with mortar in between them, the lines and shadows quite accurate and consistent with a fixed direction of light, the perspective lopsided but nevertheless fairly convincing. The face of a mountain loomed up behind it, and a tiny mountain goat was perched on an outcropping, seeming to peer off into the distance. I threw the broken chair and calendar into my trash pile, but kept the drawing, slipping it in among the legal papers pertaining to the house.

Off the main room was a sitting room which faced Phoebus Road and the forest; it took up the southeast corner of the building and was not as large as the main room. Here was an overstuffed, velvet-upholstered sofa, which had been water-damaged and which stank, and so out it went. There was also a book, a storybook for older children that seemed to have been checked out of, but never returned to, a library. The spine was missing, exposing the glue that bound the pages together, and the front cover bore only an embossed illustration: a young man, wearing tattered clothes and an expression of grave concentration, climbing up a flagpole. His hand was extended, his fingers mere inches from his goal, which was a piece of wind-tossed cloth tied to the pole's apex. This, too, I saved.

The house's ground floor also contained a smallish study or sewing room, and a large dining room, which was next to the kitchen, in the northwest corner. These rooms were empty, though a crystal chandelier hung in the dining room, just north of center. The space underneath it was bounded by four slight depressions in the pine floor, as if a heavy table had long stood there, and the floor between them bore a haze of scrapes and gouges, evidently made by chairs being pushed toward and away from the table.

I have to admit that I found these markings strangely upsetting. Nothing, of course, could have been more ordinary—the evidence of a family having shared countless meals—yet I found myself enduring a small shiver of unease. Did the family ever imagine, as they sat together around the table, that this room might someday be empty of everything but cobwebs and dust? I tried to conjure in my mind the sounds and smells that once filled the room, but nothing came to me: the image I formed of the family was that of thin, gray figures, silently hunched over a dark mahogany table, their eyes closed, their hands hanging inertly at their sides. And I pictured them covered with white sheets, as if in storage, and the sheets furred with decades of dust.

In any event, I shook off these thoughts and set to work with gusto, obliterating with my sander the markings that gave rise to them. I don't know what came over me—I am not of a particularly imaginative cast of mind. At any rate, once the boards had been sanded, I felt much better, and I was able to complete my work on the lower floor by the end of the day.

That was Wednesday. Thursday morning, when I arrived at the house from my motel, I found the electrician waiting for me, leaning against his van, looking at a magazine. Some of winter's chill had returned, and one would have thought it would be unpleasant to stand still. But the electrician seemed content. He was a stocky man of about sixty, and he wore a clean tan jumpsuit, a hunting cap with earflaps, and a pair of fingerless gloves. He held a tall silver thermos in one hand, and sipped directly from the screw top, eschewing the cup, which appeared to be missing.

He barely spared me a glance as I pulled up, and it was only when I had gotten out of my car and approached him directly that he deftly slipped the magazine into a pocket and shook my hand. "Mr. Loesch? Paul Hephner. Call me Heph."

"Thank you for coming, Heph."

He tipped his head toward the house. "Bought the place, didya?" he asked.

"That's right," I said. I began to move toward the door, to preclude conversation. "Come on in."

At the threshold, Heph slipped a pair of paper covers over his boots. The boots were impeccably clean, but I appreciated the gesture nonetheless, not yet having sealed the floors. "I'd like you to check the fuse box and the wiring," I said. "The basement door—" But the electrician was already there, nudging my rock aside with an impatient foot.

"Careful on the stairs," I called after him, peering down into the darkness. The circle cast by his flashlight bobbed, revealing a dirt floor and crumbling walls.

I stood upon the top step, listening to him move about. There was the scrape of something being dragged, a clank.

"Have you found the fuse box?" I said.

"Yalp," he shouted. "Don't worry about me, Mr. Loesch. Just you go about your business."

"All right, then," I said.

My work today would be to sand the upstairs floors, so I took a deep breath, lifted the sander, and hauled it up the steps. Each creaked deeply under the weight, but none threatened to break. As poorly maintained as the house had been, it was sturdy, and I felt a renewed confidence in my decision to buy it.

There was little to be cleared away in the bedrooms. A moldering ottoman, and a bureau that had warped and split; a small jewelry box, empty, sitting on a windowsill. In the smallest of the four upstairs rooms, I found another drawing, evidently by the same hand that had sketched the castle I'd found the day before. It was affixed to the wall with a carpet nail, and hung right next to a window. The view through the window was of the entirety of the land I had bought, and the drawing was of that same view. But the artist had altered the landscape, adorning it with fanciful details. In place of the rock that served as the centerpiece of the real landscape, there was a castle—clearly the same one as in the first drawing. Flags flew from the towers, and musical notes hung over the scene, as if some kind of celebration were under way. The sky was dotted with what I thought at first were birds, but upon closer inspection turned out to be friendly dragons, and the trees were heavy with fruit. I removed this drawing from the wall and added it to the sheaf of house documents.

After several tries, I found a working outlet in the hallway, and with my extension cord was able to use the sander in every room. In spite of the sawdust, the house seemed brighter and cleaner with the floors sanded; the boards lightened and showed their grain as I ground them down. I got through one small bedroom and part of another before I was interrupted by the electrician, whose presence in the cellar I had forgotten. I turned off the sander and asked him how things were going.

"Welp, Mr. Loesch," he said, "you got some surprisingly okay wiring down there. The cloth insulation got worn off here and there so I want to replace some of that. And I put in fuses and tested your outlets for you and they're all working now, but if you want to be safe I think you ought to let me put in grounded ones for you. And if you want to put the money in, I'd recommend we do a circuit breaker box. Your fuse box there is working okay, but it's rusted half through. And in my professional opinion you could stand to get a dehumidifier going down there."

I thanked Heph and told him that I would go ahead with his recommendations.

"Can't get to it all till next week, Mr. Loesch, but I can do it all in one day for you, maybe Wednesday, let's say?"

"Wednesday will be fine, Heph."

"Glad to hear it, Mr. Loesch. You'll be safe using the electricity until then. One other thing, though."

"Yes?"

"It's a while until warm weather, and it's awful cold outside today. Looks like there's still propane in your tank, too. You want me to try turning on the furnace?"

"Sure, Heph," I said, "that would be helpful."

I followed him down the stairs and into the kitchen, where he took off his paper boot covers and plunged down into the darkness. He seemed to expect me to follow, but I hesitated, as before, on the top step. When he reached the bottom, he turned to me. There was light down there now, apparently from a bare ceiling bulb, and so his flashlight was holstered on his belt.

"Ya comin', Mr. Loesch?"

"No thanks, Heph," I said. "I'll wait here."

He frowned. "Welp," he said, "if you poke your head down, anyway, I can show you how to get 'er going if she goes out. The pilot light, I mean."

I realized that there could be no reasonable explanation for my reluctance to follow, so I braced myself with a hand on the wall, and slowly moved down the stairs. After half a dozen steps, I lowered myself to a sitting position. Heph looked at me, puzzled, and not without some amusement. But I took a deep breath and looked around the cellar.

It was not any different from any other cellar of its era. The floor was hard-packed dirt, the walls stone, their whitewashed facing dry and crumbling. A single bare bulb hung from the ceiling next to a large, filthy

furnace. A heavy door, like that of a safe, was open in the side of the furnace, and wide black ducts snaked out in every direction, to disappear into
the floor joists above.

"This used to be a coal furnace, see," Heph said. "There's still coal dust
all over the place here. Somebody converted it to gas." From his pocket he
produced a packet of matches. "You want to come see how to do this, Mr.
Loesch?"

"No thanks, Heph," I replied. "You just show me from there."

Heph leaned in the little door, and I heard a metallic scrape. There was
the snick of a match against sandpaper, and the quiet gust of a gas flame
igniting. Heph pulled his head from the door and shut it tightly. Beyond
him, behind the furnace, the cellar seemed to disappear in its own shadows; no wall was visible.

"So alls you have to do now is go on upstairs and turn up the thermostat," he said.

"Heph, may I ask you something?"

"What's that?"

I pointed over his shoulder. "Can you see what's back there?"

He frowned and turned around. "Mr. Loesch, I don't believe I see anything at all back there."

"There's no wall?"

Heph laughed. "I'm sure there's a wall there, Mr. Loesch." He came to
the stairs and climbed up, stepping neatly around me. At the top, he put
his boot covers back on and beckoned for me to follow. I did so. We went
into the large front room, where an old thermostat was affixed to the wall
beside the door. It had the coppery look of an art deco building facade,
with an old mercury thermometer running up the center, like a vein of
blood.

"You want I should go ahead and give you some heat, then?"

"Yes, please do, Heph."

He reached out and turned the little thumbwheel at the bottom of the
thermostat, and immediately we heard a clank, a pop, and a rumble as the
gas caught fire. A few seconds later, musty air rose from the heat registers and filled the room. I felt, for a moment, as though some animal had
awakened underneath us, that we were enveloped by its hot breath, and I
suppressed a shudder.

Or perhaps I didn't quite suppress it, because a wry smile played at the corner of Heph's mouth. "You planning to live alone here, Mr. Loesch?" he asked.

"That's right," I said, sounding, I'm afraid, rather uncertain.

"Lots of character in an old place like this."

"I suppose you could say that."

He stared at me for a moment, and I stared out the window. HEPHNER ELECTRIC, read the sign on the door of his van. In spite of his friendly manner, the electrician was making me somewhat uncomfortable. His backwoods charm and colloquial speech did little to dispel my sense that he was observing and testing me, gauging my reactions to his supposedly innocent comments and questions. Though his motives did not seem hostile, he put me on my guard. I wanted him to leave, and when I cleared my throat, he took the hint. "Welp, see you Wednesday, then, Mr. Loesch," he said, and, having brought my dormant house back to life, walked out the door.

THREE

It took me most of the next week to finish the floors and walls. To seal the floorboards, I buffed in a carnauba wax blend, and the result was a pleasingly light-colored finish with a dull, almost pink, glow. After long consideration I painted the interior walls pale yellow, to match the exterior, and refinished the kitchen floor with black and white linoleum tiles.

It may seem improbable that I should be able to accomplish so much in so little time, and I will confess here that it is not without pride that I so present myself. As I believe I have said, one area of my expertise is infrastructure—its creation, maintenance, and repair—and the tasks required for the renovation of a house happened to fit neatly into my particular skill set. The fact is, I would have been perfectly able to replace the old wiring myself. But Heph had made electricity his career, and so had all the necessary tools at his immediate disposal. It was only for the sake of convenience and safety that I brought him into my temporary employ.

Over the days leading up to his return, I strove to complete my basic renovations and began to think about the weeks ahead. There were things I wished to accomplish. One was to move myself out of the motel and into the house. I was growing weary of the motel's sterility, its numbing sameness, and I had come to resent the dull and frustrating drives to and from the city of Milan. The time had come to equip my house with the basic furnishings necessary for living, and occupy it in earnest. In addition, I had spent many stray moments during my labor gazing out the windows at the woods, and had become eager to explore them. I wanted especially to trek to the large rock, and find out if it could be climbed. Perhaps, as well, the creek that formed the northeast border of my property harbored trout—and doubtless the woods were home to any number of deer, which I could hunt, and which could serve as food. I hoped to minimize my trips to town for provisions, and so I was determined to dig and sow a garden, and perhaps to find and pasture some small animals, goats I supposed, for their milk. It was with considerable excitement that I contemplated buying myself some hiking equipment, guns, and fishing gear, and placing an order for good, dark soil and compost from the garden center in Milan.

And so it was with some determination that I worked on the floors and walls, and, as I have implied, I finished them within one week. I also ordered, and accepted delivery of, a suite of basic furniture from a catalog. My only other contact with the outide world during this time came in the form of phone call.

So engrossed was I in my work and in the contemplation of the work to come, that when the caller identified herself, I had no idea at first who she was. "Andrea from Barris and Haight" is what she said, and it wasn't until she added "The law firm? About the abstract?" that I suddenly remembered our conversation of the previous week.

"Yes, of course, Andrea!" I said. I wiped the sweat and dust from my face and walked out to the stoop to talk.

"I'm calling you back about the crossed-out name in your abstract," she said. "I'm afraid we've been unable to find the name. All copies of the document that are in our records are crossed out, just like yours."

"I see."

"I wish I could have been of greater help."

I could detect, in Andrea's voice, a great relief—as if she had expected the call to be contentious, and now believed it wasn't going to be. I decided to pursue the matter further.

"You might recall, Andrea, that I merely asked why the name was blacked out, and who is responsible for having done so. I am quite concerned about this meddling in my affairs."

She said, perhaps a bit uncertainly, "I have no other information for you, Mr. Loesch."

"But didn't you do any further research? At the Henford town offices, for instance?"

Now her voice fell into the slightly awkward pattern of rote memory—she had anticipated this question and had prepared an answer. "I'm sorry, the town offices had no other information, either."

This sounded to me like a lie. "Is that so?"

"I'm afraid it is."

"What would you say," I asked, "if I told you that I had been in touch with the town offices, and asked if anyone had been in to research those records, and been told that no one had asked for them in quite some time."

She seemed flustered, but her answer was clear. "Whomever it was you spoke to, Mr. Loesch, it could not have been the person my colleague spoke to."

"And who was that person, Andrea?"

"I don't know, since I wasn't the one who did the research."

"Which of your colleagues did the research?"

"Mr. Loesch," she said, her voice hardening, "if you wish to know more, you will have to investigate it yourself. We didn't find the information you wanted. I'm sorry."

"So am I, Andrea, so am I."

"Good afternoon, Mr. Loesch."

The line cut off before my "goodbye" could leave my lips.

Heph arrived as promised on Wednesday to replace the fuse box and wiring. He nodded appreciatively at my work. "Didn't do all this on your own, didya, Mr. Loesch?" he asked.

"Yes, I did, in fact."

"I can hardly believe it," he said, and I chastised myself for thinking that I detected in his voice a touch of irony. He crouched down on his haunches and rubbed his fingers lightly against the floor. "Waxed this, didya? How many coats?"

"Five."

He nodded. "Real good," he said. "Real good." Then he stood up, his joints cracking, his hands on his hips. He was wearing the same getup that he had worn last week, but the jumpsuit was light blue this time, and the earflaps on his cap were tied together over the dome, their ropes intertwined in a neat bow. "Yalp," he said, "it's real nice to see a house come back from the dead, as it were."

"It does feel good."

"Nobody been up here for a long time. I remember hunting down in the bowl there."

"You mean on my land?" I asked.

He narrowed his eyes. "Welp, it wasn't your land then, now was it. We used to go shooting deer. Gave it up though. Too easy to get lost."

"Really?" I asked, gazing out the window. "It's not so much land."

"Too rough. No paths. And it's a bowl, see, you get all turned around." He waved his hand in the air, dismissing the very concept. "Not much to shoot anyhow."

"I'm sorry to hear that," I said.

"Oh, you'll come across something or other," he said. But it seemed disingenuous, and I let the matter drop.

Heph disappeared into the basement, and soon I began to hear the clanking and scraping of his labor, accompanied by a cheerful whistle. I stood rooted to the spot for some minutes, staring out the window, and a great exhaustion and sadness seemed to come over me, like the sliding of a white sheet over a dead man's body. The landscape appeared to blur, and I felt a tightness in my throat. It was the whistling. Gentle, round, with a deep vibrato, it carried no recognizable tune, yet was deeply evocative. It pulled me out of the here and now, and carried me off to some other, watery place, where I floated, paralyzed, unhappy and slightly afraid.

After an indeterminate interval, Heph emerged from the cellar, evidently to retrieve some supplies from his van. His boot covers crunched quietly against the floorboards, a sound akin to that of autumn leaves. When he saw me standing at the window, he stopped.

"Mr. Loesch!" he said, as if shocked and disappointed. "Are you still standing there?"

"Yes, Heph," I said without turning. "I seem to be in something of a brown study."

The electrician was silent for a moment, and though my back was to him, I imagined that he was nodding sagely. I found myself wanting, very much, to trust him. "You know, Mr. Loesch," he said, "it seems to me you've been working awfully hard. Maybe you ought to reward yourself with a little break. Me, I like to sit back and read a good magazine. Or treat myself to a good lunch."

"It's too early for lunch," I said.

"You've lost track of time! Why, it's nearly noon!"

I looked at my watch, and somehow the motion of my arm broke my reverie at last. "You're right, Heph. Maybe I will take a break."

"Seems to me all you been doing these past couple weeks is getting ready. You got to go live your life some."

"Well put," I said, blinking the haze from my eyes. The woods sprang into focus, each green bud visible on the trees.

Yes—perhaps Heph was right, whatever his motives for his comments. Perhaps the life I had led so far was, in fact, nothing more than a long period of wandering, after having been led astray, years before. Perhaps my judgment had been clouded. The thought, of course, was deeply frustrating, for if it were so, then I had wasted a great deal of time and effort. But I was not yet old, and there was much I could accomplish, if only I could take my first steps onto the correct new path. Maybe that path began here, in these woods.

Heph lingered behind me a few moments more, as if to make sure he had gotten through to me. Then he continued on his way. I waited until he had collected his supplies and returned to the cellar, and then gathered myself and walked out to my car.

I hadn't intended to make much of my trip into town. But, as it happened, the closer I got to Milan, the more excited and enthusiastic I became. Heph's words rang in my head—it was time to stop preparing and start living. It was cold today, but soon the warm spring weather would arrive, and I would go out into nature, and be a part of it. I found a sporting goods store and picked out a tent and sleeping bag, a modest fishing rig, and a pair of lightweight, waterproof boots—a far cry from the heavy, bulky footwear I was accustomed to. I then treated myself to a lunch at the local Chinese buffet, where I discovered that I was hungry beyond measure. Time and time again, I loaded my plate with steamed white rice, sweet orange-flavored chicken, fried pork dumplings, and spicy beef and vegetables, only stopping when I literally could no longer consume another bite. It occurred to me that I had been neglecting my nutrition, and had probably lost a great deal of weight over the past two weeks. As I sat there digesting, in a slightly dirty booth near the slightly dirty window, beneath a buzzing neon sign, those weeks seemed like a mere hiccup in time, a transitional period that had now come to a close. This greasy, sumptuous meal was the line that divided that period from the rest of my life, which, for the first time in recent memory, I was ravenously eager to begin living. I staggered, packed with food, out to my car, then drove to the grocery store and bought enough provisions for two weeks. I also bought seeds, tools, plastic fencing, and posts at the garden center, and arranged to have the junk in my yard hauled away. I have a very large car, but the rear was full, all the way to the ceiling.

I arrived back at my house as the sun was setting. Heph's van was gone from the lot, and his bill, complete with a self-addressed envelope for payment, was wedged into the crack between the door and its frame. Inside, the house was warm and inviting, and filled with slanting evening light. It was dinnertime, but I had eaten enough to last until dinnertime the next day. I realized suddenly that I did not want to leave—that I was going to sleep here tonight, for the first time. I called my motel and settled over the phone; I had left nothing in my room. When I hit END, I realized that I had made the break. I was living here now, in my house on the hill, and felt, at long last, that I was ready.

I have to admit that I had great difficulty getting to sleep that first night. A mind accustomed to stimulation, and left without, will create its own— and in my empty house, in the moonless, deathly silence of night, mine was madly racing into the early hours. The house creaked in a wind, and the furnace shuddered and clanked as it regulated the temperature. I thought that I smelled flowers, and then gunpowder, and then burning wood. Ghostly flashes burst at the edges of my vision. I believed, several times, that someone was walking stealthily through the rooms, and I crept downstairs, knife in hand, to investigate. But no one was there, and I never discovered the source of the sound, if there had ever really been one.

Worse yet, when at last I did fall into an uneasy, shallow sleep, my dreams were strange. I stood in a desert as a sandstorm swirled around me. I collapsed in exhaustion, cupping my hands around my mouth to keep the sand from my lungs. Then I was digging, digging like a dog with both my hands, and I uncovered a wooden trapdoor, which led to an iron ladder. I climbed deep into the ground, eventually dropping into a tunnel, lit by bare incandescent bulbs and supported by thick wooden beams, like an old mine. The walls slanted, the ceiling sagged, and I walked through the maze of corridors in search of the source of the voices I heard—familiar voices, those of people I knew, though I couldn't tell who. And then, suddenly, the voices were behind me. I was leading those people somewhere, but I couldn't turn to see who they were. They chatted and laughed: only I understood the grave danger we were all in, that death lurked around every blind corner, and I tried in vain to quiet them. There was light ahead, and heat, and terrible peril, and the rifle I carried had turned to rubber, and then to something like licorice, because I was eating it, ravenously, as I had eaten my lunch at the Chinese buffet. I woke before dawn with tears in my eyes and my hand in my mouth, having actually drawn blood in a semicircular pattern of marks, like the rough stitching on a rag doll.

But daylight soon began to trickle through the windows, and the dream faded away into abstraction. The terror and madness that made it so real now seemed like ridiculous clichés, the scar on my hand a small embarrassment. I sat on the floor, rested my arms on the sill of the east-facing bedroom window, and watched the sun come up over the trees. The forest was still gray, but green had begun, ever so faintly, to creep across its surface, like a mold. The sight of it filled me with determination and excitement. I rolled up my sleeping bag, put on my clothes, and packed a bag with fruit, trail mix, dried meat, and a bottle of water. It was time to go for a hike.

Considering the amount of time that had passed since the house had last been occupied, the edge of the forest where it met the yard was strangely well defined. The house gave way to hard-packed gravel and dirt, which sloped down into rough, woody weeds and shrubs; then, about forty feet from the northeastern corner of the house, the treeline began, a wall of tightly packed maples, birches, ashes, and pines. The trunks were high and narrow, the light beyond them dim despite the scant foliage. Peering into the forest, I could make out a tangled canopy of thin branches overhead. Heph was right—it was indeed rough. I walked back and forth along the treeline, searching for, if not a path, then perhaps the ghost of a path that must certainly once have existed. The deer, at the very least, had to have a way in and out. But no entry point looked better than any other, and so I took a deep breath, raised a leg high into the air, and stepped in at random.

Almost immediately I became tangled in a thicket. Thorns and burrs caught at my pants, and saplings snapped against my face. I half-closed my eyes and ventured forth, my boots ripping and cracking the tangle below. I gripped the tree trunks and pulled myself along.

After about ten feet, the going became easier. The heavy shadows of the woods discouraged low brush, and I was left with only deadfall to contend with. To be sure, the deadfall was a problem—variegated, chaotic, and covered over by dead leaves and moss, it formed a second ground surface above the real ground, which was visible only in small patches. It would have been impossible to step from one of these areas to the next, as with rocks in a stream; they were too haphazard, and too far apart. Instead, I was forced to make my way by balancing on broken branches and slick patches of slime. The potential to trip, fall, or twist an ankle was very great, and my frustration quickly grew. I was forced to direct 90 percent of my attention toward the problem of staying upright and not hurting myself, when what I really wanted was to get a sense of the geography of my woods. Imagine my surprise and anger when I turned to find that I could still see the house behind me—the treeline was barely thirty feet away!

Still, I persisted. I believe powerfully in succeeding at something the first time, no matter how challenging: the first try sets the tone for all subsequent effort, and a failure now would dampen my future morale. So I forged on. After a time, the ground began to level out, and I had the sensation that I was moving uphill; but a break to get my bearings told me that this was merely an illusion, brought on by the difficulty of the terrain. I opened my water bottle and took a deep sip, disappointed in myself for succumbing so soon to my thirst. With a sigh, I reshouldered my pack and forged on.

I have an excellent sense of direction, and had learned in much more perilous situations than this one that it could be counted upon in challenging circumstances. But as I trudged through the forest, I began to get the uncomfortable feeling that I had lost my way. There was no evidence that this was so, although my house was far from view now and the sun invisible behind thick clouds. Nevertheless, the woods had taken on an unrelenting, almost unnatural sameness, the trees evenly distributed, the ground uniformly impassible; and it was with some considerable embarrassment and frustration that I realized I had not brought a compass with me. I am afraid I swore under my breath, there in the silence—and silent it was, for I had seen no living thing, not a single squirrel or chipmunk, since I crossed over the treeline.

I was relieved, then, to discover that the ground had begun to slope downward again. From my house on the southwest corner of the land I had set off to the northeast, and this decline was likely to represent the approach toward the center of my property. That would put the rock somewhat to my right. Satisfied that this was so, I sat down on a fallen log and began to eat my lunch.

I had been seated for about ten minutes, my back resting against a tree trunk, when I had a peculiar experience. I had closed my eyes for a moment, in an effort to gather myself for the next few hours of walking, when I heard a noise—the sound of a branch brushing against something, then snapping back, followed by the crack of a twig. I slowly turned my head, so as not to startle whatever it was that had made the noise, and opened my eyes. About fifteen feet away, blinking in the gray light, stood a doe.

It wasn't an ordinary deer, however. Save for its hooves, nose, and eyes, it was entirely white.

Now, I should add here that such animals are not rare in the greater Milan-Gerrysburg area. Indeed, they are one of our region's only claims to fame, and a small fame at that. The deer are not albino—their eyes lack the pale pink hue common to such animals, and they are not known to suffer from the health problems associated with albinism. These deer are normal, save for the color of their fur. They are thought to have come into being as a result of a genetic mutation in a herd that once lived within the fence of a large, abandoned military depot. Over time, the white color became dominant, and soon the entire herd, isolated by the fence, was white.

Eventually, in places, the fence collapsed, or was knocked down by vandals, and the herd slowly assimilated back into the greater population. And so, though they were uncommon, these deer were often seen in our township, and were evidently much beloved by local residents.

But it wasn't merely my sighting of the white doe that accounted for the peculiarity of the moment. It was that, somehow, I recognized *this particular deer*—the one that was now placidly staring at me through the crowded alley of tree trunks. I couldn't have said what it was about the animal that was familiar—what set it apart from other, similar animals I had seen in my life—nor could I even have identified what parts of any deer tended to differ from individual to individual. I merely understood, instinctively, that this was *my deer*, and that the animal *wanted* me to see it.

I want to make it clear that I am not the kind of person who subscribes to half-baked, magical ideas. I do not believe in portents, or omens, or signs. On the subject of an omniscient deity, I am firmly agnostic, confident only that the existence of such an entity is beyond knowing. So it is with some trepidation that I advance the idea that I had some kind of special connection to this doe. Nevertheless, I have been trained to do what I am told, and to report the facts as I find them, and the fact is that, as I sat on a rotting tree trunk in the middle of my leafless wood, something did indeed pass between me and a solitary white deer, and I felt—I am afraid to say—a profound *rightness* in the encounter, along the edge of which played a very faint hint of fear.

Soon, I became uncomfortable staring at the white doe, so I closed my eyes, leaned my head against the tree behind me, and waited for it to leave. I turned over the incident in my mind, attempting to make sense of it. After a time, I opened my eyes, and the deer was gone.

It was tempting to consider the possibility that what I had just experienced was some kind of hallucination or dream. Indeed, I was very tired after my journey to the center of the forest, and it is certainly possible that I had, at some point during my respite, actually dozed off. But I did not feel refreshed, and had no sense of time having passed, and thus was able to renew my confidence that what had just happened was real.

This episode in the woods, however, was about to come to an end, on the heels of a second peculiar event, one that, furthermore, made me feel quite foolish. As I gathered my things and stood, I thought I heard a sound, a kind of rushing rumble, and I detected, once again, a bit of motion through the trees, opposite the direction the deer had come from. The motion was up on the ridge to the north, and for a split second I felt a deep terror: the motion was incredibly fast, much faster than any animal, and the noise strange, mechanical, out of place in this eerily calm wood.

But then, suddenly, I understood. It can't be, I thought—but it had to be. I tramped across the incline, then hiked up the little hill that terminated in the ridge, and when I arrived I saw that I was right. What I had seen and heard through the trees was an eighteen-wheeler. I was standing on the shoulder of a paved road.

I stood for some minutes, trying to puzzle out how this was possible. I had begun at the southwest corner: my house. I had walked northeast, then turned due east, and descended into what I believed to be the belly of the lot. The rock, I was certain, was not far away, and slightly to the southeast. But here I was, standing on a road.

My excellent sense of direction had utterly malfunctioned. I didn't even know what road it was I stood on, nor had I any idea which direction I should walk to reach my house. I chose left, and soon discovered it to be the correct choice, as a road sign revealed itself only a hundred yards beyond a small rise. I had been on Nemesis Road, and now neared its intersection with Phoebus. The northwest corner of the property. This meant that I had never strayed far from any road, and had walked due north once my house was out of sight.

My walk down Phoebus Road was swift and disheartening. A personal and professional skill that had meant a great deal to me now appeared to be gone. Was it my age? Such things, however, could be fought against, and defeated. I resolved that I would not grow complacent, and sacrifice my talents to the onset of middle age. I would retrain myself in the woods, and regain my former strength. By the time I drew near the intersection with Lyssa Road, some of my enthusiasm and self-respect had returned, and I almost relished the period of hard work and recovery that was to ensue. I had faced greater challenges before, had been forced to fall back, reassess, and redouble my efforts: surely I would succeed here, as well. Despite my exhaustion, my step was a bit lighter, my thoughts less dark. The project of my life was back on track.

Thus engaged in thought, I did not notice the pickup truck in my drive until I had nearly reached my front door. The sight pulled me up short: I didn't recognize this vehicle. It was nestled up next to my SUV, dwarfed by it, in fact—a small, rusted-out red Nissan with a missing tailgate. I had no idea who would possibly want to pay me a visit, or could even know I was here.

I did not have to wait long to find out. I approached the front stoop still peering over my shoulder at the truck, and so almost tripped over the woman sitting there, lazily arrayed like the tongue of my house's red maw.

She was gray-haired and thin, in her late forties or early fifties, and gave every impression of a person battered by experience. She wore an old pair of jeans, a dirty tan hunting coat over a gray hooded sweatshirt, and a pair of frayed running sneakers. One leg was stuck out straight, resting on the steps; the other was folded up under it. Her hands lay on her knees, one of them with a lit cigarette poking out between two fingers. The lines in her face were deep, and her expression was partly hidden by her long, thin, dry hair; but her face nevertheless betrayed a familiar combination of emotions: surprise, amusement, judgment, concern. She carried about herself an air of superiority, in spite of her clearly low social station, and I felt myself succumbing, inexplicably, to her implied authority before she even opened her mouth.

It was not until she spoke my name that I understood why. She had changed a great deal in twenty-five years, but that rough, animated voice was the same as I remembered. It belonged to my sister.

FOUR

"Eric," she said, with the hint of a smile.

"Jill," I said simply.

We gazed at one another for several seconds, calculating. There was, I suppose, a moment when, if one of us had moved to embrace the other, this period of suspicion would not have had to occur. But neither of us did, and so we stared, studied, considered. The hint of a smile dwindled to a ghost, and I'm afraid my enervation must have shown. I wanted nothing more than to go inside and lie down. It would be hard to deny that Jill and I were not particularly happy to see each other, and we made no effort to hide the fact. Only after this mild mutual enmity had been established did our bodies and faces relax, and Jill stood up, and I invited her inside.

"The door was unlocked," I said, as she passed over the threshold and into the living room, still empty of furniture.

"You might have taken me for a thief," she said. "Figured you might shoot me or something."

She inhaled deeply from her cigarette and blew smoke up toward the ceiling.

I unshouldered my pack and let it fall to the floor. "I'd appreciate it," I said, "if you would not smoke inside the house."

This elicited a smile. "That's my little brother," she said. "I guess you don't have an ashtray. Maybe you could find me a plate."

I went to the kitchen and beckoned for her to follow. She took a seat at the little round wooden table I had bought, and I found an old china plate in the cupboard, one that had been here when the house was abandoned. I considered sitting down with her, but something kept me standing. I leaned against the stove and crossed my arms over my chest.

"Two chairs," she said, stubbing out her cigarette. "Expecting somebody?"

"The table came with two chairs."

"Right."

We stared at one another for several minutes more. Of course I recognized my sister now: the thick, high, arched eyebrows; the long chin; the narrow shoulders and nervous blinking. But it was clear why she had failed to register at first. Living had changed her. She was older than I, but that did not account for the difference. Whereas I had staved off the worst effects of aging with exercise, self-discipline, and healthy eating, Jill had indulged herself from an early age, abusing her body, sleeping irregularly, and running with a dissolute, irresponsible crowd. It was obvious, to look at my sister now, that she had continued with her unsavory ways, and had suffered for it. To be perfectly honest, I pitied her.

As for the many years we had remained out of touch, it is impossible to lay blame at her feet or mine. But she had not, to the best of my recollection, given me any reason to desire her continued love and friendship. She appeared only briefly at our parents' funeral, and if I remembered correctly, she was under the influence of drugs and alcohol. Even then, at twenty-four, she had already begun to age beyond her years, her face wan, her hair lank, and her eyes heavy and underslung with blue. What I saw now, in my kitchen, only confirmed what I might have imagined, had I ever had the desire to imagine it. Hers was clearly a wasted life—for my sister was not an unintelligent woman, nor had she always been cruel or apathetic. In fact, I harbored memories of her comfort, her companionship, when we were small children. I remembered the way she would hold me in her arms when I cried out of misery or fear, the way she stroked my hair and told me everything would be all right.

I assumed that she had never left the area, and asked if this were so. Her response was a rough cackle.

"Oh, Jesus no, little brother," she said. "I was out west for years. That's where I was when Mom and Dad bought it. I used to send you postcards, remember?"

I didn't remember any such thing. But I lied that I did, to encourage her to continue, which she seemed eager to do. People, in my long experience, want to talk. They may believe they wish to keep secrets, and they may believe that they are capable of doing so. But the truth is that secrets exist to be revealed; and it is usually very easy to find the combination of words that will cause them to emerge.

My sister continued. "I was out in San Francisco then. But one of my boyfriends moved north—he got a job at a little school up on a mountain. I lived there awhile. Then I drifted. I lived in Oregon and Montana. I ended up meeting a fella at a music festival. He said he was from around here. Eventually we got married and his mom broke her hip and we came back here to take care of her. But she died."

"You're married?" I asked. There was no ring on her finger.

"Dammit, Eric, let me finish. We tried having a baby and it didn't work out, I had a miscarriage. And after that we figured out we didn't really want to be together anymore anyway. So we divorced, and I took up with Hank."

"Hank," I repeated.

"Yeah, my boyfriend. Man friend." She snorted. "He's got a spread out on Julep Hill. He's a big hunter. So I live with him. I've been there like ten years. So in answer to your question, little bro, no, I left the area plenty. And I happen to be back. Just like you."

"I see," I said to her, although I did not regard our respective returns to be comparable. "How did you know I was here?"

"Somebody saw you in town."

"Who?"

"A friend. And then I asked around."

"Hmm."

"Which leads me to the big question," she said.

I waited for her to ask it, whatever she thought it was.

"Eric."

"Yes?"

"What in the hell are you doing here?"

It was very like my sister to overdramatize such a question. But the fact was, my decision to move back to the Gerrysburg-Milan area was of no concern to her, and I did not intend to discuss it. Saying so, however, would merely intensify her questioning. I wanted her to leave. So, instead, I gave a curt reply.

"I needed a change," I said.

This explanation managed to elicit laughter. "So you come *here?*" she said. "Beautiful."

"The land is affordable, and I know the area well."

"Yeah, you can say that again!"

"I don't understand."

She frowned, tilting her head. "Never mind," she said. And then she averted her eyes for a moment, shifted in her seat, and looked up at me again. I was taken by surprise: her face was sober now, pained, and for the first time she appeared to me as a genuine adult. When her eyes again met mine, it was by the force of great effort and determination.

"Eric, look," she said. "I want you to know that . . . I understand. About what happened. And, you know. I'm here for you."

Anger was beginning to well up in me, and I struggled to tamp it down. The tone Jill had assumed was intensely familiar: that of the wise older sister, the protector, the paragon of selflessness and care. Did she have even the slightest idea how pathetic, how manipulative, she appeared to me now? The illusion of maturity that had tricked me just moments ago was torn away, and she was revealed for what she was: needy, self-absorbed, and small.

"I'm sorry, Jill," I said, my jaw tight. "But I'm afraid you don't understand at all."

She opened her mouth to speak, closed it, exhaled slowly through her long nose. She turned to gaze out the kitchen window and appeared to gather herself.

"All right," she said at last. "Maybe I don't understand. But I know."

"You may think you know something. But you know nothing."

Now her lips tightened, and she shook her head, as if to say, "Why do I bother?"

I knew the gesture well, and it shames me to say that I lost my temper. The kitchen chair I stood beside found its way into my hands, and I lifted it three inches and banged it, with violent force, into my new linoleum floor.

"Enough!" I said to my sister, between clenched teeth. "Get out of my house."

"Eric—" she began, but I would not hear it. I would not hear another word of hypocrisy from my sister's mouth. The lies she had tortured me with—about our childhood, about our parents, our sad, doomed parents—would not be compounded. I knocked the chair to the floor with my open palm, and the pain that shot up my arm and into my shoulders registered as a kind of pleasure.

"Out!" I said. I suppose I was shouting. My sister stood up, trembling, and I must admit that I expected her familiar sneer to have taken its usual place on her face. But all I could find there was unhappiness and fear. Fear of my reaction, perhaps. But when a person has lived a life like hers, a life of promiscuity, rootlessness, and substance abuse, resentment and fear tend to replace all reasonable and proper emotions, and the world becomes your enemy.

She crept around the edge of the room, never once taking her eyes off me. When she passed through the doorway, I followed, into the hall, into the front room, over the threshold, and onto the stoop. There I remained, making sure she left. I watched her walk to her truck and open the door.

"I'm sorry, Eric," she said to me. "I was only trying to help you."

"Your kind of help is of no use to me."

The fear was gone from her face now, supplanted by mere sadness, no doubt at the miserable life she had resigned herself to, and to which she was about to return.

For a moment, she appeared ready to say something. But in the end she climbed into the truck and drove away. I stood on the stoop for a long time, watching the truck recede into the distance of Lyssa Road. When finally it disappeared from sight, I waited there in the spring air for the tightness in my throat to subside.

By the time I turned to go back into the house, darkness had fallen. I had left no lights on, so I groped my way to the banister, slowly climbed the stairs, and stumbled into bed. I had only time to consider how little difference there appeared to be between sleeping and lying awake in darkness, before I fell soundly asleep.

The next morning, I woke to a new stiffness in my joints and an overall sense of disappointment and embarrassment. My failure in the woods and anger at my sister the day before had thrown my mind into disarray, and I felt the need to change tack. I would work inside the house, I decided—continue my improvements and try to enjoy the simple pleasures of labor.

I took up my pencil and clipboard, made a list, and drove to Milan, and the hardware store. My hope was not to have to encounter the tall, thin clerk who had affronted me some days before, and at first, when I pushed my cart in through the automatic doors, I thought that my hope would be realized. The only clerks visible were a couple of young women.

But fifteen minutes later, when I approached the checkout line, there he was. The store was quite crowded, despite the early hour, with middle-aged men wearing tool belts and sports-team-branded sweatshirts. Local contractors and builders, no doubt, preparing for their day's work. I wheeled to the back of one of the young women's lines, pretending not to see my nosy acquaintance. But in a frustrating trick of fate, the man in front of me had some intractable problem involving his company charge account, and meanwhile the tall clerk's line quickly dwindled to nothing. He looked up at me from his register and signaled for me to pull into his lane.

I would not be so rude as to refuse. With a heavy heart, I did as he suggested, and began to unload my items onto the counter.

"Morning, Mr. Loesch," he said.

"Hello," I replied, surprised. Had I told this man my name? Perhaps he had remembered it from my credit card. I noticed that his name tag read RANDALL. But I declined to use this information.

To my temporary relief, Randall did not speak as he dragged my purchases over the price scanner and packed them into plastic bags. The credit card machine, however, took its time accessing my account, and as we stood waiting, he said to me, without turning, "You met a friend of mine the other day."

Determined not to become annoyed, I replied with as much cheer as I could muster. "Is that so?"

"Mmm-hm," he said, nodding. "Paul Hephner. The electrician."

"Oh yes. Heph. He seems very good at what he does."

"He's the best there is," Randall agreed. "We go way back. Hunting buddies."

"I see."

The cash register, at last, kicked back into life, and a receipt slid out silently from between its metal teeth. Randall tore it free and set it on the little transaction platform before me, along with a pen.

As I signed my name, he said, "You a hunting man, Mr. Loesch?"

"Not really," I admitted.

"Just as well," he told me, accepting the pen and receipt. He tucked my copy into one of my sacks and faced me, his arms crossed. "Those woods are a bitch to get through. And there isn't much there."

I transferred my bags to the cart and prepared to leave. "So you've hunted on my land," I said.

"Tried to." His eyes narrowed slightly.

I was free to leave, if I so desired. Nevertheless, and despite my reluctance to encourage this man in any way, I couldn't resist making a small inquiry.

"Let me ask you something," I said. "When you explored those woods, did you ever reach the rock outcropping?"

He seemed to relish the question. A small smile stole over his gaunt face, and he crossed one leg over the other and leaned back against his cash register. "Oh, I remember the rock you mean. Practically a little mountain, isn't it? Just sticking up over the trees?"

"That's the one."

"If I recall, there was some talk of making our way to it, that day."

"Yes?"

His smile spread into his eyes, and it was clear that he was enjoying playing with my expectations. He stroked his chin, gazing into space, pretending to think.

"But in the end," he said finally, "we didn't bother. Too much trouble."

"I see." I heard, in my own voice, more disappointment than I would have liked to betray.

"Don't know that there's anything to see, though. It's just a rock, I'd imagine."

"Of course."

"You enjoy your renovations, Mr. Loesch." I detected a bit of irony in his mode of address, and it was true, he was some years my senior, and by rights ought to be calling me Eric. I briefly considered telling him to do so in the future. But I had wasted enough time already, and I did not wish to further erode the wall of privacy I had erected between us. I thanked him curtly, and wheeled away, my muscles aching.

It was a bright, breezy day, and a wind carried with it a balm, a round moistness with a hint of warmth. It was perhaps this warmth that had caused an odor to begin drifting through the rooms of the house. I suppose I had noticed the odor before—a flat, dank mustiness—but it was only

now that it had grown intense enough to demand my immediate attention. To this end, I had included among my purchases from the hardware
store a bag of quicklime, a bottle of antifungal spray, a respirator with several sets of filters, and a package of extra-heavy-duty plastic garbage bags.
I would find whatever it was that had grown moldy, and I would throw it
away.

In the back of my mind, however, and creeping ever closer to the fore,
was the understanding that I would have to work in the cellar, under the
disheartening glare of a single ancient bare incandescent bulb. This inevitability was causing me distress, and the distress grew more powerful with
every passing moment. I unloaded my car, removed the respirator from its
package, screwed in the filters, and adjusted the straps, taking as long as I
possibly could, and all the while feeling my heart beat faster and harder,
and my head fill up with toxic fog.

Allow me to state that I am not a coward. Indeed, I am a man of some
considerable courage. This is not a boast, merely a statement of fact. I have
faced great dangers in my life, have stared death in the face and not backed
down. But those dangers were clear and well defined, and my superior skill
in the areas of planning and prevention were able to protect me against
harm. My impending journey into the cellar, meanwhile, was something
different. There was no reason for me to fear it—indeed, I had been living and working above it for some time now, and had neither heard nor
seen anything that would indicate danger. But reason did not come into it.
My fear of the cellar was irrational, and there was nothing I could do that
would erase it. I would have to carry it with me, bear it upon my shoulders
as I worked, endure it until my work was through.

The time had come to act. But I dawdled for at least an hour more, making a pot of coffee, drinking a cup of it, checking the glazing on the windows,
examining the winter-bare landscaping plants around the house, for buds.
Eventually, though, I grew annoyed with myself. Where was my discipline,
my self-control? A strong man, I told myself, did not hesitate in the face of
his fears; rather, he took note of them, dismissed them, and got on with the
task at hand. Disgusted by my weakness, I went back inside, put on my respirator, took up my supplies, and trudged down the rickety steps.

The steps were painted red, which paint had worn away in the middle
of each from decades of tread. They creaked and bowed under my weight.
My hands were full, and anyway there was no handrail, and I took each

step with great care, making sure each foot was firmly planted before trans-
ferring my weight to it. In this way I descended gradually, until at last I
stood on the bare packed-dirt floor.

The smell here was stronger, of course; I could detect it in spite of the
respirator. My breaths inside the device were hot and damp; I had to draw
them more deeply to pull the air through the filters. The cold crept up underneath the cuffs of my pants, and the furnace, a monolithic, mound-like
protuberance in the ground, snaked its black tentacles all across the room.
It appeared to me like a giant mushroom, some massive death cap, and as I
stood regarding its great dark enormity it emitted a thunderous *clank,* and
a hacking *whoosh,* like a sudden gust of wind. I could see the blue glow of
the gas flame etched around the edges of the door, and I felt something
turn over in my chest. Perspiration began to leak out of my pores, under
my arms and in my crotch, and inside my boots my feet began to itch. I
realized, belatedly, that I ought to have urinated before I came down here.
But that would have to wait. I gritted my teeth and, supplies in hand, moved
forward into the darkness.

The basement was laid out in a large square the size of the house, and
had not been subdivided in any way. Enormously thick wooden beams supported the floor joists above, with the furnace in the center. The stairs had
led me down to the south wall, and the light bulb was southwest of the furnace, illuminating the new circuit breaker box that Heph had installed.
Foolishly, I had neglected to bring down a flashlight—but with my eyes adjusted, I could make out the north and east walls behind the furnace, and
knew I would be able to see well enough to clear out the moldy trash.

My heart thudding, I took a few tentative steps north. I felt my entire
body tighten, the skin squeezing the bones, as if it were trying to shrink me
to nothing. My jaw, tightly clenched all this time, began to spasm, and I
struggled to keep my teeth from knocking together. But I continued, taking
one step and then another, my hands cold and trembling, my head pounding, my face swollen and irritated from the nylon straps of the respirator.

And then a familiar emotion took hold of me and my trembling sub-
sided. Heat coursed through me. I gripped the lime bag and spray bottle
tighter, crushing them in my grip, and vulgarities began to pour from my
mouth.

It is a well-known truth that fear gives way to anger—we have seen it,
for instance, in those diagnosed with a dangerous illness, or among citizens

of an occupied state during a time of war. But in my case, the transformation was immediate. My irrational fear melted in the face of an equally irrational rage. I cursed the slovenly, careless people who had left things in my basement capable of growing mold; I cursed poor Heph for forcing me halfway down the stairs. I denounced the forest and its cruel rejection of me, its master, and I spat and seethed at the thought of my sister, the devious whore, for interfering in my life after ignoring me for so long. In short, the world was my enemy: it had driven me here, to this sanctuary, and, not having had enough, it had forced me into its bowels to clear away the miserable reek of its past. And so, fueled by hate, I made my way across the near-lightless space to the far northeast corner, where a jagged lump reshaped itself into a pile of cardboard boxes, each slumped, eaten away by fungus, and spilling books through its ruptured sides.

I gathered up as many of the books as I could carry, and then, my teeth tearing the insides of my cheeks, the taste of blood on my tongue, I roared up the stairs and out the back door, to fling their infernal rot into the brutal spring sun. I made many trips—a dozen, I'd say—growing angrier with each return, until at last I howled at the limp stinking cardboard that remained, bellowed as I scooped it up and hugged it to my chest and hauled it out into the light.

By the time I had opened the box of lime and begun dumping it on the floor, my anger had weakened, and with that task completed, my fear returned. I had time for a few spritzes of the antifungal spray before, wracked by terror, exhaustion, and spent emotion, I dragged myself at last up the creaking stairs to the bathroom. There, I tore off my mask and my clothes, spreading dust and scraps of clotted, putrid paper all over the floor, and stepped into a scalding hot bath, where I cleaned my wounds. I had gouged the back of one hand and an ankle during one of my desperate tears up and down the stairs; my face and scalp burned with scratches from who knew where, and my muscles ached from the tension at last released. From the bath I tumbled into bed, shivering beneath the blankets, and I slept until late afternoon. Then, at last, I dressed in clean clothes, tidied up the bathroom, and went out into the yard to transfer the ruined books to the trash pile.

There were several dozen of them, both hardcover and paperback, largely destroyed by the purple-black mold that had grown on them. The mold had permeated their pages, fusing them together into bulging, spongy blobs, and I carried them gingerly now, eager not to sully myself. Two of them, however, had largely escaped corruption, and after a moment's consideration I set these aside. My constant renovation work had precluded the need for anything to read, but now that I had some leisure time, I could use a good book or two. The books seemed to be on the subject of human psychology—one of them was called *The Malleable Mind;* the other *Shaping Behavior.* I would not characterize my own cast of mind as intellectual, and these books did indeed appear to be quite dense and technical in nature. But I had never been one to resist a challenge, and of course there was nothing else to read, aside from the children's book I had found in the sitting room. I brought these books back inside, and cleaned them up as best I could. Then I completed my work outdoors, washed my hands carefully, made myself a modest dinner, and, as the sun disappeared from view behind the hills to the west, turned in early to bed.

My plan had been to open one of the rescued psychology books at random, and read it until I fell asleep. And so I picked up *The Malleable Mind* and turned it over in my hands. Though largely undamaged, it was nevertheless redolent of the cellar, and my lips curled at the smell, and a small tremor of unease ran through me. But I was able to master myself, and I let the book fall open on my lap. The page began,

> presumption of inviolability must be negated. To this end, subtle adjustments were made to the subject's comfort and autonomy by creating a physical dependence upon the experimenter. Specifically subject was requested to bring a bag lunch to the testing location, then told it would be placed in a nearby office, from where it was "inadvertently" lost. Experimenter then promised food would be provided, which promise was then "forgotten." When subject requested promised food, the experimenter renewed his promise and then again forgot. Water meanwhile was provided for the subject that was slightly discolored and had a bitter flavor. When asked about the water, the experimenter pretended to take a sip and subsequently insisted that the water tasted fine, and that as for the color, it was always like that and nobody else ever complained.

It was clear almost immediately, however, that the book would not have the intended effect. The writing was not especially boring or difficult, as I had anticipated, but its subject matter did not sufficiently interest me to

justify my continuing to read it. Indeed, I felt a stubborn irritation and became agitated enough to toss it with some force into the corner of the room.
I suspected I would do the same with *Shaping Behavior,* should I have bothered to open it, so I got out of bed, went downstairs, and collected the children's book I had found while cleaning.

To my surprise, the children's book was quite absorbing, and I read it
with great enjoyment as a rain began to drum against the windows of the
house. It was the story of an orphan boy, raised by an old woman, who is
sent into the world to find his destiny, with only a sack of simple items—a
whistle, a hat, a coin—in his possession. A suspicious stranger tempts the
boy in an effort to convince him to give up these meager items, but the boy
resists, and eventually uses them to aid him on his journey. The whistle, for
instance, summons, as if by magic, a group of helpful animals, including a
dog, a bird, and a salamander. In a mysterious city of gold, the boy meets
a serving girl, who joins him in his travels, and in time they are trapped
in a frozen wood by the stranger, and are only able to escape thanks to the
salamander, which melts a hole in their prison using its uncanny ability to
radiate heat. Though its pleasures were unsophisticated, the book offered
a character with whom I was able to identify, and a portrayal of bravery
and self-reliance that corresponded very closely to my own values. I wished
only that I could send the book back in time, to my younger self, in his
moments of greatest need.

But such fantastic notions were pointless to contemplate, and I pushed
them away and soon succumbed to sleep. When I woke, I was greeted by
an extraordinary sight. The rain that had begun to fall during the night had
frozen, and the woods outside my window were heavily coated with ice.
All the way to the rock, the trees were gleaming gray, the buds encased, the
branches sagging beneath the weight.

Amazed, I dressed, shouldered on my coat, and went outside. Already,
in the dawn light, the air was growing warmer, and the ice was slick and
dripping, and the boughs chattered against one another in the balmy
breeze. I took a few steps past the treeline, into the gloomy shade, and the
air there was cold and crisp. Above me light was filtering dimly through
the glassine ceiling of branches, faintly shifting, much as I had imagined
the frozen branches to have done in the storybook. The wood seemed very
much alive, as if it were coming awake as I had only minutes before.

I remained there, in the bramble, until the ice began to break and rain to the ground around me. Then I stepped out into my yard and listened. The wind blew, the ice fell, and the branches sprung up, their buds again revealed. I felt a deep, nervous excitement, and my fingers and toes began to itch. I was confident now: I would go back into the woods, and I would find the rock and climb to the top.

FIVE

That day, I decided to leave my hill in order to handle some financial business, and to purchase some additional tools and provisions for my trek back into the woods. I drove into Gerrysburg, parked on the town square, and walked across the park toward the bank.

Perhaps it was the season, or a renewed sense of optimism about my impending adventure, but I thought that downtown Gerrysburg looked considerably nicer and more lively than it had when I was arranging to buy the land. What businesses there were, were just opening for the day, and a few energetic-looking people strode along the sidewalks. The trees here, perhaps influenced by lower elevation and the artificial warmth of civilization, were free of ice, and had advanced farther into leaf than the ones in my forest. And the park was tidier, appearing to have just been cleared of trash. A woman stood before the war memorial, gazing soberly at the list of names, and above her the American flag flew at half-mast, for no apparent reason.

I passed the real estate office and the ice cream parlor on my way to the bank, and so it was appropriate that fate should arrange for me to see, standing and chatting in the middle of the lobby, Jennifer the real estate agent and Jeremy Pernice, the ice cream parlor's proprietor. In Jennifer's hand was a cell phone, which she gave the impression of just having hung up; Jeremy was holding a naugahyde zippered bag, the kind small businesses use to deliver their daily deposits. Their conversation appeared animated, and they seemed to know one another quite well. In a general spirit of camaraderie, I approached them and said good morning.

Jeremy Pernice reacted at first with momentary confusion, and then his face settled into an expression of friendly interest, as he recalled who I was and how we had met. He glanced at Jennifer, as if to gauge her reaction.

To my disappointment, Jennifer's face registered irritation; then she smoothed her features into a mask of forced apathy. It was she who spoke first, primly returning my good morning without addressing me by name. It was obvious, of course, that she was still angry from what she had perceived, weeks before, as rudeness on my part. But since I had no control over her feelings, nor over the extent to which she acted upon them, I could only treat her with the same geniality and politeness I employed with Jeremy Pernice.

"I hope business is good for both of you," I said.

Jeremy held up his deposit bag in halfhearted enthusiasm. "Could be better, could be worse," he said.

"And you?" I inquired of Jennifer.

"Fine," she replied. I nodded, accepting her answer, though I knew that, thanks to me, this had so far been a better-than-average spring, at least financially. Having spoken, she quickly looked away.

I turned to Jeremy. "Well, I wish you continued good luck," I said. "I have some errands to run, but perhaps I'll stop by later for a snack."

"That would be fine," he said.

With that, I continued to the unnecessarily convoluted maze of ropes that led to the teller window, where I waited in line behind an old woman. After a moment, I heard footsteps behind me, and found Jeremy Pernice standing there, turning his bag over and over in his hands.

"Everything going all right for you out on the hill?" he asked me. It was clear from his expression that his curiosity was intense, and that he was trying, and failing, to suppress his avidity.

"Oh, yes," I replied. "I've largely completed my renovations. It's a lovely house, and a wonderful location."

"I guess you're getting to work, then?" he asked. "On . . . whatever it is you're doing?"

"I suppose you could say that."

He waited, obviously hoping I would continue. But, eager as I was to be a good neighbor, I was not interested in discussing my activities with him. Luckily, the old woman completed her business at that very moment, and I was able to move to the teller window and attend to my own business without Jeremy Pernice's interference. The teller, however, a middle-aged woman wearing a large, stiff permanent, seemed unusually attentive, watching me fill out my forms with a disconcerting level of interest. I wondered, idly, if she was a friend of Jennifer the real estate agent's, or of Jeremy Pernice's; if they had told her about me, speculated with her about my doings. Perhaps Jeremy was standing behind me right now, watching her reaction to my financial activities. The thought irritated me, and I vowed to give him a piece of my mind, should this prove to be the case. But by the time I was through, he was gone; indeed, the bank was empty of customers. As I returned to my car, I ventured a glance into the ice cream parlor, and saw Pernice behind the counter, talking to his employee, the girl I had met there weeks ago. The two looked up as I passed, and stared at me with obvious curiosity.

I drove to the sporting goods store and found a nice, sharp hatchet, a collapsible saw, and a compact one-man tent with a waterproof rain cover. I then summoned a sales clerk—a muscular, outdoorsy-looking young man— and asked him what I would need in order to do some rock climbing.

He leaned back slightly, crossed his arms over his chest, and asked, "What kind of rock climbing?"

"Oh," I said, "just your standard rock climbing."

"Going up the Adirondacks?"

"No, no, just climbing locally."

"So nothing too challenging, then," he said.

I found something vaguely insulting in his manner—an overconfidence and imperiousness that I doubted were supported by actual life experience. To move the conversation along, I said no.

The young man led me to the climbing supplies, and instructed me to buy ropes, carabiners, a type of anchor he called a "draw," climbing gloves, and a pair of specialized shoes. I gestured toward a small rack of smooth plastic helmets, and asked him if I shouldn't buy one of those, too.

"Nah," he said.

"Really?"

The young man shrugged. "Nobody uses them."

"What protects them," I said, "from a fall?"

"Not falling," was his reply.

It is perhaps a fault of mine that I find it difficult to conceal negative emotions from those who have elicited them, and rather than make a futile attempt to do so, I now chose to make my feelings known directly. I placed my hands on my hips, looked the sales clerk straight in the eye, and assumed the attitude of authority to which I was accustomed.

"I regard your cavalier attitude toward climber safety to be foolish in the extreme," I said. "I knew a young man about your age, at one time under my immediate supervision, who held similar views regarding the recommended safety equipment of his trade. He was in the thrall of his own youth and strength, and believed himself to be invincible. Any realistic assessment of the dangers he faced would have shown him the folly of this position, but he refused to make any such assessment, and the result was disaster. He was killed."

The clerk's smug expression slowly dissolved as I spoke, and reconfigured itself into one of affronted anger. When I was through, he wordlessly reached over my shoulder, plucked a climbing helmet from the wall, and shoved it into my supplies-laden basket. "Any other questions?" he inquired coldly.

"None."

His mouth fell open again, as if to speak; the muscles of his face tightened, and his eyes snapped into focus. But a woman came up behind him and tapped him on the shoulder with a question about a skateboard, and he thought better of whatever it was he had been planning to say.

For my part, I calmly walked to the counter and paid.

When I emerged from the shopping plaza that housed the sporting goods store, I saw that it was already past noon. The sky had clouded over again and a light rain was falling. There would be no time for me to return to the hill, prepare my equipment, and embark upon my expedition today, and the weather was serving as a further disincentive. Thus, I was left with a "free" afternoon.

I decided that I would return to downtown Gerrysburg and treat myself to lunch and an ice cream. And indeed, it was toward downtown that I now aimed my car. When I reached Main Street, however, I did not turn left, the direction that would lead me to the town square. Rather, I turned right. The road brought me past rows of dilapidated homes and empty shops, and to the cul-de-sac that served as the termination of both Main and Jefferson—the street I grew up on. I turned onto Jefferson and slowed my vehicle, peering closely at each house, the warped and peeling clapboards, the rusted wrought-iron railings, the cracked and crumbling cement stoops. Some of the bright canvas awnings that I recalled from the days of my childhood still remained, decades out of style, grayed and stained by the years.

At the end of the third block, where Jefferson crossed Madison, the street turned to dirt. When I was a boy, it had continued for three blocks more, and ended at a small body of water officially designated Reese Pond but popularly known as "The Swamp." Those blocks were gone now, the pond filled in. The abandoned high school stadium site was all that remained, a large area of churned-up ground surrounded by bent and crooked chain-link fence. Hillocks of excavated earth bore violent little clumps of spiny weeds. Pieces of rebar rusted in puddles, and the burned-out husk of an old car slumped in the center, its wheel rims blackened and mired in the wet ground.

I parked at the side of the road and circled around the fence on foot until I reached a flattened section. Slowly I paced out the distance from Madison, looking over my shoulder as I went. A few moments later, my boots half sunk in mud, I stood on the site of my childhood home.

It had not been a large or impressive house, 414 Jefferson. But it was here that I had formed my imagination, and developed, in solitude, the skills I would one day strengthen and refine into my professional accomplishments. It was here in the backyard, in the garden shed, that I learned how to use tools, and how to build, modify, and repair the accoutrements of childhood play. I maintained, and eventually customized, my bicycle; I built a ramp and, later, a bicycle stand, using my father's arc welder and some scavenged aluminum pipe. It was from my father that I inherited my handiness and organizational acumen—he served for many years as the head custodian at the SUNY in Milan. My mother, meanwhile, was often tired and weak from the unhappiness that today we would call chronic depression, and left me largely to my own devices.

I developed a reputation among the neighborhood children as a solver of problems, but except for the occasional request to patch a ball or adjust a pair of skates, I had little association with them. I preferred to keep to myself. That shed was my sanctuary, both from my mother's mood swings and from my sister's mockery and intransigence, and there were times when I spent the entire night there. The only member of my family who ever visited me in the shed was my father, and his interactions with me there were only, as far as I could tell, coincidental to his real aim of retrieving a hammer or other tool from the elaborate and useful pegboard rack I had made.

One side of the shed had been taken up by deep, painted pine shelves, and I had left this area entirely to my father's possessions. Most of these were magazines—back issues of handyman and do-it-yourself publications, and (I eventually discovered) a small cache of pornography, about which he seemed to have entirely forgotten. There was, however, one curious item shoved into a shadowy corner of the shelves: a handmade hardwood box about the size of a large dictionary. The box was held shut by a heavy latch with a lock on it. I was curious about this box, of course, and attempted many times to figure out what it held. It was rather heavy and solid-feeling, and it made no sound when shaken; the hinges, latch, and lock were extremely sturdy and well fitted. The only way into it would have been to break it, and my curiosity was never so great as to drive me to that extreme. Every now and then my father would enter the shed—he never knocked, as he rightfully regarded the shed as his, and my tenancy a condition of his generosity and good will—and remove the box from the shelf, and at these times I would always study his face for clues to what was inside. It was almost always in the evening when he came to take the box, and usually when my mother was asleep and my sister out somewhere, carousing. He would always return it within the hour.

Over the course of my childhood, I must have spoken with my father many, many times. But these exchanges are vague in my memory, his deep voice little more than a smear of sound. Instead what I recall is his silent presence, and my own reciprocal silence. I would not call it companionable, but neither would I refer to it as tense; our closeness was never deliberate, though we made no effort to avoid one another. But neither did we entirely ignore each other. We were like two discrete parts of a personality, taking up residence in the same brain—our proximity was unavoidable but we had little to say.

For all that, however, I never truly felt I understood my father. I do not fully understand him today. There were, however, times when I felt like I *was* my father, when I could sense his blood flowing through me, his expressions on my face, his anxious, hangdog stance in my bones.

But now, ironically, he felt very distant. And when I returned to myself from my reverie, and looked around at the gray skies and muddy ground, I could sense my memories draining away, pouring through me like rain off a mossy roof and into the earth. I was no longer sure about where I was standing—perhaps this wasn't the former site of our house, after all. Perhaps we'd lived closer to the swamp—or maybe farther in the other direction, nearer to Main Street. In any event, it was all mud and weeds now.

I returned to my car and drove away. And after several false starts, I was able to find the municipal cemetery where I had last seen, and argued with, my sister, before her recent appearance at my house. It was at the edge of town, on a woody rise around which the county highway curved. Unlike the church cemeteries that dotted our town, this one was ill cared for, the grass long and gone to seed, the ground littered with dead branches and trash blown from the road. The headstones leaned, and the graveled paths were cut through by runoff. It took some searching, but I was able to find my parents' graves. They were not buried together. My mother's bones lay beneath a willow tree. This is not as idyllic as it sounds, because the tree was old and half dead, having apparently been split decades before by lightning; and just beyond it ran a low, cracked, graffiti-covered cement wall, over which the road could clearly be seen and heard. Her stone was simple, bearing only her name and dates: 1937–1981.

My father was buried behind the crumbling cinderblock bunker where the groundskeeper, if there even was one anymore, kept his supplies. His grave was marked only by a cement slab, half-buried in the ground. The dates were identical to my mother's.

I did eventually discover what was inside the mysterious wooden box. The police found the box standing open on my father's workbench in the cellar. It was lined with velvet, and bore a depression the precise size and shape of the pistol that killed my parents.

As I drove back to the hill, rain began to fall in torrents; but by the time I got home and unpacked the car, it had ceased, and the sun emerged. The ice that had covered the trees that morning was gone, melted away in the warm rain. The front that brought the storm was balmy, and by the time I was ready to go outside again, the temperature had risen to nearly sixty degrees.

It was 2:00 p.m., leaving me time enough before darkness fell to perform an exploratory walk around the edge of my property. I recalled having been hungry before my unanticipated trip to Jefferson Street, but oddly my hunger had passed, and so I left at once, loading a few light provisions in my pack. I wore a thin waterproof jacket, a pair of running shoes, and a baseball cap; a pair of binoculars hung around my neck. It would be an easy walk, as I planned to stick to the roads, searching carefully for any former trail that could lead me to the rock.

The first leg of the walk was downhill. I left the lot in front of my house and took Lyssa Road in long strides, keeping to the northern edge, my feet crunching in the gravel. I could hear water bubbling in the ditch on the other side. A hawk circled overhead once, twice, three times, then moved on. And once I saw the face of a doe peering out from the trees to the south.

But mostly I kept my attention on my own property. I was looking for any evidence that a path once existed, some entryway to the interior that I could trace on my upcoming venture. I kept in my mind, as I walked, some sense of the location of the rock, relative to where I stood; and, given my long experience in the area of land use, I believed I had a very good sense of its direction at all times. Every once in a while I peered into the woods, or took a few steps beyond the treeline, but I found nothing on Lyssa Road to suggest there was a clear route. The deadfall, as on the hilltop, was barely penetrable, and I could see patches of wet, glistening marsh in those few places where no branches lay. The storm, no doubt, had made even worse what was already a nearly insurmountable problem.

I reached the end of Lyssa road quite promptly, and made a left turn onto Minerva. My experience there was more of the same. No paths, and no clear forest floor. I did pass a roadkilled squirrel, its snout dark with blackened blood, lying on the shoulder, and I pushed it into the dirt with my shoe, so that nature could reclaim it more quickly.

Soon Minerva Road began to climb, and I passed over the creek that cut off the corner of my property and ran underneath the pavement. Thus, it was not long before I arrived at Nemesis Road, which I turned onto with a renewed sense of purpose. The road ran downhill for a time, crossing once again over the creek, and I made my way deliberately to the lowest point, diligently checking for anything remotely resembling a footpath. Once again, there was nothing.

It wasn't long before I reached the road's lowest point, and it was here that I felt despair begin to seep into my body. My legs and back were aching, my head had started in with a gentle pounding, and my mouth was dry. I had foolishly neglected to bring a bottle of water with me, and so couldn't eat the jerky and trail mix I had packed.

Worse, the entire endeavor—trying to find the rock—suddenly seemed childish, idiotic even. What, after all, would I do when I got there? Climb up it, yes, but then what? I would stand atop the rock, and look out at the same view my bedroom window offered, except not quite as dramatic. Then I would climb back down and go home. And after that? I would just . . . live. In solitude, and to no particular end. In that moment, my entire existence seemed utterly futile, and I saw for the first time just how aimless, how pointless, it had become.

I don't know where this train of thought would have taken me, had I not then heard a noise from the road before me. It was a vehicle, coming up over the rise, a pickup truck. It coughed and wheezed, as if having to struggle to make it to the top—and then, as it crested the hill, it roared to life and came rolling toward me.

I moved onto the shoulder to allow it to pass, and then began to trudge up toward the intersection. The truck was about a hundred yards ahead, and picking up speed. And then, without thinking, I stopped.

For my work, specifically my often tense interactions with other people, I had been compelled to develop a sixth sense. Not an actual sixth sense, of course—rather, a heightened sensitivity to the information I gathered through the five normal senses. A careful observer, I discovered, can learn to predict what another person will say or do; and with practice, one can steer that person's thoughts and actions in beneficial ways. I don't know what it was about the driver's face that alerted me—he appeared in every way to be the typical resident of the area, with a filthy "trucker" style cap shading sallow, thin cheeks and a long drooping mustache—but I was suddenly wary, my muscles tensed.

And then it happened—just as it was about to pass me, the pickup swerved, barreling straight toward the verge where I stood. I leaped off the road surface and into the trees, where I tripped on the deadfall and crashed to the ground. From behind me I heard tires squeal and gravel spray, and the high, mad cackle of the vile redneck driver. I lay there, my hands scraped, my ribs bruised, and listened as the pickup struggled up to the corner of Nemesis and Minerva. I cursed under my breath, and then louder, and that's when I heard a twig break, and I looked up, into the forest.

It was the white deer. It had turned, leaping, at the sound of my voice, and now stopped and looked back. It was perhaps twenty yards off, gazing at me over its shoulder. Slowly I stood, not once taking my eyes from the animal. I brushed myself off, watching it watch me. One minute passed, and another. And then it bounded off to the southwest, stepping through the rotting branches. It turned once more before it disappeared, and I understood that this was a sign—that the deer was showing me a path to the rock.

Gingerly, I stepped out of the woods. I paced back and forth along the treeline, and after a few minutes found a suitably large stone, which I hauled up onto the road surface and placed on the shoulder, as a marker. Doubtless it would still be here tomorrow, but I stared hard at the trees, forcing myself to remember their arrangement, just in case.

I had my entry point. And indeed, the deadfall here did seem somewhat thinner than elsewhere, and the ground less saturated. I closed my eyes, recalling what I had just witnessed, the white deer hopping, with weightless ease, from one island of ground to the next, and vanishing into the shadows. Tomorrow, I told myself, I would do the same. I would walk down Nemesis Road, find my marker, and follow the deer.

SIX

At 7:00 a.m., after a breakfast of bananas, grapefruit, and oatmeal, I stepped out my door and into the pink light of morning. The sun was low and blinding on the far horizon, the sky streaked with high cirrus, and the air, though cold, was heavy with birdsong and the promise of warmth. I descended the porch steps and crunched across the lot, burdened with gear: my backpack bulged with food and water, a rolled-up tent, climbing supplies, and my compass and binoculars. On my feet were a pair of waterproof boots; lashed to my pack were the climbing shoes and helmet the sneering sporting goods clerk had grudgingly sold me. I had slept well, better than I had at any time since my arrival on the hill. I'd risen at dawn and watched the sun rise behind the rock as, tacked beside my window, the child's castle drawing served as an inspiring symbol of the endless possibility of adventure.

I marched north on Phoebus Road, retracing, in reverse, my route back from yesterday's reconnaissance. The pavement, cracked and uneven, was still damp from the rain. I tested my boots by splashing through puddles—though my canvas trousers, tucked in and laced fast, were soon dotted with wet, my feet remained warm and dry. I was alert to the possibility of oncoming traffic, the disturbing encounter with the rusted pickup being fresh in my mind, but my overall mood was one of excitement and confidence. Any passerby, watching my progress along the treeline, would have seen a man who appeared younger than his years, a spring in his step and a sense of purpose in his stride. I leaned forward and, pacing my breaths like a swimmer, plunged forward, as if on a mission of great importance and priceless reward.

After my turn onto Nemesis, it took less than ten minutes to reach the entry point I had discovered the day before. The marker stone was still in its place, the pattern of tree trunks precisely as I recalled. I lifted the stone and tossed it into the weeds at the roadside. Then I took one last look at the brightening sky and plunged into the woods.

In spite of the brilliance of the day, and of the trees' nascent foliage, I was instantly enveloped in gloom. The temperature dropped fifteen degrees, the light winked out, and a sense of unease began to insinuate itself in my mind. After four or five careful steps into the forest, I peered over my shoulder at the world I had just left. I could make it out, of course—the shoulder, the pavement, and the woods on the other side—but already it seemed impossibly distant. Indeed, it was as though I had been cast back in time to the middle of January.

I suppressed a shiver. My sense of dread was nothing but foolishness. It wasn't so dark here that my eyes couldn't adjust; nor was it so cold that my bushwhacking efforts would fail to warm me. Nevertheless, I found myself in the grip of a creeping despair, a premonition of exhaustion and failure.

This was not the state of mind I was accustomed to, at the outset of an expedition. But one does not fight the battles he wishes to fight; he fights the battles that find him. I would do my best to ignore my foul mood and physical discomfort, and plunge ahead as I had planned.

The white deer, I recalled, had fled southwest, and so it was in this general direction that I began to move. As before, the going was slow. Branches that appeared sturdy snapped underfoot, plunging my legs deep into mire; clumps of humus that seemed insubstantial harbored heavy stones, sending me sprawling onto the saturated ground. Low-hanging boughs scraped my face, or released a torrent of water as I ducked beneath them, chilling my scalp and neck.

But I would not be, and was not, deterred. I struggled forward, for hours it seemed, and I did not look back until I felt that I had made sufficient progress. Indeed, when at last I did turn around, there was no sign of the road I had left, and no noise from passing traffic.

In fact, there was almost no noise at all. The forest had insulated me from the raucous birdsong I heard when I left the house, and whatever creatures the wood concealed were silent.

By now the sun was likely overhead, but the light that came down through the branches was gray and weak. The trees were tall here, extraordinarily so, and it was difficult to imagine this land ever having been farmed, as the title abstract had suggested. I took a break underneath a towering fir, to catch my breath, get my bearings, and confirm my route to the rock.

But my mind, in defiance of my aims, grew cloudy and began to wander. I suppose that, given my exertions since I left the road, and my singleness of purpose up to this point, unfocused thoughts were to be expected, and even perhaps welcomed. But I was not used to them and did not wish to indulge them. I have learned that there is nothing more dangerous than a mind that strays from the task at hand. Of course, here there was no immediate danger, and I could not have been said to be working; but old habits die hard, and this was one I had hoped to preserve.

It was unclear to me whether these muddled thoughts were the result of my uncharacteristic musings upon the past which I had indulged the previous day, or if they indicated a general ailment of which yesterday's thoughts were also a part. In any event, that indulgence was proving to have been a mistake. I tend to align myself against the present cultural obsession with the past—I am not interested in the ethnic and geographical origins of my family, nor in the circumstances of my parents' meeting, nor that of their parents, whom anyway I can barely recall. I do not like to reminisce about my own childhood, or remember pleasant moments in my life. I don't keep journals or photo albums, and in general am not prone to reflection at all. I make my most important decisions according to the facts on the ground, and do not allow the past, or some sentimental interpretation of it, to interfere with my present actions. Furthermore, once I have made a decision, I abandon all resistance to it and act upon it immediately. This process rarely fails to deliver the results I need, and when it doesn't, the consequences are never worse than those that would have befallen me if I had failed to act at all.

However, it would be wrong to imply that my visit to my parents' graves was of no significance. The same instinct that I had long relied upon to accomplish my work had driven me to the cemetery, in defiance of what

I thought I was supposed to be doing, and I had to trust that there was some practical purpose, at this juncture in my life, to revisiting the past. Perhaps it was this apparent contradiction in my personal philosophy that was muddling my mind and causing me to feel tired, exhausted even, to a degree far in excess of that which the day's physical efforts would seem to have justified.

As I considered these things, I felt my head slump against my shoulder, and all my analytical acumen dissolved. I did not fight the onset of sleep—if my body and mind required it, then I would allow it to come, would even welcome it.

It was with some considerable disappointment, then, that I found myself waking instantly into the same moment that I had left. Or so it seemed. My muscles did feel somewhat more stiff, and the light appeared to have changed. I blinked, and dragged myself to my feet. My pants were wet from the humusy ground and a pressure exerted itself on my bladder. I relieved myself into a patch of moss, then looked at my watch. It read 9:04. For a moment, I was puzzled—even if I had nodded off only for the barest second, the time was surely past ten. A second glance at the watch revealed the problem: the second hand was not moving.

Such a misfortune was highly improbable. My watch, a military-grade stainless-steel timepiece with sapphire crystal, waterproof to 200 meters, was nearly indestructible, and I had never once neglected to wind it. I spun the crown, and felt, instead of its familiar mainspring resistance, a sickeningly smooth, freewheeling rotation. Somehow, in defiance of all logic, the watch was hopelessly broken. I tried to remember what I had done to it since I set out earlier that morning, and came up with nothing. There was no anomalous occurrence that could explain its current state. This was a watch that had had the leg of an oak desk set down upon it, that had been run over by a truck, and here it had ceased working through no greater violence than the swinging of my arm.

With a sigh, I shouldered my pack and gazed about, taking stock of the situation. I needed several seconds to find the sun through the branches of the conifers that now surrounded me; once I did, I determined that it must be past noon. According to my compass, I had been traveling in the right direction, and now I aligned myself with it and continued on my effortful way.

After walking—or, to be precise, struggling—for fifteen minutes or so,

I began to experience yet another new phenomenon, one to add to my exhaustion and equipment failure. It was, inexplicably, fear. The sun, already dim, had slid behind a cloud, and the gloom of the forest had deepened; the silence that had at first seemed an aid to concentration now merely felt strange, alien. Where were the insects, the animals? The one creature upon which I had come to depend in these woods, the mysterious white deer, was nowhere to be seen, and the trees, in their towering inertness, seemed to be closing in on me. I braced myself against the trunk of one to adjust my sock, which, soaked through in spite of my new boots, had doubled over on itself, and my hand slipped, and I tumbled into the mud.

It was there, lying on the ground, with a sharp twig digging into my calf and my filthy fingers numb with cold, that I allowed myself to grow angry. A low growl formed deep in my throat, rose to my tongue, and transformed itself into a scream of rage. I leaped to my feet, straightened my pack and hat, and rushed headlong through the thicket, crushing branches beneath my boots. I felt my face flush and sweat break out on my forehead, and my mind seized upon the most recent object of anger that it could find: my sister Jill.

Murder. That's what she accused our father of: murder-suicide. She believed, or claimed to believe, that he had shot my mother in cold blood, using the gun he had kept hidden in the velvet-lined box in his shed, and then turned the gun upon himself. To my dismay but unsurprise, it was this same interpretation that the police had chosen to believe, as did the few acquaintances my parents had had.

Of course my father had killed himself. There was no question of that: when his body was found, the gun lay inches from his hand, on the floor beside the overturned chair he had sat down upon to do the deed.

But my mother's death was another matter entirely, and I refused to believe that my father, for all his flaws, would ever have taken the unimaginable step of murdering her. It was true that they had fought, that their marriage was weak. And there was no denying that the same weapon which killed my father had killed her as well.

That, however, was the only evidence of murder, and there were ample grounds for believing that my mother's death had, in fact, been an accident. Take the gun, for instance. It was an Enfield No. 2 Mark 1, a British firearm of 1930s design, commonly used by the French during the Second World War. This gun was a revolver, practically an antique, and at such an advanced age, and in the hands of such an inexperienced user, must have been spectacularly unreliable. Adding to this was the fact that, on the table he had been sitting at when he died, there lay a greasy cloth, a bottle of lead remover, and a bronze barrel brush. My mother, meanwhile, was found crumpled in front of the sink, into which water was still running when a neighbor discovered the bodies. She was wearing her striped kitchen apron and her hands were wet. Obviously, my father had been cleaning the Enfield (which I later learned he had brought home from his postwar service in the army) while my mother stood nearby, washing the dishes. While he was reassembling and loading the weapon, it had gone off, the result of either a malfunction or his own error. The shot had killed my mother, and my father, driven to despair by the horror he had inadvertently caused, raised the gun to his head and shot himself.

Such a scenario seemed likely to me at the time, and even likelier the more I learned about weapons and how to handle them. But the police were not interested in my interpretation of events, and my sister even less so, and it was about this subject that we argued on the day of their burial. Now, crashing through the underbrush, I pictured my sister's flushed young face, rubbery with drink; I imagined punching her over and over, as I might have done—but restrained myself from doing—on that day, and her nose running with blood. The face changed to that of the ruined woman she had become today, laughing at me in my own home, a cigarette dangling from a corner of her mouth. *How dare you impugn my father?* I said to her in my mind, and soon I was saying it aloud, shouting it as I leaped the deadfall and splashed through the mud: "How dare you! How dare you!"

It was as I was screaming this that the ground gave way beneath me and I tumbled headlong into darkness.

I landed on my side, and my head soon followed, thudding against a smooth stone lodged in the mud. I was not knocked unconscious, but the wind was driven from me, and it was at least a minute before I had gathered myself enough to determine where I was and what had happened to me.

I was lying at the bottom of a pit approximately ten feet deep and six feet in diameter. It was very quiet here, and cold, with snow and ice still covering the ground, and the walls near my head hoary with frost. The pit gave the impression of having been dug with hand tools, not by a machine, and the walls had been scraped smooth and any protruding rocks or roots removed. Slowly, carefully, I tried to get to my feet. My head throbbed, my neck ached, and my muscles, bruised by the fall, protested. But I was able to stand; and, bracing myself with my hand against the earthen wall, I gently probed the painful spots to determine if I had broken any bones.

To my relief, the answer seemed to be no. There were many tender areas around my midsection, and it was possible I had fractured a rib, but no debilitating breaks were apparent. I was, I knew, lucky. I had allowed my emotions to overwhelm my good sense and had made a tactical error. In less benign circumstances, a mistake like this might have resulted in more serious injury, even death. I took a minute to catch my breath, and to stifle my feelings of embarrassment and inadequacy. Then I turned my attention once again to my surroundings.

Scattered about the floor of the pit were the remains of the false ground cover I had fallen through: a few broken twigs, some pine boughs and stones, and a lot of leaves. More startling, however, was what poked out of the ice and snow underfoot: thick branches, carefully whittled sharp, and positioned to do grievous harm to anyone or anything that should land on them. Most of these branches had slumped over and lay on their sides, but some stood straight, and it seemed a minor miracle that I hadn't landed on one. I might have been killed.

The sharpened sticks had provided me with another piece of luck, I could see now: they could be driven into the dirt walls of the pit, and used to help me climb out. Having noticed this, I wasted no time. I tugged several out of the snow, along with a palm-sized flat stone that had fallen down with me, and began to pound them into the earth. Ten minutes later, I heaved myself up and out of the pit and lay panting on the damp forest floor.

The relative warmth of the surface was a great comfort, and I tipped my head back onto a mossy log and took a moment to think. Two things were clear to me. One was that this was a trap intended for men, not animals. There were easier ways to kill a deer, for instance; and even if a prospective hunter wished to use a pit, he would not have to dig it nearly so deep. This begged the question of who, then, had dug the pit, and why— but I had more important things to do at this point than to indulge in idle speculation.

The second obvious thing was that this trap was not carefully maintained, and might even have been entirely forgotten. The circle of false floor I had crashed through had developed its own layer of natural humus;

it had been very well built, and had lasted a long time, perhaps a decade or more.

Surely, no one had come this way in years. Nevertheless, I suddenly felt paranoid. I jumped to my feet, body crying out in protest, and looked around me. I saw nothing and no one, save for the trees. The sun was lower in the sky, and a faint fog appeared to be rising up from the ground, but that was all. No one appeared to be watching.

I realized that the going would be rougher now, that the bruises and scrapes I had just endured would grow more painful as the hours passed. I briefly considered returning to the house. It seemed so inviting to me: the roaring furnace, a hot bath, a comfortable bed. But I have never been one to indulge in creature comforts; the only real comfort was success. I straightened my pack on my shoulders, consulted my compass (mercifully unbroken), and continued on my way, stepping more carefully now, with my eyes locked on the treacherous ground.

I made it another hour or so before I stopped. The sun had sunk further, and its slanting rays no longer found their way through the canopy above. In addition, the fog had thickened, and it had become difficult to see clearly more than a few feet in front of me. And finally, my fall was beginning to take its toll, with exhaustion and pain overwhelming my conscious thoughts. It was time to make camp for the night.

I found a lightly wooded area and began to clear it of debris. This proved more difficult than I had anticipated, as my rib cage ached, and the years of deadfall had become intertwined and grown through with vines. I made heavy use of my small hatchet, hacking away at everything that could not be pulled apart, and half an hour later I had managed to create a large circle of bare ground. The earth was very wet, of course, but I had packed a thin tarpaulin, and I laid this out carefully where I wanted my tent to go. The tent, a water-resistant one-person pod with inflatable headrest, came together without difficulty. By now it was nearly dark. I made a quick circuit of the area around my camp, gathered up as many dry or semi-dry branches as I could find, and built a small fire. When at last I had it blazing, I unpacked my food and sat down to a meal of trail mix, dried meat, and water.

Where, I wondered, did the time go? It seemed to me that it had only been a few hours since I'd left my house, yet somehow the entire day had managed to pass me by. Furthermore, I was puzzled once again by the apparent disconnect between the amount of time I'd spent walking and the amount of ground I ought to have covered. It took only an hour to circumambulate the entire wood on paved roads. Even allowing for the thick underbrush and mud, I ought to have been able to traverse the area twice over by now. Perhaps I had been walking in a circle—but the compass suggested the contrary, and I couldn't remember encountering the same piece of terrain more than once.

These thoughts led nowhere, and my mind entered into the same state of confusion it had suffered earlier in the day. I looked up and found that the fog was impenetrable now: it reflected the light of my fire back at me, as if I were sitting in an igloo. The silence of the forest, already unnerving, had deepened, and a shudder ran through my weary body. The only thing to do was sleep, and hope that the fog lifted in the morning.

I removed my boots, crawled into my tent, unpacked my sleep sack, and slid deep into it, shivering and aching. A tightness in my throat suggested that, as if my misfortune were not already great enough, I might have contracted a cold. With a deep sigh, I closed my eyes and tried to plot out the morning's progress. But the fog that blanketed the woods crept quickly into my conscious mind as well, and I was soon fast asleep.

I woke with a start in the night, as if from a frightening dream—though I remembered nothing of it—and cried out, in part from fright, in part from pain: my bruises and lacerations ached in earnest now, and my tent was eerily illuminated by the campfire's remains. I paused a moment, caught my breath, calmed my racing heart. The pain was sharpest just below my left kidney: I probed the area, certain now that I had cracked at least one rib. I was just about to lie back down, to ease myself back into sleep, when I heard a noise outside my tent.

I froze. There was another sound, a rustle of brush. And then the light changed: it flickered and dimmed, and slowly a shadow appeared, elongated, on the tent wall. An animal.

For a moment, I was terrified. And then the animal moved, and I could see that the distorted shadow was that of a deer. I let out breath, and the shadow raised its head, and it bounded away. I heard its footsteps on the wet ground, and the cracking of twigs, and then silence returned. Reassured, I closed my eyes.

When I opened them again—mere moments later, it seemed—the tent was flooded with daylight. Effortfully, I unzipped the tent door, crawled outside, and stood.

The fog had lifted. The air was clear. Directly in front of me, about fifty feet ahead, visible between the trunks of trees, stood a solid wall of stone, reaching up beyond the canopy and out of sight.

SEVEN

I resisted my instinct, which was to run to the rock without hesitation. Instead, I broke down my tent, rolled it into my pack, and removed my climbing shoes, gloves, and helmet. Faintly trembling, I scattered the remains of the previous night's fire and covered them over with dirt; then I sat down and scraped the mud off the soles of my mostly dry boots with a twig. At last I shouldered my pack and strode calmly to the rock, taking care not to trip and fall.

The work of breaking camp had loosened my stiff muscles, but the scrapes and bruises from my accident had ripened, and I winced with every step I took. My blood, however, was flooded with adrenalin, and my fingers and toes were warm. Above the forest canopy, the sun shone brightly. I imagined myself basking in its light when I attained the summit, and a shudder ran through me, a quiver of excitement that I did not fully understand, nor wish to. My mouth went dry, my palms were moist, and my skin prickled with anticipation.

In a few moments, I had reached the monumental stone. Its face was nearly sheer; it was smooth, and cold to the touch. Its composition was utterly unlike the brittle shale that comprised most of the local landscape; rather, it appeared to be nothing less than an enormous granite boulder, a massive foreign ship that had sailed here, fifteen thousand years ago, on a sea of glacial ice. I pressed my body to it and tipped my head back, enduring a wave of nausea and pain. The swollen knot on my forehead throbbed.

Between the trees and the rock I could make out a blinding blue strip of sky, which a small white cloud slowly traversed. The wall was very high, and footholds were few. There was little chance I could scale it, given my age, lack of experience, and aching ribs. As important as confidence in matters of personal safety is an understanding of one's own limits, and there was no question that this climb was beyond mine.

I began to walk counterclockwise around the rock, hoping that the southern face would offer a clearer path to the top. For the first time since I entered the forest, the going was easy: the rock's huge shadow disinclined vegetative growth, and the ground at its foot was flat, dry, and clear. Within a few minutes, then, I could see that my hopes would be fulfilled. The sheer face gave way to a pronounced slant, its angle decreasing gradually as I moved along. When at last I reached the southernmost point of the rock, it became clear that its overall shape was similar to that of a boot, with a low "toe" end sloping upward to a steep "ankle" at the north. I would likely have little difficulty until I reached the ankle—indeed, I was able merely to lift my foot and hoist myself directly onto the "toe" without even using my hands.

Nevertheless, I took my time, alert to the possibility of further injury. Here on the lower end of the rock, there were deep fissures where lichens and hopeless maple and pine saplings grew. Smaller boulders were seemingly held to the face by will alone, and I was eager not to upset them; depressions in the stone held pools of slimy green water in which I made certain not to slip.

As I rose up out of the woods, the air seemed to clear, and I breathed more easily. I was still underneath the long morning shadow of the trees, but the sky was full and blue above me, and my aches and pains receded in a wave of enthusiasm and hope. And a further detail caught my attention: a conifer, as tall as thirty feet, which appeared to be growing directly out of the solid rock. It was the last major feature before the rock arched skyward at the "ankle," and I made my way toward it, eager to discover how this natural wonder had come to be.

A few moments later, I stood before the tree. I am no arborist, but it appeared to me to be a member of the family Pinaceae, a common pine, with broad flat boughs of short, sharp needles, and large, woody cones. It stood in a wide depression in the rock, which in defiance of the odds had developed its own miniature ecosystem—a bowl of humus-covered soil rich with mosses and smelling strongly of vegetative fecundity. There was even a small subdepression, perhaps three feet in diameter, partly attached to the main one, that was filled with rainwater. The water looked extraordinarily clean, rippling gently in the breeze and reflecting sky, and I had to resist the strong (and probably dangerous) impulse to kneel down and drink deeply from it. Instead, I removed my canteen from my belt and took a few sips.

I walked slowly around the tree, marveling at its singularity, until I noticed something incongruous lying half-buried in the compost, something small and yellow and unnaturally straight. I crouched at the edge of the depression and pulled it from the soil. It was a pencil.

Specifically, it was an inch-long stub, the sharpened end blunted by use, the eraser end missing entirely. It was the kind of pencil you might find at a library, in a cup on top of the card catalog, or at a miniature golf course. It was aged by the elements, but not much: the process of its subsumation into the earth had only just begun, with the paint still largely intact and the wood only beginning to grow soft. As I had upon escaping from the pit, I stood up straight and looked around suddenly, as if someone might be watching me, assessing my reaction.

Of course, this was silly. The pencil might have been dropped here at any time in the past few years. It could even have been left by a crow. And while these woods were fairly remote from any large town, they lay bounded by paved roads, in the middle of an inhabited region of the state. In fact, I should have been more shocked, on this little expedition, *not* to have encountered some human artifact. But given my solitude over the previous twenty-four hours, and for that matter over the preceding several weeks, coupled with the alarm and injury I'd suffered in the pit, it was only natural that a hint of paranoia should once again steal over my consciousness. I chuckled at my all-too-human reaction and slipped the pencil into my pocket. Then I turned to the "ankle."

It was a monolithic chimney of solid rock, rising about seventy feet from where I stood; and while its face was hardly as imposing as the north face of the rock proper, it still presented a considerable challenge to the amateur climber. I breathed in and out, assessing its surface, plotting a path of ascent. Its angle was approximately seventy-five degrees, a not inconsiderable grade, but surmountable. The stone here had suffered more from the elements than its northern counterpart, giving me a distinct advantage, in the form of cracks, outcroppings, and ledges. I paced back and forth, examining the surface from every possible vantage point, and after ten minutes or so of consideration, a clear route presented itself to me.

I pulled on my gloves, changed into my climbing shoes, and fastened my helmet. After a moment's thought, I laid my pack down on the rock, next to the pine tree. Though I had filled it judiciously, to avoid excess weight, the pack was large, and its absence from my back gave me new confidence. I flexed my fingers, stretched my arms over my head, and took hold of a crack in the rock.

Within a few minutes, and despite my injuries, I had climbed twenty feet into the air. The hand- and footholds I had spied from the base of the wall had proved even more effective than I had dared hope; up close, the rock face was everything a climber could desire. I paused to catch my breath on an outcropping, and, with one hand wedged into a crack, I hazarded a glance over my shoulder. I had nearly reached the forest ceiling. Below me the pine tree betrayed a slight lean to the south; I saw my pack lying forlornly on the ground beside it. The sun was on me now, and I was sweating; the air would doubtless reach sixty degrees today.

But every moment I held on still required an expenditure of energy. And so I continued, finding a hold for my left hand and pulling myself up another few inches.

At this point the going became rough. The rock provided few handholds, and my fingers scrabbled over the surface, desperate for purchase. Several times I had to move back down, pull myself laterally across the face, and seek another route. I had one frightening moment when I was certain I would fall: what I thought was an outcropping on a ledge proved to be no more than a loose shard of stone, and I was thrown off balance when it broke away. But my other handhold was secure, and I suffered little more than a racing heart.

It took the better part of an hour, but soon I realized that I was near the top. The grade dropped off precipitously, and I was able to scurry up the last ten feet on all fours. The sun beat down, warming the weathered stone, and I collapsed upon it, grateful and exhausted. I had reached the summit.

When my heart had calmed and I was breathing easily, I took a sip of water and got to my feet. The view around me was indeed spectacular—but, as I had imagined, no more spectacular than the view from my window. I could see over the trees at last, all the way down the valley to the distant steeples, rooftops, and power towers of Gerrysburg. It was the loveliest day since I'd arrived, and it gave me special pleasure to be able to enjoy it here, on the rock I had eyed with curiosity for all these weeks.

I turned then to look back, to the west, toward my house. Even from this distance, its roof appeared dark and tidy, the edges straight, and I felt a sudden and surprising upwelling of pleasure at the work I had done. Perhaps it was my exhaustion and pain; perhaps it was the weather, or my emergence from the woods into the light—but the sight of that roof, peaked tightly against the cloud-studded blue, moved me quite nearly to tears. I took in a deep, grateful breath at my good fortune.

My mood thus buoyed, I began to walk around the summit, looking down into the woods below; and this is what led me to make a discovery that could only be regarded as astonishing. The summit was a slightly convex cap of smoothly weathered stone approximately fifty feet in diameter, and as I have said, I knew that the western face was a sheer cliff, and the southern a gentler slope, the "ankle" that led to the rock's "toe." I had not, however, yet explored the northern and eastern faces. I was pacing in a clockwise direction, beginning from the west, and so as I rounded the northern edge (more cliff, it would appear) I was able to peer over the eastern lip to the forest ceiling. Except that what I saw there was not that gently undulating sea of trees. Rather, I saw what first appeared to be a peculiar, peaked cap of stone. I stepped closer to the edge, eager to have a new stimulus for my troubled mind, and looked more closely. There was not one such outcropping, I observed; there were three, plus a fourth that was shaped like a box. They were all connected by a high stone wall, and were not natural formations at all.

I was, in fact, gazing down at the ruins of a castle.

EIGHT

It was, in its design, much like the fifteenth- or sixteenth-century castles popularly portrayed in movies and on television, with towers on three corners and a keep on the fourth, all connected by a curtain wall. Inside the wall, opposite the keep and pressed into the corner, stood a large stone building with small, barred windows; it appeared to open out onto an L-shaped yard with a rough flagstone floor. To the outside of the southern wall was attached a kind of vestigial barbican, which, in the absence of a moat, appeared to serve as a grand entrance. Of course, the entire thing was significantly smaller than a real castle—it was a reproduction in miniature, though quite large in comparison with a regular house. Were it to stand in an otherwise normal neighborhood, it would be perceived as a highly eccentric mansion.

Having given the castle a cursory examination, I revised my perception of it as a "ruin." Rather, the castle was unkempt—the flagstone yard was overgrown with shrubs and saplings, which partially concealed broken pieces of equipment made of wood and metal. The equipment gave the yard the appearance of a playground or outdoor gym now fallen into disuse. The crenellation of two of the towers was crumbling, with many stones missing, and the third, which stood over the main building, bore the remains of a conical slate roof, now caved in. For all that, however, the structure could be made habitable with a little bit of work, and for a moment I grew excited imagining such a project, the supplies I would need, the steps

I would take, the time it would consume to complete them. And then I remembered the survey map that had been included with the title abstract to the property, and the cryptic hole in the middle of it, beside the rock. I lay on my stomach and poked my head out over the edge. The castle's western wall had been built mere inches from the eastern cliff. There was no question in my mind. I did not own the castle.

I lay back on the rock, closed my eyes, and thought. The castle belonged to someone, and this person had been blacked out in the title abstract. The law office handling the land sale had not been able to locate the name, or had been unwilling to. Should I wish to purchase the remaining property, then, would I have to undertake a search for this person, to find out if he or she were still alive, or if the land had been passed on to family? The prospect of doing so made me uneasy.

The fact was, if I didn't own that plot, my work on the land would be incomplete. This was all the more true, given what I knew to be standing there. The "missing" land, and the castle, seemed to me like a sore, a wound, in my property; and a wound untreated could of course taint the flesh around it, could kill the entire organism. It bothered me greatly that Jennifer the real estate agent, and the firm of Barris and Haight, should subject my residence here to this impurity, this small corruption. I began to grow angry.

But then, I reasoned, what was the point? There was nothing to be done about it now. I took several deep breaths, clearing my mind of these dark thoughts, and decided instead to explore the castle.

My descent was no less challenging than my ascent had been—more so, even, as I was forced to look down to find the hand- and footholds. Luckily, I remembered more or less where they were, and so, with great care, slowly made my way to the bottom of the "ankle." I passed the little grotto, with its lone pine, and continued to the "toe," which I slid down without difficulty. I then proceeded around to the eastern face, where the castle stood.

It was quite cleverly concealed, I could see now, by a thick stand of pine trees, similar to the one on the rock. Even now, with the deciduous portion of the woods not fully in leaf, I could not make out the castle at all, until I was nearly upon it.

I reached the barbican first. It was the approximate size of a large garage, with two arrow-slit openings flanking a large, eight-foot wooden door. The door had not been fashioned to appear "old," but was clearly custom-made from very heavy timber, with crude iron strips holding the pieces together. Its hinges were as large as a man's foot, and they were heavily rusted, as were the enormous latch and padlock that held the door closed. I stepped up to this entrance and tried the handle. The door, of course, did not budge. Indeed, it might as well have been part of the wall, so tightly was it shut. I pushed my fingers into the cracks along the top and sides, and felt no jamb—the door had to be at least three inches thick! I moved aside a few feet and reached up toward one of the arrow slits. I could touch it, I discovered, only if I jumped. So I ignored my aches and pains and leaped, catching hold of the opening. Finding some purchase on the mortared stones with my climbing shoes, I scrambled up far enough to peer through the slot—but alas, there was nothing to be seen but darkness. The only indication that there was a room there at all was the scent of dampness and mold.

I dropped to the ground and continued to walk around the building. My impression of the curtain wall's great height had not been incorrect: it was twenty feet tall, and sheer, and no windows broke the uninterrupted surface. Only the towers and keep bore windows, and they were far too high to see into, except the few that framed a small rectangle of sky. Soon, I had made my way back to the rock on the north side, and I had seen no other point of entry.

It was at this time that I realized I was growing hungry, and that I had brought very little food with me—certainly not enough for a second night in the woods. The time was likely to be late afternoon, and the sun would not last long; if I wanted to leave for the house, the time to do so had come. I would eat some fruit and meat, and drink my water, and then begin to find my way back.

My pack, however, had been left behind, by the grotto. So I returned to the "toe" of the rock, clambered up once again, and walked in the afternoon sun to pick it up. I was astonished to discover that it was gone.

I closed my eyes, trying to remember precisely where I had left it. Unless my injuries had addled my mind, the pack had been lying on the northern edge of the grotto, in the shadow of the pine tree, half in and half out of the humus. I crouched at the spot and examined the ground: yes, the pack's impression was still visible, and several smears of soil trailed six inches or so in the direction of the "ankle."

When was the last time I saw it? I must have glanced down at the grotto as I was scaling the rock; surely I would have noticed had it been gone. It must have been taken while I was on the summit, perhaps during my few minutes of repose in the sun. Certainly, I was distracted by my discovery of the castle; the safety of my pack was the last thing on my mind.

What, then, had taken it? Though the forest had seemed to harbor very little wildlife, it seemed clear that the thief was an animal, drawn to the pack by the scent of food within. If this were the case, then the pack was probably not far away: the animal had likely dragged it to a sheltered area, forced it open, and taken the food, leaving the rest behind. Acting upon this deduction, I began to search the area, peering into each fissure on the rock's surface, and then, when this tactic proved futile, making a careful circuit of the edge, to see if the pack lay on the ground below. I found nothing. I then climbed down off the "toe," and made a careful examination of the surrounding ground, penetrating about fifty feet into the forest in every direction.

Forty-five minutes of concerted effort left me with nothing, and little sunlight remained for my journey back to the house. The time had come to give up the search. I drew a deep breath, and prepared to make my way out of the woods.

The most immediate consequence of my pack's disappearance was the loss of my boots, which had been tied to one of its straps. I was wearing, remember, climbing shoes, helmet, and gloves. I had stripped off my fleece jacket, as well, and stored it in the pack; and while I still wore a long-sleeved climber's shirt, the material was thin, and not very warm, out of the sun. I had to act fast, and find the road quickly.

It was then that I had an idea. The castle, mysterious as it was, had to have been built in a more or less conventional way. That is, supplies would have been needed: scaffolding, tools, mortar. The stones it was made of surely came from somewhere other than the woods—they had to have been purchased from a quarry and delivered by truck. So at some point, the woods must have been penetrable by such a vehicle. I knew, of course, that none of this area harbored old-growth forest. But there had to be a strip of land—a former road—where the forest was thinner than elsewhere. With this in mind, I once again walked around the rock, my eyes attuned, this time, to the ghost of a road.

And with the light dying behind me, I found it. It led east, a barely perceptible tunnel through the trees. Saplings had grown up through it, mature trees had fallen across it or leaned into it, but it was there, easy to miss unless you already knew it existed. Immediately I began to walk. The difference underfoot was obvious now: the ground was hard-packed and much drier beneath the leaves and branches, and the going was swift. In places, the road had veered to one side or the other, in order to avoid a particularly large tree or, in one place, a six-foot-wide boulder, presumably left here by the same glacier that had deposited the rock. But these diversions were minor, and the road righted itself easily after them.

The light in the forest, meanwhile, had dimmed to brown, then gray, and would soon be gone entirely. I picked up the pace, careful not to trip over some hidden obstacle, and just as I thought I could no longer walk safely in the dark, I found myself standing before a rise that gave way to gravel, and then pavement. I had reached Minerva Road.

As I stood on the road surface under a deep purple sky, all of the past two days' anxieties and injuries came crashing down upon me at once, and I felt a deep ache over every part of my body. My journey had proved far more dramatic and upsetting than I had anticipated, and had left me with more questions than I had when I embarked upon it. I turned once more to the woods, to mark the entrance of the former road. It was obvious, now that I knew it was there—the road was flanked by the trunks of two maples, each leaning toward the other, forming a kind of natural gate. The weeds and saplings between them had caused their significance, upon my initial circumambulation of the forest, to elude me. I would not forget them now. I sighed heavily, then turned south and began, under the darkening sky, my final trek back to the house.

It was full-on night when I felt the crunch of driveway gravel under my feet, and made my way to the front stoop. There was mail in the mailbox; this I removed, and I laid my hand upon the knob, and prepared to go inside. A hot bath was on my mind, a nutritious meal, and a warm, comfortable bed. I turned the knob, walked into the house, turned on the light, and shut the door behind me.

I stood there in the hall, perfectly still, for several minutes, listening. For what, I didn't know. In any event, there was nothing: not even a mouse or a rat, or a squirrel scampering across the roof. Only silence. After a minute had passed, I relaxed my muscles, let out breath, and headed for the kitchen. And at that moment, a tremendous *clank* sounded underfoot, and a thundering *whoosh,* and the house trembled, and I shouted, jumping into the air and dropping my mail all over the floor. I was pressed, terrified, to the wall, synapses popping in my head, when I realized that I had merely heard the furnace switching on. I slumped to the floor and rested my head in my hands. It had been a long two days.

With effort, I rose to my feet, went to the kitchen, and prepared a makeshift meal of fruit, cheese, and stale bread. I ate it with animal desperation, stuffing the food into my mouth and choking it down with large gulps of water. I hadn't realized how hungry I'd been. When I was through I fixed another helping, and then another. At last I was sated: time for a bath. I turned the thermostat down and paused at the foot of the stairs, again irrationally unnerved; and after chastising myself for my fear, I switched on the landing light and climbed to the second floor. I threw open the door to each room, to each closet, revealing nothing but stale air. I opened each upstairs window several inches, to let in the spring; then I drew my bath, undressed, and lowered myself into the heat.

I performed a long, indulgent wash, scrubbing my hands and upper arms with extra vigor, making certain that I was clean. When I was through, I dried myself, went to the bedroom, and put on my pajamas. I was exhausted and eager to sleep; and yet unease again crept over me. The bedroom window hung before me, the same I had gazed at from the summit of the rock that afternoon. High and uncurtained, ready to let in the light of dawn, it revealed nothing but blackness now. I went to it. The glass, reflecting the bedside lamp, was creased with age. I threw up the sash as far as it would go and looked out into the moonless night, trying to make out the rock. But it was invisible now, blending with the forest that surrounded it.

At last I closed the window and turned out the light. I ought to have dropped off to sleep immediately, as I had many times under far more stressful, indeed terrifying, circumstances, but instead I lay awake, listening to the silence. Every now and then a car or truck could be heard passing in the distance, but otherwise there was nothing, and the small sounds of the house as it cooled took on ominous significance. The rhythmic tick of the dormant furnace, slowing gradually, would give way at any moment to a deadly explosion; the old timbers settling against themselves creaked like the careful footsteps of an assassin.

And then another sound gradually impressed itself upon my consciousness, so faint at first against the ambient roar of the air in my ears that I wasn't even certain I was hearing it. It was a whine, as of air escaping through a narrow opening, a kind of keening, which gradually resolved itself into an intermittent animal cry. It was the sound of solitary despair, a high, drawn-out weeping, a noise made by a creature, man or beast, not to draw attention but to console the hopeless self.

I had heard this sound before, in the place I had worked before I came here, the sound of men without hope crushing their misery into a tiny space in the throat, from where they could not prevent it escaping, even in sleep. It chilled me, brought me fully back to wakefulness, and I sat up in bed, the covers falling from my bruised body. Where was it coming from? I held my breath, strained at the sound, but now, as if in response to my motion, it had seemed to stop.

A few moments later, I again lay down, and as the minutes passed, I became convinced that the sound was a product of my imagination. My eyes closed, my breathing slowed, and I felt myself pulled toward sleep. And then I heard it again.

I was certain it was there. I could feel a sympathetic cry gathering at the back of my own throat. It was human, this sound. It was real. I tried to isolate it in my mind, to shut out everything else, my heartbeat, the sheets against my flesh, the ringing in my ears. There was only the sound, and my perception of it. Where was it coming from?

Outside, I thought at first. Something, or someone, was outside, perhaps in the woods, suffering. I got out of bed, willing lightness out of my heavy body, slowing myself nearly to motionlessness. Five minutes until one foot touched the floor, five more for the other. Five minutes to cross the room and another five to open the window. I thanked myself for having sanded down the frame and replaced the sash: the pane slid up smoothly, without rattling or creaking. I leaned forward, poking my head out into the cool air, and listened.

Nothing but the slow and heavy wind, flowing through the trees. Had the crying stopped? I carefully pulled my head back in: no, there it was. It was in the house.

I paced across the room like a glacier, my bare feet sticking to the boards, then peeling off again. I reached the door, turned the knob, and pulled.

There. I could hear it more clearly now. A long, high, mournful wail, followed by a pause, as if to draw breath. I opened the door far enough to admit my body, then lifted my left foot and took a single step into the hall. In the deep quiet of the house, the creak the floorboards made was like a rifle shot. The crying stopped. I froze.

I remained frozen for five, ten, fifteen minutes. The sound did not resume. I let out breath. Where on earth had it come from? It was in the house, to be sure. I repeated my room-to-room search and again found nothing. The house was empty, and against all reason, I was more awake than I had been in days. What was more, I felt dirty again, my mouth sour and sticky, my underarms redolent of sweat. I went to the bathroom and took another bath, then brushed my teeth a second time. Afterward I returned to my bed, anticipating a sleepless night, and even reached out to turn on the bedside lamp. But my hand never made it. My body, evidently, had overruled my mind, and I dropped off to sleep without difficulty, and dreamed of nothing all night long.

NINE

The first thing I found when I came downstairs the next morning was yesterday's mail, scattered on the floor in the hallway. I remembered now that, frightened by the furnace, I had dropped it there the night before. Raising my eyebrows at my own foolishness, I gathered it up, then went to the thermostat and turned the heat back on. The furnace clanked to life. The sound was identical to the one that had so terrified me, but now of course it was no more alarming than the birds singing outside. I went to the kitchen, put a pot of coffee on to brew, and sat down at the table with my letters.

My credit card bill had arrived, bearing the costs of my home renovation. I was pleased to find them to be below my budgeted estimate. There were some papers from the bank, and tucked with them into the envelope, a promotional refrigerator magnet. I was surprised to see an official-looking letter from out of town, and after examining it for a moment, I chose to set it aside for the time being. There was also what appeared to be a card from my sister, and though I felt my face tense up as I took it in hand, I went ahead and tore it open.

The card bore a fairly innocuous reproduction of a painting of a twelve-point buck, backlit by a rising run, perched on a rock outcropping, majestic mountain terrain all around. As far as I knew, deer did not tend to stand high upon rocks—this was the purview of mountain goats and bighorn sheep, I thought—but the image was pleasant enough and enabled me to take a neutral stance to the card's contents.

Interestingly, though, it was not the substance of my sister's message that struck me most powerfully. The message itself was not noteworthy—she apologized for her cavalier attitude during her brief visit to my house and offered her emotional support and friendship for "dealing with your troubles," whatever that was supposed to mean—but the handwriting made me sit up and pay attention.

With the coffee maker burbling quietly behind me, I remembered the last time I had seen my sister's rushed, angular scrawl. It had been in her diary, which I had read when I was thirteen. There was a period of time when Jill had seemed to be sleeping somewhere different every night—at the homes of friends, no doubt so that she could have free access to the boys and men she was known to be having relations with at the time. I admit that I would often snoop in her bedroom when she was gone, in the precise hope that I would find her diary there. But until this particular night, she had always taken it with her to her sleepovers.

This time, however, she had forgotten, and I sat on the edge of her un-slept-in bed, reading as quickly as I could. And I had been right to rush, because she actually came home to get it, launching herself from the back of a car out of which loud rock music was blaring, and stomped up the stairs to snatch it from my hands as I read. She actually struck me, as I remember, and I struck back, and it took my exhausted mother to pull us apart. In fact I seem to recall my mother ending up on the floor, weeping, and me helping her up and leading her to bed.

But it was the diary itself that truly rankled, as it contained all manner of lascivious fantasy about my father, horrible desires and distasteful proclivities that she had invented for him, clearly to satisfy some deep, childish need to blame others for her own failings. Even at thirteen I understood this—Jill was always rather transparent, pathetically so, and God forbid that someone close to her should suggest that her actions were motivated by self-deception, or a need to relieve herself of responsibility for unfortunate things she had done. Of which, as I have said, there were many.

This is not to suggest that I regarded my father as a paragon of virtue. He was not—indeed, I would be the first to admit that he was deeply flawed, emotionally stunted, and of course extremely careless. But to make the insinuations my sister did in her diary was simply wrong, even if they were, ultimately, for her own private consumption.

Sitting there at my kitchen table, I was not especially happy to revisit these memories. I have already established that I am not one to live in the past, and I feel that the anger which results from recalling past injustices is among the most impure of emotions, and damaging to heart and soul. But it was not my sister's fault that her handwriting happened to bring these recollections to mind, and I had to admit that, misguided as they may have been, the words of her apology and offer of friendship were sweet, almost touching. And so I took the unusual step of affixing the card to the refrigerator with the magnet from the bank, if for no other reason than to inoculate myself against the effect her handwriting imposed upon my mind.

By now the coffee was finished, and I poured myself a cup. All that was left of the mail, aside from the official-looking letter, was a thin white envelope without any return address. My own address was neither typed nor printed, but written, in a neat, precise hand. I carefully opened it, and unfolded the single sheet of paper within.

The paper bore only three words, in the same hand as that on the envelope: *Doctor Avery Stiles.*

I had no idea who had sent me this cryptic message, but the sight of those words caused my stomach to turn over. I sipped my coffee, in order to calm it.

The handwriting was not one I recognized, and I cast about in my mind for whose it might be. There were very few people who knew where I lived—my sister, the employees of the real estate agency, the lawyer's office. Heph the electrician, Randall from the hardware store, Jeremy Pernice. And, of course, whomever those people might have told about me—though it seemed unlikely that my purchase of the house and land would qualify as gossip worthy information.

I studied the envelope and paper once more, and determined that the handwriting was liable to be a woman's. And after a few moments, I had it, or thought I did: it must be the girl from the law office, the one who had insisted that my land's previous occupant could not be identified. Perhaps she meant to indicate that Doctor Avery Stiles was that occupant! I got up, retrieved my land-purchase folder, and located the office's number.

"Barris and Haight."

"Hello, Andrea?"

"Yes?"

"This is Eric Loesch."

There was the slightest hesitation before she said, "Yes, hello, sir!"

"Andrea, I'm calling about Doctor Avery Stiles."

Again, a pause. "I'm afraid I don't know who you mean."

"I realize that you don't wish for your employers to know that you told me his name. But perhaps you could answer yes or no to a few questions."

The pause this time was longer, and when she spoke, her voice had changed. It was more pliant now. "All right," she said.

"This is the man whose name was blacked out on the title abstract?"

"Yes," came the muted reply.

"Do you know who this man is?"

"No . . ."

"Do you know why your employers wanted to keep this information secret?"

"I'm afraid not."

"Will you meet me," I asked, "to discuss this further?"

She sighed. "I don't know if that will be necessary . . ."

"You'll need to eat lunch. May I treat you?"

"No, I don't . . ."

"Or coffee. Or just a moment of your time. I'll tell you what. Meet me at 12:30 at the end of Jefferson Street, by the abandoned football field. You may stay in your car. I'll just pull up beside you. I just want to ask you some questions."

The wait for a reply was very long, this time, but her voice, when it returned, was resigned. "All right." And then, as if someone were walking by, she said brightly, "That will be no trouble at all!"

"I can't thank you enough, Andrea. I'll see you then."

"Goodbye," she said, and hung up.

Her car was there, a little red Volkswagen with a crooked front fender. She had parked on the side of the road just before it turned to mud, and was facing south, toward town, presumably to reserve the possibility of a quick getaway. Frankly, I was surprised. I had assumed that she had no good reason to meet with me, and expected to have to stop by the law office to draw the information out of her. I pulled up slowly, giving her a friendly wave as I approached. As if by reflex, she waved back.

We rolled our windows down. Her car was filthy from the April mud and rain, though the sun shone today, as it had during my adventure on the rock. Having the taller vehicle, I was forced to lean down to speak to her, and she to tip her face up.

By any standard, she was a lovely girl, with wispy blond hair framing a face the shape of an ash leaf. Her eyes were gray, and her small pursed mouth betrayed her nervousness, and perhaps a fierceness that I had not, to my surprise, detected over the phone. She was dressed for work in a silk blouse and woolen skirt, but was huddled inside a ski jacket, despite the warm weather. A small diamond glinted on her ring finger, and I wondered what kind of man had managed to catch her. I smiled and thanked her for coming.

"I don't have anything to tell you, really," she said.

I merely nodded, remaining silent. It is the rare interlocutor who can bear to leave a silence uninterrupted.

She let out breath and trained her gaze out the windshield of her car. A pop station was playing quietly on her car radio. "So yeah," she said.

I offered a gentle prompt. "Doctor Avery Stiles?"

She spoke without turning back to me, her voice full of resolve. "He was some kind of weirdo in the sixties," she said. "Like a psychologist? He taught at the college but then got kicked out. That's what they said anyway. I never heard of him."

"Who's 'they'?"

"My boss, Mark."

It was clear by her tone that she didn't like this Mark—her presence here, I could see now, was an act of rebellion against him. I chuckled gently, as though to suggest that we all knew a Mark or two, and that it was right to stick it to them.

"Why didn't he want me to know?" I asked.

Andrea turned to face me, a sour look on her face. "Beats me what his problem is," she said. Her voice, freed from the constraints of the workplace, was very different from the one she used on the phone—casual, and a bit crass. "I asked why it was blacked out on the abstract, and he looked at me like I ought to just keep my little mouth shut and mind my own business. He just said, 'Mr. Loesch doesn't need to know that.' So now I was curious, right? So I asked him why you didn't need to know. And he said, 'I'm sure he's well aware that the land used to belong to Avery Stiles.' And when I kept looking at him, he said, 'I don't know what Eric Loesch thinks he's doing out there, and I don't want to be involved in it.' And that's all he would say."

"Interesting."

It was she who remained silent now, gazing at me with annoyed anticipation. "So you don't know who this guy is?" she said, finally.

"No, I don't," I said.

"And you're not doing something weird out there?"

"No," I answered, though I was unsure what, in Andrea's view, would constitute weirdness. "Tell me something, Andrea," I went on. "Did it seem to you that your boss knew something about me? That he had some prior knowledge about my life?"

She thought about it a moment. "I guess so."

"But you don't know what, exactly?"

A note of anxiety had begun to creep into her voice. "What," she said. "Are you some kind of crazed killer?"

"Oh, I wouldn't say crazed," I joked.

Andrea, however, didn't find it funny, and her face betrayed a moment of real fear before she shifted, quite deftly, to her previous sour expression. "So can I go now?" she asked, feigning nonchalance. "Honestly, that's all I know about this."

"Yes, of course," I said. "You were good to come. Thank you, Andrea."

She wasted no time rolling up her window and driving away.

I allowed my car to idle while I considered her words. Her employer must have remembered the drama my family experienced when I was a young man, or perhaps he had heard something—doubtless something incorrect—about the more recent events I had been involved in. Either way, his suspicion of me was unjust, and his desire to distance himself puzzling. This was not the first time I had been unjustly accused, however, and it was unlikely to be the last. I decided to put this affront behind me, and see what more I could learn about the "weirdo" whose name Andrea had uncovered.

I drove to the Gerrysburg Public Library and parked in the lot beside it. I remembered the library well—when I was a boy, it had also housed a museum of local history, which had eventually been eliminated to make room for more books. The parking lot had been expanded at some point in the past, but the asphalt was cracked and patched now, with bits of it scattered around, heaved up by winter.

Inside, the library was much as I had remembered it, except that the card catalog was gone, replaced by a bank of computers. This transition had clearly taken place some time ago, however, because the computers were old, and two of the four bore handwritten placards reading OUT OF ORDER. There were also a pair of newer computers, above which hung a sign marked INTERNET. A dirty-looking man sat at one, playing video chess; at the other a teenage mother typed furiously while her baby slept in a nearby stroller.

I strode up to the circulation desk, where an old woman was using the telephone. She appeared to be calling patrons who had books on hold. I waited patiently for her to finish her conversation, and when she did, she looked up with an inquiring expression. She appeared energetic for her age—which I estimated to be about seventy—and her gaze was bright and clear.

"Good afternoon," I said. "I'm trying to find out information about a particular local resident, whom I'm told lived here in the 1960s."

"I've lived here all my life," the old woman said. "Perhaps I know this person."

"He was a psychologist named Avery Stiles."

The old woman's expression didn't change, but her focus seemed to deepen, as if she had ceased looking at my face, and was now trying to see what lay behind it. "I see," she said. "I do think I remember such a person. A bit of a radical, maybe? I seem to remember some trouble."

"I'm told he taught at the college."

"That may be so. Have you tried an internet search?"

When I said I hadn't, the librarian suggested I go wait for a computer to free up. Meanwhile, she would do a bit of low-tech sleuthing for me. I thanked her, then walked over to the computer area. A lone wooden chair appeared to have been designated the internet-waiting seat. Beside it stood an easel, and propped up on it, a hand-lettered list of rules. 30 MINUTES PER PERSON, read one. SILENCE MUST BE OBSERVED. NO OBJECTIONABLE INTERNET CONTENT.

I waited several minutes before the teen mother noticed me. She had been typing furiously, working on what appeared to be an e-mail, and peered furtively over her shoulder. Her expression was grim, her complexion wan and blotchy. On her cheek was a brown patch of the sort commonly associated with addiction to certain illegal drugs. I offered up a small smile, which the girl rebuffed, or perhaps didn't see.

A few minutes later, the girl closed the browser, got up, and grabbed the handles of the stroller. She stalked past me, her lips moving. I took her seat and reopened the browser.

Avery Stiles psychology, I typed into the search box. A list of hits scrolled down the screen. Most of these appeared to be false matches—someone named Avery, someone named Stiles, a mention of psychology somewhere nearby. But a few did indeed seem to be the Avery Stiles I was looking for. These were mostly class lists—archived information about graduates of various schools. Stiles evidently had attended the University of California at Berkeley and the University of Pennsylvania, where he received his doctorate in 1958. Another entry had him as an assistant professor at SUNY Milan the following year. Still another referred to "the sad story of Dr. Avery Stiles."

I clicked on this one and brought up the entire article. It was part of a recent paper written by a sociologist, a woman named Lydia Bulgakov, also of the local SUNY. The paper seemed to be a study of academia itself as a social system, and the various ways that students and professors could find themselves marginalized within it. The section that mentioned Avery Stiles was near the end, and was something of a summary; "the sad story of Avery Stiles" was alluded to casually, and without explanation, as if the reader was expected know what story Professor Bulgakov was referring to. There was no other such reference in the paper.

I was about to navigate back to my search results when I sensed someone's gaze, and I turned to find the chess-playing man leaning over, reading the screen of my computer. He was tall and thin, perhaps sixty years old, and wore enormous square-framed eyeglasses with thick lenses. Mostly bald, he nevertheless had let his gray hair grow quite long, and it hung around his head in a fringe. He appeared quite mad.

"Hello," I said.

He turned to me, squinting. His mouth hung open, and his eyes, magnified by the glasses, looked wounded, affronted, though not by me.

The man was certainly harmless; nevertheless, I found his gaze to be disturbing, and a strange unease spread over my body. I felt weak and slightly sick to my stomach. I asked the man if I could help him with something, and his only response was to turn abruptly back to his chess game.

Clearly there was nothing more to be said or done—this small incident was over. And yet I heard myself say, "I asked you a question."

The man's response was immediate. He froze, his hands poised over the keyboard, and began to tremble. I could see his eyes; they were darting spasmodically from side to side, as if he were receiving an electric shock. For some reason this reaction made me angry, and I dug in.

"When you've invaded someone's privacy," I said, "and then that person asks you a question about what you're doing, you are obliged to answer that question." My voice, I'm afraid, was quite strident; I was well aware that I was overreacting, but I felt powerless to stop. "I wanted to know if there was anything I could help you with. Is there?"

The man shook openly now; his aluminum-frame chair rattled beneath him and his head hung down over the keys. He was blinking, and his lips moved wordlessly.

"Answer me," I said, between clenched teeth.

"Sir?" came a stern voice.

"Answer me."

"Sir!"

I turned. It was the librarian. She was holding a small cardboard box in her hand, and her lips were pale and pressed tightly shut. She looked older than she had at the counter.

"Leave that man alone," she said. "He is doing no harm."

I stared at her.

"I found this for you," she said. "The information you want might well be here."

She held out her hand, and I accepted the box. She returned to the desk without waiting for thanks, and when she arrived there she glared up at me over the tops of her glasses.

The box contained a roll of microfilm. I closed the internet browser, stood up, and went to the back of the stacks, where the microfilm viewers were kept when I was young. They were still there, exactly as I remembered them, and both seemed to be in working order.

It took me several minutes to recall how the machines operated, but soon I had the roll of film installed, and pages of text and images were zooming across my field of vision. They belonged to the *Milan Times* newspaper, the only "local" paper Gerrysburg had ever had. This roll was from 1965, and after a few minutes of idly scanning the pages, I realized just how much there was to read, and how long it was going to take me. I heaved a deep sigh, and winced as the pain in my head flared up—I had a large bump, just above the hairline, from my fall into the pit two days before, not to mention my aching ribs—then I scrolled back to the beginning and began, methodically, to read every single headline.

1965 was a year of relative calm and prosperity in the area. There were, of course, war stories, but for the most part the paper focused on local news: businesses opening, a school renovation, a fire, a blood drive. As I read, I tried to remember what my own life was like then. A small child, I must have played outdoors, watched television, listened to adults talk. But nothing came to me. I could remember, vaguely, what my mother looked like—the chignon she wore in those days, and her tired beauty—but I could recall nothing specific. Indeed, the more I thought about it, the less I seemed able to remember. The earliest memory I could come up with was the one I have already mentioned, working in my father's shed and wondering about the box that contained his gun. But I was very nearly a teenager then. Surely there was something more.

I had to catch myself from falling into reverie—it was easy to lose focus, doing such dull work. In the end, though, it was during such a reverie, when I was gazing blankly into my past, or lack of it, through the still image of a random newspaper page, that I realized I had happened upon the information I'd been looking for.

It was an obituary, its headline no more than a single name: Mary Killian Stiles.

Mary Killian Stiles, 37, passed away Monday, at her home in Town of Henford. Mrs. Stiles was born in East Rutherford, New Jersey, and has lived in the Milan-Gerrysburg area since 1958. She is survived by her husband, Dr. Avery Stiles, a clinical psychologist and professor of psychology at SUNY Milan. She is predeceased by a daughter, Rachel.

TEN

There was no mention in the obituary of how Rachel Stiles had died. But it seemed to me that Doctor Avery Stiles's story was very sad indeed. I rewound the microfilm and turned off the reader, then went to the circulation desk to return the box to the librarian.

She accepted it and set it aside, then gazed at me with great seriousness over the top of her eyeglasses. "Don't you remember me?" was her question.

"It was you who gave me the microfilm an hour ago," I replied.

My answer seemed to take her by surprise. She smiled, and raised a single eyebrow.

"You're Eric Loesch, aren't you," she said.

"Yes, I am."

"I've been working here since you were a small boy," the librarian went on. "Your mother used to bring you here. I'm Mrs. Hill."

It was clear from her tone that she hoped this name would ring a bell. But it did not. I have never been comfortable with white lies, but the librarian had been helpful to me, and deserved my good will, so I smiled and took her hand. "Mrs. Hill!" I said. "I'm sorry I didn't recognize you. It's been a very long time."

"You wanted to build a moon base," she said. "I remember, all one summer, you couldn't have been more than seven or eight years old, all you wanted were books on engineering and space travel. I quickly ran out of books for you—I actually ordered more. Some of them are still here."

"I never knew," I said truthfully, "that you had gone to such lengths for me."

"I would talk with your mother sometimes, as you worked. I recall she said she had no idea where your brains came from. She said you were the smartest person she had ever known."

This came as a great surprise to me—my mother had never told me anything of the sort. I wondered, briefly, if this Mrs. Hill might actually be suffering from some kind of senile dementia, if perhaps she was confusing me with another patron. She asked me if I had been able to put my smarts to good use.

"Yes, of course," I said.

Now the old librarian averted her eyes. Her fingers found the countertop and drummed idly there. "Eric," she said. "I want to tell you how sorry I am for what happened to your poor parents."

Quite suddenly I wished to leave. "That's kind of you to say."

"I . . . I wish there was something I might have done. I considered your mother a friend."

"I'm sure she felt the same way about you, Mrs. Hill. But I really—"

"I knew that all was not right. But I didn't realize how terribly, terribly desperate—"

I brought my hand down on the counter with what I'm afraid was excessive force. The sound made the librarian jump, and I spoke perhaps more loudly than I had intended. "That's quite enough, Mrs. Hill!"

"I beg your pardon . . ."

"Thank you for your assistance with the microfilm," I said, and turned toward the door.

It was, then, the sight of the door itself—large, oaken, and divided into fifteen glass panes—that brought back to me the memory of coming to the library with my mother that summer, the moon landing summer. We would come here, and Mrs. Hill would bring my books to me, and I would make my plans in a marbled notebook, my plans for the moon base which I intended to send to President Johnson. And my mother would talk to Mrs. Hill, or read magazines, or go outside and smoke, and when it was time to leave we would walk through that heavy door, summer sunlight blasting through the panes, and walk to Pernice's and eat our ice cream cones in the park. We would sit side by side on a bench, and I would tell her about the work I was doing, about the science that I was trying to understand, and the wind would pick up her hair and blow it into my face, and she would laugh and tie it back behind her head. Or it was raining, and we would run from the library to Pernice's, and my mother would drink coffee and the rain would stream down the window beside her. My sister was off somewhere with her friends, my father was at work, but neither of them ever came up in our conversations; they weren't on our minds at all.

All of this I remembered as I strode toward that door, as I pushed it open and emerged into the cold wet April air. I crossed the parking lot in the rain, much as I had in memory, got into my car and started the engine and sat there, waiting for the heat to come on, to take the fog off the windows. It took a long time, and when I finally pulled out of the library parking lot, my face was still wet.

It was difficult to find anywhere to park at SUNY Milan. The buildings were low, and cracked cement was everywhere, and I struggled to find the visitor lot on the water-damaged campus map. Eventually I flagged down a passing university policeman and he told me where to go.

The department of sociology was housed in a long brick structure that resembled a passenger train, its wide windows tinted against the sun and sealed shut. The building directory hung just inside the double doors, and it led me to the far end, where the office I sought was located. PROFESSOR LYDIA BULGAKOV, a sign read, followed by a schedule. I read the schedule, glanced at my watch, and sat down in a nearby chair to wait.

An hour later, a figure appeared far down at the end of the hall and strode toward me on strong, compact legs. She was rather short, in her late forties, with broad hips, narrow shoulders, and a wide, round face surrounded by wild gray-black curls. A pile of books and papers was balanced in her arms. She appeared puzzled by my presence, and offered me an appraising glance as she drew a set of keys from a skirt pocket and unlocked the office door. I heard the thump of her schoolwork hitting a desk, and then her head appeared around the jamb. "You're here to see me?" she asked.

"Yes."

"Then come in."

The office was small but comfortable, with bookshelves concealing the cinderblock walls, and several table lamps filling the room with warm yellow light. Lydia Bulgakov sat down behind a large metal desk and gestured to a chair beside it.

"I thought you would be Russian," I said, taking a seat.

"I am Russian."

"Your English is unaccented."

She nodded. "My family immigrated here when I was ten. I have been told that my accent returns when I have had a glass or two of wine, but I suspect this is wishful thinking on the part of my acquaintances. And you are?"

I told her my name. "I have come to ask you about a former colleague of yours, a man named Avery Stiles."

She shook her head. "Not a former colleague. He was gone years before I came here. I was still a child, in fact."

I told her about the article I had found, and the allusion to his "sad story." I said that I had found his wife's obituary and wanted to know what other information she had about him. I asked her these questions respectfully, deferentially, as I sensed a certain self-confidence in Professor Bulgakov, a haughtiness even, which my usual methods of questioning, it was clear, would do little to penetrate.

Professor Bulgakov nodded, leaning forward. She was very serious, though I gathered that this was her general manner, and not a reaction to the subject at hand. She said, "My understanding is that, in the wake of his family's deaths, Doctor Stiles gradually withdrew from the university community, stopped publishing his research, and became difficult to understand. He had been working on operant conditioning, following some of the work of B. F. Skinner, but his research became strange and his funding evaporated. He was retired early after an incident with a student, and he left academia and apparently moved away."

She was an excellent speaker, curling her lips around each word as if she were tasting it. Her enunciation was precise. Clearly her late adoption of English had prevented her from taking it for granted; her speaking skills were a source of considerable pride.

"What kind of incident with a student?" I asked, trying not to appear too eager.

"A young man. He was a volunteer for one of Doctor Stiles's studies, and not long after his visits to Doctor Stiles's lab, he entered into a paranoid, delusional state and tried to kill another student. The young man later admitted that he had been taking LSD. But reporters also learned that he had been one of Doctor Stiles's test subjects, and they seized upon this detail, which subsequently captured the public's imagination. Once reporters realized what an eccentric Doctor Stiles was, they played up this angle, and he became known as a violent madman."

I asked if his studies were, in fact, violent or cruel. The question seemed to make Professor Bulgakov uncomfortable. She let out a small grunt and adjusted her position in her seat. "Perhaps," she said at last. "You have to remember what life was like during that era. The Holocaust was still recent history. The Vietnam War was under way. Experimentation with mind-altering drugs was a strong cultural theme. As far as I can tell, Doctor Stiles was working on depriving and confusing his subjects, removing them from their social context. He wanted to see how quickly a person could be broken down—how strong his personality actually was. I'm sure it will come as no surprise to you that many people can be broken down very quickly."

There was a silence as I digested what she had said. She settled back into her chair. Finally I leaned forward, placing my fingers on the edge of her desk. "What do you mean by that, exactly?" I asked.

She arched an eyebrow. "Well, the human mind, in spite—"

"No—you said, 'It will come as no surprise *to you*.'"

She stared at me.

"Why should that come as no surprise *to me*, Professor Bulgakov?"

"I'm sorry," she said. "I don't understand."

"I am wondering what you think you know about me that would make you believe that."

She appeared puzzled for a moment, perhaps in earnest, perhaps not. I realized that I was testing her, to find out if she were testing me. Perhaps, on some level, every human interaction was a psychological experiment.

"All I meant," she said slowly, "was that, in the wake of the sixties, and of our military adventures abroad, most intelligent people have absorbed the idea that none of us is ever very far from emotional collapse." When I offered no reply, she went on. "Our personalities are complex, but the animal instincts they conceal are stronger, and not very far below the surface." She met my stare and said, "Don't you agree, Mr. Loesch?"

"Yes, I do," I answered.

"You are dissatisfied with my explanation."

"No, no," I said. I must have appeared lost in thought, because I had been trying to figure out how Professor Bulgakov had learned my name. Had I introduced myself? Surely I had. But I couldn't remember.

Suddenly it was I who felt uncomfortable. I pulled back from the desk, rubbed my hands together, and stood up to leave. "Well," I said. "Thank you, Professor. You've been very helpful."

Lydia Bulgakov appeared surprised at my sudden change in demeanor. "By all means," she said, frowning.

I nodded once, then turned toward the door. As I was about to pass through it, she called out, "Mr. Loesch?"

"Yes?"

"Is everything all right? I hope I haven't given you some wrong impression."

"What kind of wrong impression?" I demanded.

She appeared to be about to answer, then let out breath and sank back into her chair.

"Never mind," she said.

I gazed at her for a long moment, by the end of which, if I was not mistaken, the faintest hint of disquiet had begun to creep into her face. It was then that I left, striding back down the hall the way I had come.

When I reached the exit, I turned for one last look. She was there, standing outside her office door, one hand on the jamb, watching me go.

Before I returned to the house, I stopped at the sporting goods and hardware stores, to replace the items I had lost on the rock. Luckily, the arrogant sporting goods clerk was not there, and I was able to buy a new pack and climbing supplies without another confrontation. But Randall was indeed working at the hardware store, and once again it was his checkout line I found myself in, with my new hatchet and folding saw.

"Well, how are you doing today, Mr. Loesch?"

"Very well, thank you, Randall." After a moment's consideration, I added, "You may call me Eric."

"All right then," he replied, placing my purchases in a plastic sack. He told me to swipe my credit card, and then he said, "Good thing we're being so friendly with each other, because there's something I want to ask you."

"What's that?" The cash register printed a receipt, which he added to my bag.

"Your name came up when I was talking to Heph the other day. He was wondering how you were doing out there on the hill. And it occurred to me, maybe you'd want to come down to the Amvets in Milan with us for a drink or three. We have a regular Tuesday-night thing."

For a moment, I was speechless. "That's very kind of you," I said at last. He handed me my bag. "So we'll see you tomorrow?"

That was not what I had meant, but I found myself agreeing. As I walked out the door, I wondered why. I did not want to socialize with Randall and Heph. I found Randall to be excessively assertive, even imperious; and Heph, though polite and amiable, hardly seemed interesting enough to be worth spending an evening with. This may sound rather stuck-up, but I am generally more than well enough occupied by my work, and do not require excessive social interaction.

Nevertheless, I had accepted the invitation. My susceptibility to social pressure embarrassed me. I sat behind the wheel for the second time that day, thinking of nothing, and it was only when someone pulled up beside me in the parking lot and peered at me through the window that I returned to myself and pulled away.

It was nearly evening now, so I stopped at a fast food restaurant and ate a cheeseburger in my car. My diet was poor, it was true, and my body was riddled with aches and pains. I had to get back onto a regimen. I wondered, not for the first time, what it would feel like to be old. Eventually, I supposed, no diet regime, no exercise regimen, would be able to obscure the passage of time. A day would come when I would not be able to repair a roof, or climb up the side of a mountain. And then climbing a ladder would become impossible, and then sanding a floor. And soon I would be helpless, and I would die. I found it difficult, however, to envision the circumstances of my death. Somehow, I could not imagine myself experiencing the kind every American hopes for—lying in bed, surrounded by family and friends, and slowly fading away into eternal rest. Indeed, the prospect seemed singularly depressing. Perhaps, if it ever became obvious that my death was imminent, and I still possessed the strength to control it, I should end my own life.

The cheeseburger sat uneasily in my gut, and I scolded myself for my indiscretion. What on earth was the matter with me?

By the time I reached the house, the sun was going down and cold had returned. I parked, climbed the front steps, and walked through the door into the darkness of the front room. I had set my bags of supplies down on the floor and was reaching for the thermostat when I experienced the same creeping unease of the night before, prompted by some faint noise from upstairs. I was convinced that someone was inside my house.

I didn't hesitate and allow fear to take root. Instead I sprang into action, climbing the steps two at a time, flipping the light switches as I went. The hallway exploded into light, and I ran from room to room, illuminating everything and throwing open the closet doors. But, as before, there was nothing. The closets were empty of all but my possessions. Beneath my bed was only dust. I did discover that I had left my bedroom window open an inch or so—perhaps a draft had been causing the door to bang against its frame while I was out.

Frustrated and exhausted, my body throbbing from my injuries, my mind racing with the day's uncharacteristic social interaction, I stumbled into the bath and, soon after, fell into bed. I dreamt with unusual intensity. A girl appeared in the bedroom doorway, long black hair framing a pale thin face. She was illuminated by a cold light without any clear source, and wore a thin nightgown of plain cotton. She could not be more than twelve years old, and I understood her to be Rachel, Avery Stiles's daughter, who had been mentioned in his wife's obituary. When she turned to leave, I followed her down the stairs and into the yard: she crossed the threshold of the woods and disappeared. Realizing that she was in danger, I gave chase. The nightgown flashed between the trees. I was quite naked; branches scratched and gouged my bare skin. I heard the girl scream, and came at last to a hole, a pit like the one I had fallen into—but it was far deeper, too deep to see into. I began to climb down, calling the girl's name, as I groped with my toes for footholds in the crumbling dirt.

At last I fell, tumbling some great distance before striking the ground flat on my back. I looked down and saw the sharpened branches jutting up through my ruined body, slick with blood, and when my head fell back I found Rachel standing above, on the edge of the pit, gazing at me with empty eyes. I woke on the bedroom floor, my head throbbing, a scream curled in my throat.

It was still night. I lay, naked on the cold wood, until my heart and breath had slowed. I felt as though I hadn't slept at all. With effort I hauled myself to my feet. Through the window came the glow of the moon behind the house; the landscape was edged with silver, the trees and rock etched against the starry sky. I am not deeply moved by beauty, and in fact may even be incapable of appreciating or even recognizing it. But there was a profound rightness to the scene outside, a natural order that the unseen moon seemed to emphasize with its clinical light. I could admire this, the ability of nature to create order out of chaos, and I stood in the window, coexisting with it, feeling some small part of it, for long minutes. Not a thought was in my head, and my dream was already half-forgotten.

But it came back to me with terrifying force when I looked down into the yard and noticed a white shape lying curled in the grass.

It was hard to make out, there at the edge of the woods, in the shadow of the house; but it had the appearance of a twisted white sheet. Could it be her? I wondered. Could the girl, the dream, have been real? I ran down the stairs, out the door, across the parking lot. The gravel scoured my bare feet and the cold air shocked my bare skin, and I made my way across the yard, the white blur looming closer.

Even when I was upon it, I couldn't tell what I was looking at. I crouched down and reached forward, expecting to feel the soft cotton of the girl's gown, her lifeless body beneath it. Instead, what I felt was bristly, coarse, like a woolen rug, and still warm, though no life was evident. In a moment, I understood. I jerked my hand away, stood, stepped back.

It was lying on its side, its legs splayed out against the grass, its head thrown back. The dead eye gleamed. It was the white deer, pierced through the heart with an arrow.

ELEVEN

At first I assumed the arrow to be a sportsman's. But when I touched it, and felt its irregular, planed smoothness, I realized that it had been handmade, from a whittled twig and what appeared, in the moonlight, to be crow's feathers. The shot was excellent—it had struck directly between the creature's ribs. There was little blood, just the barest stain around the wound, far less than one might expect from an animal with its heart pierced, and I wondered if perhaps the hunter had treated the arrow with poison.

And how had the deer come to rest here, at the edge of my yard—and why? It couldn't be chance that led it here; its presence could only have been deliberate, a signal to me. I knew now with certainty that my pack had been stolen by a human being, not some hungry animal. I stood and scanned the impenetrable treeline. Was this hunter, this thief, watching me now? My flesh rippled with fear and disgust, and I felt, for the first time, utterly exposed.

I mastered myself, however, and went back inside with slow, deliberate steps. I dressed. It was a quarter to four—sleep, it appeared, was finished with me for the night. I went out the back door, grabbing a shovel from the vestibule, and returned to the white deer's corpse. In the few minutes I'd been away, it seemed to have deflated somehow, its one visible eye sunken, its fur lusterless. The body had cooled. With another glance at the treeline, I took a few steps back and sank the shovel into the sod.

The soil here was clayey and resisted the blade, but I had faced far greater challenges, and persisted in my work. In an hour I had made consider-able progress, and when dawn arrived, the hole was dug. I went inside and drank a glass of water, then returned to the grave. I wiggled the arrow: it was stuck fast. After a moment's thought, I went back to the kitchen, found a pair of rubber gloves, and put them on. I then removed my new knife—it had replaced the one stolen over the weekend—from my new pack, and carried it outside. I made several cuts in the deer's flesh, radiating away from the arrow's shaft, and in time I was able to wiggle the weapon free. I held it up before my eyes. The tip appeared to have been fashioned from scrap metal—stainless steel, it seemed, perhaps from an old kitchen knife. It was roughly cut, and uneven, but the blade itself had been care-fully whetted and was clearly very sharp. I brought it inside, rinsed it off under the faucet, then left it to soak in a mixture of hot water, dish soap, and bleach. I would scrub it more carefully later, using a brush—I didn't want to risk the same fate as my deer.

Back outside, I took two of the animal's hooves in my hands and dragged it into the grave. I'd dug the hole three feet deep, and hoped this would be enough to discourage scavenging creatures. I shoveled the dirt back on top, tamped it down again with my feet, and replaced the sod. The mound was considerable and would likely remain so for a long time.

I completed my cleaning of the arrow, then sat down at the kitchen table to examine it. It was, to be sure, a peculiar artifact. The maker had found a remarkably straight twig, cut it to a length of thirty-six inches, stripped it of bark, and sanded down the knots, perhaps with a rough stone. He had care-fully split several crow's feathers, slotted the shaft, and inserted them with impressive straightness, apparently without glue. The same was true of the tip, which, as I had surmised, was made of a kitchen knife—the beginning of the word JAPAN was actually visible, engraved on one side—cut to the shape of an elongated chevron and ground to a stunning sharpness. A very small, crude hole had been bored in the shaft and through the blade, and a precise little peg had been fitted to hold the metal in place. I tugged at the tip, but it would not budge. The arrow was solid.

I set it down on the table and considered. Clearly, anyone who lived in this area would have no trouble buying as many arrows as he wished. Indeed, I had admired the bow-hunting supplies at the sporting goods store, and briefly considered buying some for myself. It was possible, of course, that the arrow maker had little money. But surely even a poor sportsman would have access to tools? The arrow appeared to have been made entirely out of found materials, and the tiny peghole, while effective, was too rough to have been made with a drill.

There was one obvious explanation, which had first occurred to me while I lay, bruised and stunned, at the bottom of the pit: that somebody was living in the woods. I had previously assumed that, if this had ever been true, it was certainly not true now. But I could deny it no more. Someone was in the woods—in the castle, quite probably—and this person had dug the pit, stolen my pack, and killed the white deer. Furthermore, it was possible that this person was the same man who owned the land to the east of the rock—the vanished psychologist, Doctor Avery Stiles.

On the face of it, the theory seemed ridiculous. A mad doctor, hiding out for thirty years in an abandoned castle? But the facts lent themselves to this strange explanation, and I had to assume, in the absence of conflicting evidence, that it was correct. Of course, Doctor Stiles would be quite old by now—nearly eighty, in fact—and it hardly seemed reasonable to think that such an elderly man could survive alone, particularly in the harsh winter climate of the region. Nevertheless, no better explanation presented itself. A crazy old man was living in my woods, and did not appear to want me around. These were the facts, and, as such, had to be dealt with.

Randall had not indicated a time to meet him and Heph at the Amvets. I assumed that this meant they would be spending quite a long time there, so I decided not to worry about being punctual. After a bath and a long nap, I went into town for dinner. I was still disgusted with myself for having eaten the fast food cheeseburger the day before, and vowed to find more nourishing fare; after driving around Milan for a good twenty minutes, I believed I had found it in a small, tidy restaurant called Vegan Delights. It occupied an unlikely corner of a parking lot that primarily served a dilapidated shopping center, and looked more like a gas station than a health food establishment, but I found several appealing items on the menu and ordered one without significant consideration.

The place was sparsely patronized by scattered collections of hippies and loners, who thoughtfully chewed their food without saying much to one another. There had been a time in my life when I had reacted to such people with deep disdain. In those days, I viewed pacifism and activism as expressions of cowardice, and had even gone so far as to pick fights with anyone who espoused such radical ideas. Indeed, I considered such people inherently, and willfully, weak—and believed that their political views were merely a convenient means of justifying their weakness. Eventually I would learn that all human beings are inherently weak, and that our efforts to overcome that weakness are little more than pathetic sallies up the face of an impossibly high mountain. As a result, I came to a somewhat more nuanced understanding of "alternative" lifestyles. But I was still uncomfortable in the presence of such people, finding them unreasonably indulgent of their frailties. Furthermore, I could feel their judgment of me: doubtless they found my trim profile, stern bearing, and unwavering gaze discomfiting. The people here tonight, however, appeared focused on their food and on one another, and I was left in peace.

Eventually my waitress, an attractive, dreadlocked young woman with hairy underarms, brought me my falafel, and I ate it while reading the day's paper, a used copy of which had awaited me in the booth. The paper was filled with inconsequential things—businesses opening or closing, town council meetings, births and deaths. I wondered, idly, why most people were so disconnected from world events, why they only seemed to care about those things that affected them directly, rather than those with broad consequences. But then again, I thought, I myself had lately been guilty of this same self-absorption.

I sighed, picking at the remains of my food. The waitress returned, asking if I was still working on it. I told her I was not. I paid, and left.

It was not exactly on a whim that I decided to visit the sporting goods store again; the possibility had lodged itself in the back of my mind earlier that day, I was burying the white deer. I pulled into the parking lot at a quarter past eight. The store was mostly empty save for its employees, who were obviously preparing to close for the night. Nevertheless, I walked to the gun counter and told the woman working there that I wished to buy a handgun. Her chin creased in distaste—the necessary paperwork would keep her here past closing. But she capitulated.

"What are you looking for?" she asked me. She was about forty, sandy-haired, with a flat, unfriendly affect. I felt very comfortable dealing with her.

"A Browning nine-millimeter," I replied. There were better firearms, but it was the Browning I was used to.

She showed me what they had: a used P-35 Mark III, and a new HP-SFS, with its improved safety. The P-35 was unadulterated by its previous owner, which was good news—I preferred to customize my own weapon, and smooth operation of the Browning required certain modifications. I told her without hesitation that I would take it, and filled out the proper papers. I was finished by closing time.

"Well that was easy," the clerk said, with obvious relief. "We'll give you a call when the check comes through."

"Excellent," I replied.

I left the store feeling much more safe and secure, even though I didn't have the Browning yet. It was the feel of it in my hand; in spite of its flaws, or perhaps because of them, it filled me with confidence. I thought of my father's Enfield then, and wondered if it had made him feel the same way. Of course, in reality, the gun did not make him safer—on the contrary, it was the instrument of his death. But I was not my father.

The Amvets was exactly where it had always been, and appeared not to have changed since I was a child. It was a low, long structure with a peak-less roof that sloped back toward the parking lot; there were no windows, save for a wall on one end made almost entirely of glass blocks. It was beside this wall that I found Randall and Heph, occupying one end of a large buffet table, along with three pint glasses and two pitchers of beer, one full, one nearly empty. They waved me over and, before I arrived, shared a hearty laugh.

"We had a bet goin', didn't we, Randy, on whether or not you'd show up, Mr. Loesch!" Heph smacked his dungaree'd knee.

"What side were you on, Heph?"

"Welp, I thought you would come! Randy thought not."

Randall offered his large, dry hand to be shaken. I obliged. "Glad you decided to join us," he said.

"Me too." I turned to Heph. "Heph, you should call me Eric, if we're going to be friends."

"All right then, Eric!" The entire exchange appeared to amuse him no end. I could see that he would make a fine drinking companion.

I sat down and poured myself a glass of beer, offering to pay for my share. The offer was quickly refused. I listened to the two of them for a short while; they talked about bass fishing. Eventually the discussion turned to local matters, and I revealed that I had, in fact, grown up in the area, which they did not appear surprised to learn. This led to the subjects of childhood pursuits and shared acquaintances. I was not especially helpful with the latter, as my family had not had strong social connections here, and as I was a number of years younger than Randall and Heph. But we knew of certain names in common, and discussion was lively until, at last, it petered out.

In the silence that followed, I watched a pair of headlights rake across the glass block wall. When I looked up at my companions, they were exchanging a meaningful glance. They saw me noticing, and quickly turned away.

"Randall. Heph," I said. "It's clear there's something you'd like to discuss with me. Though I'm flattered you wanted me to join you tonight, I never doubted that you had an ulterior motive. What is it?"

Heph seemed abashed by this little speech, but it appeared to give Randall some resolve. He sat up a little straighter and said, "Well, we know about all that happened to you. And we just want to let you know we're behind you, that's all."

To be perfectly honest, I had imagined this would come up. I was not, however, interested in discussing it. "That's very kind of you," I said.

"So it was you then, was it?" Heph said suddenly. "Randy said he was reading up on the internet and all that. Seemed to me there's gotta be other people called Eric Loesch in the army, right?"

"No," I admitted. "That was me."

Randall was gazing at me with a strange intensity now. I turned my beer mug around and around on the tabletop.

"You're not drinking your beer," he said.

"I'm not much of a drinker," I replied.

"Ahh, on the wagon. Sorry about that."

I said nothing, though his characterization was not entirely accurate. I did not have a drinking problem from which I was recovering. I simply did not enjoy excessive indulgence in alcoholic beverages.

Heph spoke up, to fill the lull in conversation. "Welp, anyway, it's you then. I'll tell you, son, I think you got a raw deal. Seems to me none of that was your fault. You were just following orders, right? You were doing what had to be done."

"I suppose so," I said.

"People on the outside don't understand what it's like," Heph went on. "They think it's all black and white! There's bad and there's good and nothing in between! But it isn't like that, now, is it! It's hard making decisions in a time of war, and when push comes to shove you gotta do your job and you gotta show the enemy who's boss, don't'cha think, Randy?"

Randall nodded slowly. He appeared to be slightly ill at ease after Heph's little speech. For my part, I realized that I would be forced to leave. There was no way to carry on with the conversation, now that this subject had come up, and I began, in spite of myself, to shift uncomfortably in my chair.

Fortunately, or perhaps unfortunately, an excuse for leaving would soon present itself. Only a few seconds of awkward silence had elapsed when I began to become aware of the health-food meal in my stomach, and the fact of its not having yet been digested. It had been quite some time since I ate; the meal ought to have been well on its way through my system. Instead, it was threatening to make a dramatic return.

"Gentlemen, would you excuse me a moment?"

Randall and Heph replied with grim nods as I rose, then walked, then walked faster, to the men's room. I pushed open the door of a stall just in time to expel my dinner into a filthy, waste-encrusted toilet. A few moments later I was washing my face with scalding hot water from the chipped and stained porcelain sink, and shivering uncontrollably. My stomach, though empty, turned over, and I returned to the stall for another round of painful release.

When I emerged at last into the bar, Heph and Randall looked up at me expectantly. "I'm sorry," I said. "I seem to have come down with something."

"You look like you just saw a ghost in there," Randall remarked.

"It was the ghost of my dinner," I managed to quip, and their laughter went some way toward smoothing over the discomfort of the moment. I thanked them again for inviting me out, and walked unsteadily to my car.

Twice on the way back to the house I was forced to pull over and endure a series of dry heaves. The shivering intensified, and it was only through the sheer force of will that I was able to keep my hands steady on the steering wheel. I staggered into the house, up the stairs, and into bed, where I began what was to be several days' discomfort and delirium.

I remember little of those days. Sometimes it was light outside, sometimes it was dark. At times I slept as though dead; at other times I rolled in my reeking, sweat-stained sheets, in an agony of nausea and pain. My head throbbed, my throat burned, and my belly ached from its exertions. At first I imagined that I had contracted some foodborne illness, but my body barely seemed to notice that the food was gone. Clearly, then, it had to be some kind of severe flu. Light exploded behind my closed eyes; I buried my head beneath my pillow, in fear of the sun. I must have managed to take some aspirin, because the almost-new bottle was half-empty by the time I came out of it; twice I woke from cramped sleep laid out on the bathroom floor. I also tried to bathe—I would wake up one night trembling in a tub full of freezing water, which I had no memory of having drawn.

When at last I came out of it, it was late afternoon, and a wind thrashed my bedroom window. I was surprised to find myself climbing out of bed to look out: the eastern sky was dark with roiling clouds, and the gusts carried a light rain that clattered against the pane like thrown gravel. I mustered enough strength to open the window an inch. The wind shouldered in, spattering the sill, and my hands upon it, with rain. Warm rain—a warm wind blowing warm rain. Relief spread through me. I was well again, and warm weather had arrived. Outside, the roof of the forest roiled like a sea, and the sunlight streaming from behind the house cast its long, strange shadow against the trees.

I shut the window and drew deep breaths there in the small, empty room. I could smell it now, my bed, my body: the sickness was gone, but its sourness, its stale spoor, was left behind. Shivering with hunger and weakness, I gathered up my filthy sheets and took them downstairs to wash; then I returned to the bathroom and bathed, scrubbing the past few days away. I dressed, went to the kitchen, and prepared myself a piece of buttered toast with trembling hands.

The toast was perhaps the most delicious food I had ever eaten in my life. The bread, thick and chewy, was flawlessly browned and crisped; the crust had been roasted nearly to burning, and it flaked off onto my tongue, releasing a full, rich, smoky roundness. The butter was sweet and half-melted, and I could feel its oily essence penetrating me, lubricating long-rusted synapses, opening up my mind and my senses after so many days of disuse. The toast was gone in seconds, and I made another piece, and a third, and a fourth, devouring them with robotic efficiency as I leaned against the kitchen counter.

Soon I was sated. But I felt no particular motivation to move. The washing machine churned and knocked in the laundry nook, working away at my bedclothes, and the afternoon sun blasted through the tiny window above it, bathing the kitchen in diffuse, blinding light. I was alone, and free to do as I pleased—and yet a strange emotion had begun to steal over me, a familiar one, that of being trapped, tested, manipulated. Scraped clean by my brief illness, I could hold up this emotion and examine it as though against a plain, uncluttered ground: in isolation, objectively. And I was given to wonder, had there ever been a time in my life when I had not been a pawn of those more powerful than I? My father, my teachers, my commanding officers? Indeed, was it even possible to live otherwise? I say this not to relieve myself of responsibility for my failings, for it was clear that, if I had always lived under the sway of the powerful, I had done so voluntarily, even eagerly. There is no comfort like the comfort of following orders. There is no relief like being relieved of agency.

In the midst of my drama of the year before, I was repeatedly counseled by my JAG attorney on the subject of what I should say during the hearings, which information I should volunteer, which I should keep to myself. I was coached at great length on how to tell my story so as to cast myself and my superiors in the best possible light, and at the time I regarded this advice as invaluable, and followed it to the letter. Indeed, the advice was correct, insofar as I was merely reprimanded and put on indefinite leave, and I ought to have felt gratitude and relief, and been proud to have made the best of a bad situation.

But then, as now, I felt this strange emptiness, this negation of self, as though there were some other course of action possible, one that might have produced a more satisfying outcome; and this possibility hounded me through my days of waiting and worry. Unfortunately, however carefully I considered and reconsidered my circumstances, I could not think of what this other course of action might be. Every day I was assured, both by my lawyer and by my commanding officer, that everything would work out fine, and the tacit assumption, which no one seemed to question, was that everything working out fine was what we all wanted. For what defendant, facing the accusations I faced, would not desire such an outcome? To be exonerated and set free in the world, to live at last in peace and quiet.

Today, in my newly renovated house, on the remote swath of forest that was mine and mine alone, I could not think of any better outcome. And yet I felt this uncertainty. That I might have assumed control of my destiny. That I might have defied my betters. That I might have saved my parents, or remained close to my sister, or averted the unfortunate circumstances that led to this drastic change in my relationship to the army.

The washing machine stopped, and I transferred my sheets to the dryer. I drank a glass of water, and stared out the living room window at the now-setting sun. When the dryer was finished, I tried to replace the sheets and blankets on my bed, and somehow, the act of stretching the fitted sheet over the mattress—tucking the fabric under each corner and smoothing down the wrinkles and folds—managed to drain every last bit of energy from my body. I fell onto the mattress and did my best to haul the bed-clothes over myself, but it didn't matter. Despite the early hour, I was asleep within minutes.

I awoke in darkness. The glowing digits of my bedside clock were miss-ing, though I could barely discern its outline looming there beside my head; I must have unplugged it by mistake while I was making the bed. And clouds must have moved in to cover the moon, because its light was missing from the sky, save for the faintest glow emanating from the mist.

What had roused me? I was entirely awake and alert. I closed my eyes and strained to hear.

There—the scrape of metal, faint and muffled, as though from some distant part of the house.

I stood up, gulped a breath, and held it. My blood rushed in my ears.

I heard it again, and this time I recognized it—the rusty steel doors that led to the backyard from the cellar. Something was trying to get in.

I considered racing down the stairs, in an effort to intercept this intruder. But something led me to the window instead, the one that faced north, the same side the cellar door was on. I parted the curtains and thumbed open the lock, and as I reached down to pull up the sash, I heard the clatter of the open door against the stone abutment that supported it.

It was, as I have said, very dark. But in the faint light of the cloud-covered moon, I could make out a figure, climbing up the cement stairs and into the yard. It was not an animal, but a human figure, and before I could discern any of its features, it vanished into the shadows of the trees. I could make out some motion in the murk—the figure was headed for the forest edge.

Without hesitation, I spun from the window, dashed down the stairs, and threw open the door. In moments, I had arrived at the treeline, in the general area where I believed the figure to have disappeared. I remembered very clearly the impassible and quite hazardous deadfall that lay all over the forest floor, and my own struggle to penetrate more than thirty yards into the trees around my house. The night was cold, and I wore no shoes—to forge ahead would be foolish. Instead, I leaned in, my hand braced against a maple, and called out, "Who's there!" I could see nothing—the darkness in the woods was total.

There was no reply. But I heard the rustle of branches. Against my better judgment, and with careful, halting steps, I moved past the tree into the blackness.

"Hello! Who are you!"

The forest was anechoic, and swallowed up my voice as neatly as a black hole. Nevertheless, I could still hear the intruder somewhere up ahead, the humus crunching under his feet.

His feet—for who else could it be?

"Doctor Stiles!"

Now the silence was deeper, longer, and pregnant with meaning. I waited one, two long minutes. And then, at last, I was rewarded with the sound of a footstep. Just one, and perhaps I was deceiving myself, but I believed it to be a step toward me. He could not have been far away, twenty feet at the most. Alarmed, I backed up, pressing myself against a tree— surely he was better equipped than I, this night, for a fight.

But his next step was fainter, and the next after that was fainter still. And soon it was clear that he had chosen not to return. I listened as the intruder retreated farther and farther into the trees. How he navigated the treacherous ground, I could not begin to imagine; but, like a creature of the forest, he moved quickly, and soon I couldn't hear him at all.

Nevertheless, I stood there several minutes more, perfectly still; and I might have lingered even later, had I not felt, quite suddenly, the horrible totality of the blackness around me. I may as well have been in the cellar, or some dungeon or cave, for all I could tell; and when I turned to leave I realized that I could not see out of the woods any better than I could see into them, and for a moment I believed I was lost.

But no. I mastered myself, and moved forward, back the way I came, my hands out in front of me, groping for obstacles. And a minute later I found myself in the yard once again, standing over the grave of the white deer; and a minute after that I was back in my moonlit kitchen, panting from the effort of the chase.

It was then I noticed that the rock I used as a doorstop had been shoved aside, and the door to the cellar hung open. The stairs led crookedly down into the darkness. Unnerved, I quickly shut the door and replaced the rock. The intruder, I understood—and it was he, Doctor Avery Stiles, I was certain—had come into the house. I cast my eyes about, trying to discern why he had come, and it was not long before I found the answer. It lay on its side in the center of the kitchen table, an object the size and shape of a box of large wooden matches. I reached out, picked it up, and held it in my hand.

It was cool to the touch, heavy for its size. Its cast metal surface was black, the paint chipped and scratched by years of careless handling. The sight of it, its weight, seemed familiar, infecting me with a vague, gnawing unease. It was, in fact, a toy—a miniature locomotive.

TWELVE

Whatever the true meaning of this cryptic object, its general intent was clear. It was a taunt—perhaps even a threat. "Look what I was able to do," the intruder was saying. "If I'd wanted to kill you, I could have." I suppose I ought to have been grateful that I wasn't murdered in my sleep. But instead, I became angry. Stiles might still have owned his little square of land behind the rock, but the rest of it, the rock itself, and this house were all mine now—fully, and as dictated by the law. If he felt that I was trespassing, somehow, on property he still thought of as his own, well then, perhaps he oughtn't to have sold it to the state. In any event, these disturbing games would not intimidate me. Indeed, I did not intend to sit still, idly waiting for his next sortie against my home, my land, and my hard-earned sense of personal well-being. If he wanted to taunt and threaten, then I could play the same game. I could deliver a threat of my own.

Thus resolved, I was tempted to gather my supplies and leave for the woods at first light, but I knew better than to undertake a difficult task while under the influence of strong emotion. Instead, I sat down at the kitchen table and made a detailed list, based upon my previous expedition, of what I might need in order to ferret out and neutralize this threat. When I was through, I lay in bed until daylight in a futile effort to sleep; in any event, I was able to get a bit of uneasy rest. By 7:00 a.m. I was showered and behind the wheel of my car.

Spring was certainly in the air on this clear, breezy day. Though the temperature was barely above freezing when I left the hill, the sun had driven the thermometer to forty-five by the time I reached Milan, and as I walked into the grocery store I felt a balmy gust sweep in from the southwest. Without a doubt, today's journey into the forest would be different—I knew the way in now, and I knew where to seek my quarry.

It was 8:00 a.m. by the time I had gathered what provisions I needed, and a quarter past when I reached the sporting goods store. The store didn't open until 8:30, so I parked about a dozen spaces away from the entrance and waited.

A few minutes later, a dented Ford Taurus spotted with primer pulled up a few spaces closer to the store. The door opened and the sandy-haired gun counter clerk stepped out. She went to the entrance of the store, pulled a key ring from her pocket, and let herself in. A few minutes later, the other employees arrived as well, and a few minutes after that, one of them appeared at the door and unlocked it. A sliding panel in the plastic business-hours chart slid aside, revealing the word OPEN. I got out of my car and went in.

I walked slowly through the store, passing down almost every aisle, to make sure I hadn't forgotten anything. In the clothing section, I chose a cap, shirt, jacket, and pants in forest camouflage. Then I approached the gun counter. In the glass case underneath it, I could see the Browning P-35 that I had chosen the week before. The clerk looked up with an expression of guarded friendliness, which dissolved into worry and discomfort as she recognized me.

"You remember me," I said.

"Mr. Loesch, hello."

"I'm surprised that I haven't yet heard from you."

She turned, pulled open a file drawer behind her, and removed a folder. "No, sorry," she said, "I was going to call you today." She placed the folder on the counter and opened it. "I'm afraid that you failed your background check."

"That's not possible," I said.

"Well, that's how it came back. I can't sell you a firearm, sorry." To her credit, she appeared frustrated and disappointed by the entire process, as though my rejection were a personal affront to her. Though this frustration seemed genuine, she was nevertheless still nervous in my presence. Perhaps she believed that I was a criminal.

"May I ask why?"

She shook her head. "I wish I could tell you. It just came back rejected, that's all. We usually get some explanation, but not this time."

"I have never been convicted of any violent crime or other felony."

"I believe you. But the government says no, and we gotta listen to what the government says."

The irony of hearing this from a private citizen was not lost on me, and I gave up the fight. "All right then," I said. I took one last look at the Browning underneath the glass counter and walked away.

I did not, however, leave the store. Instead I went to the hunting section and began to examine the archery supplies. It was still early, and few customers had yet come in, so it was not long before a salesclerk approached me.

"Can I help you?"

It was, unfortunately, the arrogant young man whom I had lectured on climbing safety some weeks before Luckily, his self-absorption appeared to prevent him from recognizing me. I told him that I was in the market for a bow and some arrows, that I intended to use them to hunt large game.

Immediately the young man directed my attention to the crossbows and compound bows, with their complicated pulleys and cams. I quickly interrupted.

"I am looking for something compact and lightweight."

He frowned. "Like, a shortbow?"

"Yes," I replied, though I didn't know the term.

"Hard to get close enough to a deer to kill it with a shortbow," he said.

"I'd like to see some."

With a sigh, he led me to a rack of compact, thin bows that appeared to be made of a composite of wood and fiberglass. They were precisely what I wanted.

"These, though," the clerk said, "you wanna get any velocity out of them, you're practically gonna give yourself a heart attack drawing them tight enough."

"That's none of your concern," I said, hefting and stretching each bow. I settled upon the one that felt most supple without seeming to sacrifice tension. I held it up. "This one," I said.

"Your funeral," the clerk said.

I chose to ignore him. "Arrows," I said. "I would like the arrows that would be the most lethal at low velocity."

This comment appeared to satisfy him, at least temporarily. He nodded. "You want something that'll take a broadhead and fly straight," he said. He showed me a package of four arrows tipped by a quartet of razor-sharp blades, and accompanied by a collapsible nylon quiver with a shoulder strap and reinforced floor. "You'll get a nice, clean kill from these, if you can get close enough." He pointed to the opposite end of the arrows. "Helix fletching, turkey feathers. They'll fly straight and true. Aluminum shaft, nice and lightweight, and pretty easy to bend back in shape, if they get bent."

"Fine. I'll take them."

"Great. Let me show you some sights for that thing, it'll help you a lot. Also you'll want some targets to practice with, and—"

"No, thank you," I said, and walked away.

I was back at the house by half past nine. The sun was full and bright now, and the temperature well into the fifties. I expected that it would be over sixty by noon, and though the woods would surely be colder, I was confident that my vigorous physical activity would keep me warm.

I was eager to embark on my mission, but first it was necessary to test my new weapon. I gathered up the bow and arrows and carried them into the yard, where I stood twenty yards back from the mound of earth where the deer was buried. The disturbed, clayey soil would be unlikely to dull the razor tips or deform the shafts. I first practiced drawing the bow and arrows from my quiver, which I had strapped over my right shoulder; next I nocked an arrow, raised and drew, then relaxed my fingers.

The arrow flew laser-straight, driving itself into the grass in front of the doe's grave. The next was high, and disappeared in the weeds at the treeline. But the next two struck home, burying themselves eight inches into the soil, and I knew that this new weapon would be at least as effective, for my purposes, as any firearm. Indeed, the bow felt so good in my hands—light and strong and perfectly balanced—that I retrieved the arrows and shot them all again. This time, three hit home, and one fell a few inches short. The accuracy of the equipment was impressive, and while I would never win an archery competition, I was certainly capable of defending myself against an enemy. I was surprised to discover that I was glad to have failed the background check, for, as effective and useful a weapon as a handgun was, it could not compare to the tactile immediacy and visceral satisfaction of the bow. I was, to put it mildly, a convert. With the muscles of my fingers and upper arm pleasurably stinging, I gathered up my arrows once again and went inside to suit up for my mission.

Fifteen minutes later, I was walking along the shoulder of Lyssa Road, my pack full and tight against my back, and my quiver nestled alongside it. A light, warm breeze swept dead leaves across the empty road; the shadows of the trees swayed in sharp relief on the pavement. I reached the corner of Minerva Road and turned left, and soon I stood at the once-invisible arch of silver maples that marked the track to the rock.

It was not without excitement that I peered now into the near-dark of the forest. For the first time since I scaled the rock, I had a challenge before me, a plan with a clear objective, and my hands and feet fairly tingled with anticipation. I could feel the years falling away from me, and my senses growing more acute, reaching far out in every direction. I felt, as I once had, like the lord of my kingdom.

I must confess, however, that my certainty was curbed somewhat by the sickness and confusion of the past week, the unexpected obstacles I had confronted, and the despair I had felt in the face of them. Was it simply that there had been a time in my life when I was able to overcome obstacles, and that time was now over? Or were these experiences merely aberrations, unexpected turns in the path to success?

In any event, now was not the time to dwell upon such things. Whatever doubts I might harbor about my purpose in life, the goal of the moment was clear—to hunt down the man who lived in the castle, discover what he wanted from me, and force him to cease his incursions into my territory.

I hitched my pack higher onto my shoulders and stepped once again into the woods.

Now that I knew the way, I had no difficulty making progress toward the castle and the rock. My hiking shoes were quiet on the mossy track, and I stepped with ease over any branches blocking my path. Within ten minutes I sensed that I was growing near, and I paused to get my bearings.

My eyes, by now, had adjusted fully to the gloom, and it was possible to detect, up ahead in the distance, the sun-drenched glow of the rock face. A roughness at its base must have been the castle. I closed my eyes and listened carefully, making sure that I was not being tracked. Hearing nothing, I turned 360 degrees, studying everything within my view. But all that could be seen was the dense foliage, and the only motion was my own. Convinced now that I had not been followed, I turned to step off the path, so that I might continue my journey under cover.

It was there that I very nearly put a premature end to the mission, and possibly to my life. For my foot had come to rest less than two inches from the paddle of an old-fashioned iron bear trap.

At first, I thought I must be mistaken about the object's identity. Such things were, as far as I knew, illegal, and at any rate were no longer in regular use. But closer examination revealed that, in fact, my foot had actually fallen directly into one of the stretched-open jaws. I backed up a step and found a stout branch, which I then used to lift off the twigs and leaves that had been concealing the device. A cursory look revealed that it had not merely been lying here for years, forgotten. The iron was clean and oiled, and the ground underneath it smoothed out, to make a flat surface.

The trap had the look of a shark's mouth, with the jaws forming a circle in the center, and two wings of folded steel, which served as springs. The springs ended in a ring which the jaws passed through; had I pressed the center paddle with my foot, the springs would have lost their grip on the base and unfolded, forcing the jaws shut. The base, a cross of iron, was attached to a chain, which had been staked into the ground with a stout peg.

It would not do to have this lying here, unsprung. I found a thicker branch and, after taking a moment to brace my feet, drove its end into the paddle.

The trap jumped off the ground, scattering leaves and dirt in all directions, and the jaws slammed shut, snapping my branch in two. I was quite startled, and may have cried out. I stood there for a few long seconds, gazing at this inert pile of metal, its lethality spent, and imagining what I might have done had it broken my leg as it had the branch. Nothing, I suppose. I might have been able to pull the stake from the ground and drag myself back to the road, where I supposed I would have waited for a passing vehicle. But by then, the trapper would likely have emerged from hiding to get a look at his quarry.

Of course this gave me an idea. I stepped back into the darkness of the trees, about twenty feet from the track, and about twenty feet east of where the trap had been set. I found a spot at the base of a tree, where a very narrow sight line allowed me to peer between two other tree trunks. It was through this gap that I could watch for the trapper.

I waited. I am experienced in remaining perfectly still for long periods of time, so this was not a problem. After half an hour, though, I decided that no one would come after all, and I stood up in order to continue on my way.

It was then that I saw him.

He did not, as I had hoped, expose himself on the overgrown track. Instead, he appeared to have been doing exactly what I had been doing— sitting twenty feet back from the other side, and waiting. I could see little of him through the trees, and what I could make out seemed little more than a pale blur against the forest gloom, a suggestion of movement, a specter. I believed I could make out a narrow frame, and long arms, as he moved out of the shadows. But then he entered a shaft of sun that had wandered down through the canopy, and in an instant he was gone, subsumed by the light.

I blinked, but my eyes had not deceived me. He was there, and now he had disappeared.

My disappointment at the failure of my ruse was now compounded by profound unease. If this was Doctor Stiles, his expertise with these woods was even more advanced than I had imagined, and his powers in them almost supernatural. Furthermore, I had revealed myself before I even reached the castle, and thus any advantage I might have enjoyed was now lost. He would be expecting me now, and would be prepared. And what of the bear trap? There could be more—or another pit, or some other danger beyond imagining. I would have to move more carefully now, calculating the likely safety of any possible route. In addition, I had to outwit and outmaneuver a once-celebrated psychologist, beating the old man at his own game.

Well, I did have the advantage of relative youth, and while I possessed no advanced degrees, I was nevertheless adept at second-guessing an enemy. It was likely that the Doctor had not anticipated this particular series of events—my almost, but not quite, falling into his trap, then springing it intentionally and spying on him—and so had planned according to other possibilities. Most likely, he would have planted his traps along the easiest route, assuming that I would fall prey to them if I missed the first. If so, he didn't know me as well as he liked to think. My own experience with stealth, and evasive maneuvering, was considerable.

I decided to proceed as I had been about to when I found the trap. Carefully, I continued southwest for some fifty yards, poking the ground

in front of me with a branch and examining the forest floor for signs of recent activity. Several times I stopped and cleared a patch of ground, convinced I had come upon another trap or pit. But each time I was mistaken.
It was better, I told myself, to be safe than sorry.

Eventually I arrived at the southeast corner of the rock—the "toe"
that had given me access to the summit, some days before. I peered at it
from the cover of the woods, waiting to see if the Doctor, or anyone else,
would pass by. Ten minutes later, no one had. The sunshine was bright and
warm—I could feel the warm air rolling off the rock and into the trees—
but I resisted its call. Instead, I continued to skirt the edge of the rock from
deep within the forest, never letting it entirely out of my sight, but never
revealing myself to whomever might be waiting in the clearing that surrounded it. It took me a good half hour to make my way clockwise to the
northeast corner, and in that time I found no traps, and saw no sign of the
Doctor.

I was facing, from my vantage point just behind the treeline, the back
of the rock's "ankle." Just to the east stood the castle's northwest tower—
one of the two lowest, and the most damaged by time and weather. The
north curtain wall led farther off to the east, while the western wall hugged
the nearly vertical cliff of the "ankle."

I say "hugged," but in fact there was a narrow gap between the rock
and the wall, owing to the natural unevenness of the cliff. This gap was
approximately fifteen feet away from where I now stood. It was mid-
afternoon, however, and the sun had sunk low enough so that the shadows
of the trees covered the clearing. If I were to make for that gap, I would
be exposed for the two seconds it would take me to cross the ten feet between the trees and the wall. But owing to the shadows, and my camouflage clothing, I believed I could make it without being detected. And
since the figure I'd spied fleeing the scene of the foiled trap had been moving in a direction that would have taken him to this very spot, it was the
last place from which he might be anticipating my approach. I decided
to take the risk. Slowly, quietly, I moved close to the edge of the clearing;
from behind a tall pine I surveyed the tower, the high cliff edge, the curtain wall. And then I ran.

Nothing happened. I reached the gap and wedged myself into it, the
quiver containing my bow and arrows chafing against my back. The gap
was even wider than I had assumed it to be, and, after moving several feet

into the darkness, I rested comfortably there for a moment, catching my breath.

It was cold in the gap, with a strong smell of fungus and dead leaves. The ground beneath my feet was spongy, and the rock face felt massive and comforting behind me. I looked up at the strip of sky overhead. A hawk crossed it, circling. The only sound was that of my own breaths.

My original plan had been to wait here for my quarry to reveal himself. But some impulse, fueled by instinct or memory, caused me to move further into the gap. The cliffside was as irregular as it had appeared from the clearing, but it was obvious now that a man could move all the way to the southwest tower from here without much difficulty. And now, as my eyes adjusted to the dim, I realized that, in fact, a man had, and did. The spongy ground was quite clean and even, covered by a bed of pine needles; a faint depression ran down the center of it, as though it was frequently tamped down by human feet. The castle wall was impressively straight, and tilted slightly inward; I assumed it must be thicker at the base than at the top, assuring that it could not be breached from the ground. I entertained, briefly, the notion that I might be able to scale the wall by pressing my back against the rock and "walking" up, but I could see this was impossible: the gap at the top might have been as wide as five feet.

I pressed on, toward the center of the wall. A cloudbank had rolled in, and was now covering up the gap with a uniform gray; the light dimmed. It was then that I made an interesting discovery.

I had just inched around a bulge in the rock face, and found that the gap just beyond it widened considerably, for a length of perhaps six feet. The ground here was well worn, particularly right at the foot of the wall.

The key detail, however, was the wall itself. Its impenetrable mortared stone face was interrupted, at knee height, by what appeared to be a block of wood, snugly inserted in place of a single stone. It was approximately eighteen inches high by two feet wide, was depressed about two inches into the rock face, and bore a large iron handle, right in the center, fastened to its surface by large bolts.

Of course. I immediately recognized the block as the way in. I crouched down and gripped the handle with both of my hands, bracing myself for a great deal of exertion. But when I pulled, the block slid smoothly toward me a full inch, spilling a bit of debris, crumbs of mortar and pine needles, to the ground at my feet.

At this point I paused, considering. I had acted with the utmost care so far today, in spite of which I had nearly lost my leg. There was every reason to expect that someone, Doctor Avery Stiles himself, perhaps, now stood on the opposite side of this very wall, with one of his homemade poisoned arrows aimed at the hole. Even if he was not, he doubtless lurked somewhere in the compound, and would soon know that it had been breached. I had to proceed with care. I looked up once again at the lip of the curtain wall, then both ways down the length of the gap. Seeing nothing out of the ordinary, I slowly slid the block out of the wall and set it on the ground at my feet.

The block was very heavy, about eight inches thick, with a handle on the inside identical in design, but less damaged by the elements. The reason was clear: as I had predicted, the wall was very thick at its foot, sheltering the handle from harm. Indeed, I discovered, hazarding a peek inside the opening, that it was at least four feet thick—so thick that it must have been difficult to detect, from inside, whether someone had moved the block.

The hole—a tunnel, really—was smooth and even, and had obviously been part of the wall's original design, rather than an afterthought dug out after construction. It was as neatly mortared as the exterior of the wall, and was more than wide enough to admit an adult male in good physical condition.

There was no need to wait. I removed my pack and quiver, ducked down, and climbed inside. I moved forward slowly, making as little noise as possible; the air grew cold as the wall closed in around me. I was reminded of my trip to the cellar of my house, and breathed deeply and evenly, in an effort to dispel my fear.

My head had soon reached the end, even as my ankles dangled out into the gap. I was looking out into a sheltered corner of the main courtyard that I had seen from the summit of the rock. A large piece of shrubbery grew directly before me, and I was reassured by the cover it offered. To the left was another wall, part of the large hall or dwelling I also remembered from before; the pieces of play or exercise equipment I remembered were also here, off to the right. I lay there for several minutes, looking and listening, and I detected no human presence besides my own.

Without further hesitation, I crawled out of the tunnel and onto a flagstone, where I crouched, ready to fight. I was, at last, inside the castle.

THIRTEEN

For all my anxiety at having breached my quarry's stronghold, I must now confess that, at this moment, that anxiety was twinned with a second emotion, one less easy to identify, and more surprising. It was a feeling of belonging, if not of actual familiarity—a sense that, though I was far from safe standing here in the castle courtyard, my presence here had a rightness, that it represented the fulfillment of some previously unknown desire. It was as though something hanging crookedly in my mind had finally been righted.

For all the peculiarity of this feeling, however, I did not have time just now to stop and consider it at length. I studied my surroundings until I was confident that I had indeed gone unseen, then I reached back into the tunnel to grab hold of my pack and quiver. I dragged them through, and after a moment's thought, wriggled in once again and took hold of the inside handle of the block. With some concerted effort, I was able to wedge it back into place from the inside. I realized that it might cause me trouble if I were to need to retreat quickly; but to leave the block lying there would signal to the Doctor, should he be outside and approach through the gap, that his fortress had been penetrated. The element of surprise was a reasonable trade for the seconds I might lose trying to escape. I did not, of course, plan to need to escape. Whatever happened, I intended to leave the castle without fear or haste.

I shouldered my belongings and slowly stood up.

The castle had appeared quite imposing from outside, but now that I had come through the wall, it seemed smaller, and less threatening. It had more of the look of a ruin, as well. Debris that had fallen from the crenellated walls was piled, seemingly untouched, around the edges of the courtyard; a few stones even lay on the roof of the building to my left. The flagstones were heaved and cracked, and weeds—even entire trees, like the shrub I now stood behind—sprung up between them. And contrary to my observations of the path outside, I could detect no clear evidence of any human presence. If the Doctor lived here, he concealed himself well. The castle looked abandoned.

I took one last visual survey of the grounds, and began to move.

From over my shoulder I drew my bow, and an arrow, which I nocked and held at the ready. I kept close to the western wall, stepping stealthily, swiftly, keeping my eyes on those obstacles in the courtyard which might conceal a man. I sidestepped along the curtain until I reached the edge of the compound; then I inched silently east. I passed underneath a small square barred window, and soon reached the corner.

The only part of the courtyard that had been invisible to me from the tunnel opening was on the other side of this corner. This would be the small area underneath the large watchtower. There was likely to be some kind of entrance into the compound, and another into the tower; if my foe lay in wait for me, it was almost certainly around this corner that I would find him. In fact, it was possible that he stood there now, his bow aimed.

After another scan of the visible courtyard, I decided upon a course of action. I unchocked my arrow, gripped it and the bow in one hand, and took a breath. There was a wooden structure up ahead, a sort of crooked, broken table around which tall weeds had sprung, and it was there that I now directed my gaze. From behind it, I would be able to peer into the hidden corner of the courtyard. I marked my decision with a quick nod, and sprinted toward the structure.

Only ten feet separated me from my goal, but my feet slipped and skidded on the crumbling flagstones, and my mad dash felt more like a labored, heavily burdened trek. In any event, I made it. I crouched down behind the wooden table and inspected my body for wounds. There were none. If an arrow had been fired, it had missed me.

I took a moment to gather myself, then peeked over the top of the table. The hidden section of courtyard was much as I had imagined it. There were open doorways, yawning into darkness, leading into the compound and tower, and a large pile of rubble that appeared to have fallen from the tower's southwest corner. There was also another wooden structure, a kind of cage, with chains and other metal apparatus hanging inside it. The sight of this object gave me pause—it had an aura of sinister intent about it, and impending danger. No one was visible anywhere, but I smelled smoke.

I chose to wait a few minutes, in an effort to detect movement anywhere on the castle grounds. As I waited, I examined the structure I was crouched behind. I could see now that it wasn't a table, not precisely—rather, it was a heavy, circular wooden platform balanced upon a roughly carved inverted wooden pyramid, the two attached by a fist-sized and tightly fitted peg. Overall it had the appearance of a very large child's top. The platform, though thick, was cracked down the center from exposure, like an old kitchen cutting board left soaking in water. The flagstones underneath it were worn down and cracked, as if from its weight and motion.

Again, I felt uneasy looking at it. It seemed to evoke some nameless anxiety or desperation, which I could not put my finger on. I began to feel as if I were being watched. I quickly shot glances up to the four towers, the walls, the roof of the rock. But there was nothing, and no one. I was still alone.

At last it was time to move on. The nearest wall was that of the watchtower, so it was there that I dashed, my footing surer this time, the journey swifter. Again I arrived unharmed. I slid along this wall, peered again into the once-hidden area of the courtyard, and slipped around to just beside the watchtower door. After a brief pause to listen, I ducked in.

It was clear that no one else was here. My eyes adjusted quickly to the darkness, and a flight of stone stairs made themselves visible before me, spiraling up into dim light. There was a strong scent of rodents, and fungus. I climbed the staircase slowly, quietly, stopping after every three steps to listen for my enemy. In this manner, I reached the top and emerged onto the broken roof.

In the minutes I spent climbing, it had begun to rain, a stinging, spitting rain accompanied by a warm wind. Gunmetal clouds were racing in from the west, promising a powerful storm. Looking down, I could make out the overgrown path to Minerva Road, and the approximate place where I had avoided the bear trap; above me loomed the barren rock. No people or animals could be seen, not to the east nor in any other direction. The wind picked up, and I felt very desolate and helpless, in spite of my commanding view of the surroundings.

A few moments later I was back in the courtyard. Again there was no one. I moved along the castle's north wall, giving the wooden cage a wide berth, and quickly arrived at the doorway that led into the compound. As in the tower, I smelled a rats' warren, and the chemical tang of mildew; but in addition I again detected woodsmoke—and a human scent, the stink of living. Fear enveloped my body like a sack, and I suppressed a shiver. My eyes adjusted to the light, and I could see now that I was in a large open room, with the blackened remains of a fire off to the center, underneath a small hole in the peaked roof. A flat stone sat beside the fire, and a small pile of sharpened twigs. It appeared that food had once been cooked here, though there was no indication that the fire was recent. In front of me and to the left, a rectangular hole was dug in the dirt floor and a flight of crude stairs led down into darkness.

No—not darkness, not quite. There was light, and not the gray light of the stormy sky outside; rather, it was a yellow light, flickering faintly. A fire, somewhere below. That was where the smoke had come from—not the dead fire here in front of me, but the one burning at the bottom of those stairs.

Slowly, I crept across the room and began to descend. Once again I nocked my arrow and held it before me. One step, then another, and another—I paused between each, listening, knowing that this must be the place where he waited. Fourteen steps, fifteen, and I was standing one step from the doorway on the other side of which burned the fire. Smoke stung my eyes. I leaned against the stairwell wall and inched my head closer and closer, until I could see the outlines of a room. A rough corner, walls of stone. A bundle lying on the ground—blankets, perhaps, brown in the dim. And a pair of shoes. Moccasins, by the look of them, sewn together out of deerhide.

He was here—I knew it. The moment had come. I closed my eyes, breathed in and out to clear my head, and then stepped forward, into the light.

The room was about twenty feet square and undivided, like the room above, and I realized that it had been hollowed out underneath the rock. The walls, as I have said, were of stone, not milled and fitted together as in the castle walls, but irregular and jagged, as if they had been found on the ground outside, or dug up during the room's excavation. The wadded-up bundle I had noticed was indeed a pile of blankets—a bed, in fact, laid right in the dirt—and the wall I faced, across the fire, was lined with bookshelves—crude, crooked planks, heavily weighted with books, their spines obscured by years of smoke. The planks were supported by the books themselves, so that the bottom few rows were hopelessly squashed and bent, their bindings ruined, and only the top two shelves' contents were even removable.

Something, however, stood in front of that wall: a small wooden table. It was old, a bit lopsided, the kind of table one might find in a child's playhouse or a kindergarten classroom. On it lay an apparently random collection of objects. Something about them—some familiar pattern in their arrangement—made me take a step closer.

As if in keeping with the table, the objects seemed to belong to a child. There was a homemade slingshot, made from a stout branch and a thick rubber band; there was a military action figure—a G.I. Joe. These lay beside a mushroom hunting guide, a small canteen, a penknife, a cigar box full of bones.

I should clarify here that the cigar box was closed. Yet I knew that it contained bones—the tiny bones of birds and squirrels, and perhaps the husks of cicadas. The box was cardboard, with a fabric-hinged lid, and it bore the name CABAÑAS above a kind of heraldic crest. The lip of the box was ragged with torn paper, which once had sealed in the cigars.

I reached out and ran my thumb along the lip, feeling the paper's uneven edge. After a moment, I lifted the lid.

It was just as I had imagined. Several skulls, some of them beaked, and a scattering of tiny thin bones. The cicadas' husks were in a separate compartment, an unlidded jewelry box, to keep them intact. From underneath the bones poked the corner of a thick, folded piece of paper; even as I reached for it I knew that it was a map, a hand-drawn treasure map, marking the places in and around my childhood home where I had concealed things that were valuable to me. The weightless bones clattered faintly as I drew out the map; it unfolded with a dry rustle, revealing the drawings and symbols I knew would be there, rendered in pencil, then traced over with calligraphic ink. There was the house, the shed; there stood the catalpa tree and the sugar maples. The trash pit, the gravel drive—it was all there, the diagram of my childhood, as I had drawn it thirty-five years before.

The smoke in the room was thick and choking; the flickering of the fire cast disorienting shadows across the walls, and I gazed down at my lost possessions: my slingshot, and my book, and my canteen. All of it was mine.

From behind me, over the crackle of the fire, I heard the small noise of a bare foot shifting against the dirt floor.

I stood and turned. It was him. He held a hollowed-out twig to his mouth and, with a terrible grin, blew. I felt something sting my face, and moved my hand to brush it away. But my hand merely hung at my side, immobile.

My knees buckled and I lost my balance; my arm landed in the fire. The old man acted quickly to move it, tucking it in close to my body, and as I lost consciousness I felt gratitude for his alertness and concern, and tried, but failed, to form my lips into a gesture of thanks.

FOURTEEN

I don't know where or how my father met Avery Stiles, but it is not difficult to imagine a scenario by which the two, working after hours on campus— my father at his maintenance chores and Professor Stiles on his research— struck up a conversation and, eventually, a friendship. My father, though cold and distant with his family, was quite amiable around others. In retrospect, this may seem strange, but as a child I never thought to question the drastic change in personality that overtook him at the hardware store, the bank, the municipal dump, when he encountered perfect strangers. I accompanied him on these errands for many years, and distinctly recall the tense silence that enveloped the truck as we drove. My father's back never seemed to touch the seat—he leaned forward, his chin out over the steering wheel his bony fingers gripped, his jaw tight, his eyes darting across his field of vision. Any attempt on my part to speak was met with a terse "Quiet," and so I sat in nervous boredom, my body rigid, waiting for the journey to end.

But when we reached our destination and climbed down from the truck, my father changed into a different person. His compact frame loosened, his forehead smoothed, his hooded eyes grew wide. When he encountered a familiar face, he initiated a handshake from ten feet away, striding forth with a confident gait and a broad smile. He chatted with great intensity, usually about the weather, or a description of some project he was engaged in, and people in town seemed to like him. You wouldn't think, looking at such a man, that he was friendless. Indeed, he appeared to enjoy broad social acceptance in our town. And then, when his errand was over, and he turned his back on his acquaintances, his face and body tightened up again, and by the time we climbed back into the truck, he had assumed his usual truculent demeanor.

I was not conscious, at the time, of harboring any particular feelings about my father's transformations. Now, of course, it is easy to imagine that I must have felt jealous, that I wished he would bestow this kind of cheer upon my mother and me. But the truth is, I don't remember feeling that way, and I don't believe I did. I didn't regard this version of my father as having anything to do with my mother and me. I thought of the cold, angry man I knew as my real father, and this gregarious fellow as a character he played. If anything, his manner embarrassed me—living as I did, I had come to regard this kind of social display as foolish and false, and though I have since overcome this misapprehension, I remain uncomfortable in my relations with others. But I digress.

Quite probably my father was very friendly to those he encountered at the college. And I suspect that he regarded himself as the equal of any professor who taught there—indeed, he likely considered himself more intelligent than the average academic, and he might well have been right. So it was not surprising that he would befriend a man like Professor Stiles, a misfit in the university community whose work had fallen into disfavor with his colleagues and superiors. He and my father were outsiders, and natural allies. This, anyway, is what I imagine may have been the case.

In any event, it came to pass that Doctor Avery Stiles was invited to our house for dinner one night, and my mother ordered to prepare some elaborate meal. I don't recall what it was we ate, but my father spent an unprecedented amount of time in the kitchen, overseeing her work, dipping his fingers into things, demanding to know what she was doing and why she was doing it. I was a boy at the time—I would guess around eight—and understood only that a guest would be coming for dinner, and that I was supposed to be on my best behavior. Largely, though, I expected to be ignored that night, because it was my sister who was the ostensible focus of the evening.

Jill was around thirteen and in the early stages of her delinquency. She had begun to smoke cigarettes—I had seen her and her friends doing it behind the school—and wear makeup, and she sulked in the presence of my parents and often disappeared when family meals were in the offing. Perhaps as a result, she had lost weight, and no longer looked like the child she must still have been. She had begun to take on the twiggy roughness that she would settle into, in her adulthood.

I didn't fully understand what my parents were talking about before Doctor Stiles's arrival at our house. But it seemed to me that Doctor Stiles had been called in to meet Jill, assess her social problems, and suggest some course of action that would "cure" her. My mother insisted that she didn't like the idea of a "psychologist coming into our house," and my father said that he wasn't a psychologist, he was a scientist, and he would "use science on her." After a while the discussion became heated, and my mother, as always, backed down. But the evening was already unprecedented, not only because a college professor was coming over, but also because my parents had spoken to each other at such length, and with such passion.

The dinner was not to work out as planned, however, because just before Doctor Stiles was to arrive, my sister went missing. My mother called her down from her room, but she was not in her room, and she wasn't anywhere else in the house, either. Her jacket was gone from the coat rack, and her bicycle from the garage.

My father blamed my mother for letting her leave, and insisted that she get in the car and go find her. But before the issue could be resolved, Professor Stiles appeared on the doorstep.

He was a tall, gaunt man with a long face, a narrow chin, and a round pair of eyeglasses. His clothes were drab and brown and threadbare, and his sparse black hair was snarled at the crest of a high, pale forehead. But he carried with him an air of quiet authority, to which my parents responded by taking his coat and leading him to the sofa, where he was handed a drink.

On the one hand, the Professor looked weak. His skin lacked color, and his arms and legs were thin as a waif's. But he moved with a precision and assurance that bespoke a great physical dexterity, and his eyes ranged around the room, absorbing, one imagined, every detail. He appeared, in fact, to hold us all in judgment—but what sort of judgment was unclear. He betrayed nothing of his opinions. Such a person had never been in our house before, and I would have been hard pressed to recall when anyone besides ourselves had ever sat on that sofa.

My parents made small talk with Professor Stiles, and he joined the conversation with ease. But his eyes, I couldn't help but notice, fell upon me time and time again. I said nothing, but I felt that I was expected to, and several times I almost opened my mouth to speak. I resisted, however, afraid of how I might sound. I had already developed a reputation at school as a quiet, studious pupil, not especially socially adept, and I wanted such a man to be impressed by me, or at least to approve. Ultimately I considered it best, then, not to speak at all.

In time, the group moved to the dining room, where a place had been set for my sister. As the meal began, Doctor Stiles glanced at the empty plate and asked, "And so your young lady will not be available this evening?"

My mother reddened, and my father grumbled something about my mother's inability to keep her in line, but Professor Stiles waved off the question with a graceful, leaflike hand. "It is of no consequence," he said.

Awkwardly, my parents returned to small talk, and we ate. Professor Stiles complimented the food, and my mother blushed again, this time with pleasure—I could not recall my father ever having complimented her for anything. It was not in his nature. But, seeing that she was under the Doctor's sway, my father said, "Avery, tell her about your work. Tell her what you've been doing."

"Ah," Professor Stiles said, setting down his knife and fork, and addressing my mother with disarming directness. "I am interested in modifying behavior, particularly in children, through a form of conditioning that I have devised."

"Oh!" said my mother, and though her tone was bright, I could tell that it was a put-on, that she didn't like this visitor and wished he would finish his meal and go away. My father must have sensed this, for he scowled slightly at the tablecloth and gripped his fork a little tighter.

"Forgive me for being obscure, Mrs. Loesch," the Professor went on. "It is difficult to distill my years of research into a simple explanation, even for a colleague. I'll put it this way." He straightened in his chair, lifted his napkin to his face, and daubed at the corner of his mouth. Then he replaced the napkin on his lap, drew breath, and continued. "You have noticed, I should imagine, the social unrest that has overtaken our cities of late, and the reactionary culture that has sprung up in protest of the war."

"Of course," my mother replied briskly.

Professor Stiles acknowledged her with a nod. "And so you are likely familiar, as well, with our failures in that war, the losses our armed forces have suffered, and the despair that has spread among our soldiers there."

He did not wait for an answer, but merely went on. "It is my feeling that we have civilized our own humanness out of existence. We are too affluent, and too soft, and many of our natural instincts have atrophied. My research means to explore how the human mind reacts when its comforts have been stripped away. I intend to recover those human skills that we have lost, to create a better soldier, and perhaps more importantly, a better citizen."

"I see," my mother said.

The smile that Professor Stiles offered in response was a sad one. He shook his head, turned to me, and winked. Then he reached into the pocket of his sport coat, lunged to his feet, and grabbed me from behind, pinning me to my chair. His arm was crooked around my neck; the tweed was rough against my throat. I felt something being pressed to my skull, just above the right ear.

My mouth was full of food, but I was unable to swallow. I heard my mother scream.

"I'm going to murder your child, Mrs. Loesch," Professor Stiles said, his voice loud but calm. "What are you going to do?"

She screamed again and again, her hands twisting her napkin, her body curling further and further in on itself, shrinking like a piece of paper thrown into a fire.

I had not yet had time to be frightened—I felt only shock and confusion. I looked to my father for help and was even more baffled to find him sitting back, his arms crossed over his chest, looking on with interest, even amusement. It was clear he was not comfortable with the situation—his mouth was taut, and the veins stood out above his ear—but neither was he frightened, or even angry. Meanwhile, my mother continued to scream.

"I'm going to kill Eric, Mrs. Loesch," he said. "What will you do? How will you save your son?"

"Please!" she wailed, rocking in her chair. She turned to my father. "Please! Brian! Please!"

"Mrs. Loesch!" Professor Stiles shouted.

"Oh, please!"

"Mrs. Loesch, look at me!"

I felt the object press harder into my scalp, and I tried to lean away. But the Professor's arm held me tight. I struggled to swallow, failed, and coughed horribly, spitting the food across the table. My father frowned.

"Look at me, Mrs. Loesch! If you want your son to live, look at me!"

I believe that lifting her head was the most difficult thing my mother had ever done. Slowly, as though she were terribly old, she turned to face the end of the table where the Professor stood over me; she gazed into my eyes and I recognized that something in her had toppled over and shattered. Her cheeks were streaked with tears, and wrinkles fanned out from the corners of her mouth. A bubble appeared at a nostril, grew, and popped.

"Look at *me,* please, Mrs. Loesch."

With a final, desperate effort, her eyes rolled up to meet his.

"Do you want me to kill your son, Mrs. Loesch?"

"No," my mother whispered.

"Mrs. Loesch, I want you to look at my hand."

She blinked, and blankly gazed at his left hand, which rested on my shoulder, holding me to the chair with casual, implacable force. I could feel the long fingers there, pressing painfully into my flesh.

"No, Mrs. Loesch, the other hand."

Her jaw trembling, she shifted her gaze to the Professor's other hand, the one holding the weapon to my head.

"Mrs. Loesch, I want you to tell me what I have pressed to Eric's head."

Fresh tears began to run down my mother's face. "A g—," she stammered, "a g-g-*gun.*"

"Mrs. Loesch. Cybele. No. *What do I have pressed to Eric's head?*"

A curious transition played itself out on my mother's features. Though she was wracked by fear and despair, she must have found within herself some well of resolve, for she focused her glassy pink gaze and concentrated on the Professor's weapon. After a moment, her eyes flew open, and her head jerked back an inch; the first stirrings of anger were visible at the corners of her mouth.

She looked up at the Professor, then at my father, who had slid down in his chair and was staring at his hands, folded on his belly. Some of the food I'd spat out had struck his shirtsleeve just above the elbow. He did not appear to notice it there.

Finally my mother's eyes returned to mine. Her gaze was cold.

"Mrs. Loesch? Tell me what you see."

She did not look at him as she spoke; her eyes remained on my face, but she appeared to be looking elsewhere, someplace far from this room. Her cheeks were still wet, but her eyes were dry now, as if the tears had been burned away. She said, "A train."

With the pronouncement of these words, Professor Stiles released me from his grip. I slumped in my chair, coughing, and found suspended in front of my face, gently held by the Professor's long pale fingers, a die-cast toy locomotive. After a moment, his face appeared beside it.

"For you," he said.

This train was something I wanted very badly. I had seen it, in fact, just that week, at the toy shop in downtown Milan, displayed in the front window along with a collection of cars that linked to it. But it was the locomotive I wanted the most. Sleek, black, with windows of real glass and a precise red and white stripe running down its flank, it was a marvelous toy. It looked nothing like a gun, of course.

It is difficult to remember what, precisely, was going through my mind at that moment. I had just been through an unprecedented experience, but I cannot say that I was ever actually frightened, in spite of my mother's apparent breakdown. This may seem like a strange thing for me to say, but it is true. My father, of course, had never moved from his chair, and had never once seemed worried as events unfolded. And there was something about Doctor Stiles's hand, the particular way it gripped my shoulder—firm, of course, nearly to the point of injury, but also somehow reassuring. I was not often touched by my parents; ours was an undemonstrative family. Perhaps I was simply unaccustomed to this kind of contact and relished it for its novelty. At any rate, I was not afraid, merely puzzled. I had no idea what had just happened, or why, and understood only that, in the wake of an unpleasant minute, I was being offered something I wanted.

I raised my hand to take the train.

"Don't touch that, Eric," said my mother.

I looked at her, my hand frozen in the air, waiting for her to change her mind. Her anger was fully realized now, enveloping her face like a mask.

My father spoke now, sitting up straight with a little grunt. His voice was quiet, cowed, and strained. "Oh, now, how about—"

"Don't touch it, Eric," she said again, and then shifted her gaze over my shoulder, to where Professor Stiles was standing. "And you get out of my house."

"Now, Cybele," my father began with a sigh.

"Out!" she spat. "You're sick. You're a sick man."

"Mrs. Loesch," the Professor said quietly, taking a step away from me. The train went with him, and I watched it slip back into his jacket pocket. "I was merely illustrating that—"

"I don't care what you were illustrating," my mother said. "I want you to leave. You're terrible, horrible. How could you do that to a boy?"

"Look at him, Cybele, he's fine!" It was my father, his open hand thrust out toward me. "He knew it was a trick, you were the only one who was fooled!"

She scowled at me, as though I had betrayed her. But I had done nothing other than sit there, waiting for it to end.

"He might have choked to death on his food," she offered weakly.

"Come on," my father said with a nervous chuckle. "There was never any chance of that."

My mother leaned back in her chair and closed her eyes, and I watched as her anger and fear gave way to exhaustion. She let out a long breath. The battle was over; she had lost.

But Professor Stiles did not return to his seat. Instead, he apologized to my mother. "Mrs. Loesch, I'm sorry. I never dreamed that this demonstration would have such an effect on you. Of course you're right; it was rude of me. I'll leave you to finish your meal in peace." My mother opened her eyes to stare at him, and for a moment I thought that she would actually insist that he stay—would get up, take him by the arm, and lead him back to his chair. But she could not capitulate so completely. She stayed where she was. Perhaps she was just too tired.

Professor Stiles patted me on the head, then walked around behind me to shake my father's hand. My father rose and accompanied him to the door. A few moments later, he returned to the table.

There was no question of finishing our meal. No one had any appetite anymore. We sat in silence as we listened to Professor Stiles's car start up and drive away.

During this interval, I watched my father change. He had sat down a defeated and humiliated man, the architect of a crashing failure. But he crossed his arms over his chest, as if gathering together the parts of himself, and began to concentrate. His brow furrowed, his lower lip stuck out, and his jaw first twitched, then trembled, and finally settled into a slow grind. As the minutes went by, his eyes regained their luster, and the angles came back into his face, and I could see that he was to emerge from his trance in a state of righteous indignation.

The transformation filled me with both pride and unease. I did not like to see my father defeated, and it pleased me to watch the life return to him. But I understood that it was my mother who would be forced to bear the brunt of this new vitality. It had only taken perhaps ninety seconds—he began to shift his body and to emit small, outraged grunts. My mother, hearing them, stiffened in her chair, sat up a bit straighter, stared with greater intensity at a meaningless spot on the tablecloth.

"A *professor,*" was the first thing my father said.

"A *distinguished professor* of psychology," he elaborated a few seconds later. "Run out of our home."

He waited a long half minute to speak again, this time to the ceiling, his head tipped far back, the tendons on his neck sticking out in sharp relief. "That's who she decided she was smarter than, *Doctor* Avery Stiles. She decided she knew better than *Doctor* Avery Stiles. Because, after all, *she* is a brilliant professor with many advanced degrees, isn't she? Isn't she?

"Oh, that's right," he went on. "No. No, she's not. She's a plain old regular housewife who didn't even finish high school. But of course she knows better anyway.

"Maybe she's just embarrassed that she didn't catch on? Maybe she's upset because *Professor* Avery Stiles *proved* how stupid she is? Maybe that's why she threw him out of her house. Because he told her a *truth* that she didn't want to hear.

"Well, Doctor Stiles is used to that. Perhaps that's why he was so polite, even after being told to *leave* our *humble home.* Because he's used to telling people things they don't want to hear. That's why his colleagues have abandoned him. With their communist ideas. They don't like being told they're weak. They don't want to hear it. They don't want to admit that the *enemy* is *them.*"

My father was shaking his head slowly, his face compressed, as though he were crushing his teeth together inside his closed mouth. My mother, for her part, was highly alert, her eyes wide, her body very still.

"I want to tell you something," he said now, speaking to her directly. He stood up, and his chair slid back and rattled against the breakfront. My mother flinched. "I want to tell you something about that man you kicked out. The man you threw out of our home—who you just expelled from our family. *That* man has no family, Cybele. You know why? They died. His daughter, his wife—they got sick and they died. He has been *alone* for *five years*. What kind of man is that, who can bear the death of his whole family? If it was me, I know what I would do—I would put an end to it all right then and there. I would just put an end to it. And don't think I haven't considered it anyway, Cybele, because I barely even *have* a family as it is. I have a daughter who's never home, and a wife who doesn't care, and doesn't respect me. And I have a son who just sits there"—his arm was thrust out now, pointing at me, and he had raised his voice nearly to a shout—"doing nothing, *saying* nothing, like some kind of goddam zombie. And whose fault is that, Cybele? Who does he get that from? Who just sits and says nothing, and does nothing, and never shows any sign of life?"

He walked around the far end of the table, past Professor Stiles's abandoned meal, and stood beside her, his hands on his hips. He was shouting at her hung head.

"It's *you*, Cybele! It's you! And what do you have to say to that, hah? What do you have to say!"

My mother was frozen now, silent, her eyes squeezed shut.

"That's what I thought," my father spat. "Eric, go outside."

I didn't hear at first—or, rather, I heard, but it was unclear that he was talking to me. I remained in my seat through several seconds of silence.

His head snapped up, the face red and folded over itself like a pug's. *"Go outside!"* he screamed, and I jumped down from my chair and ran out the door.

It was a lovely evening in early spring, a bit cold to be out without a jacket, but I intended to keep moving, and would likely feel no particular discomfort. The sun had set, but there was still light in the near-cloudless sky, enough to see by until I reached the streetlights. I walked the three blocks down Jefferson, turned onto Main, and strolled into town; the closer I came to the park, the busier were the streets—there was Pernice's; there was Old Gerry's Diner. The marquee above the movie theater entrance was illuminated, and high school boys and girls were lined up there for tickets, the boys pushing one another and laughing, the girls huddled into little clusters, whispering to one another. Some kids a little older than I were playing touch football in the park, and I went to a bench and sat down to watch them. On the sidewalk in front of me, a crow was eating a dropped piece of bread.

I woke up shivering to the sound of a man's voice. "Son," the man said, but it wasn't my father. It was a policeman.

"Shouldn't you be going to bed about now? Where do you live?"

I blinked. There was a bit of drool on my face, which I wiped with my sleeve. "Jefferson Street, sir," I said.

"Well, what are you doing here?"

"Going for a walk, sir."

The policeman was short and heavy, and the gray hair underneath his hat was cut close, in the military style. He leveled a skeptical look and said, "You're not walking, son, you're sleeping."

"I just . . . I fell asleep."

"Your parents know you're here?"

"Yes, sir."

The policeman sighed. "C'mon," he said. "I'll give you a lift home."

"I can walk, sir," I said, getting to my feet. I began to inch around him. I noticed my shoe was untied, but that would have to wait.

"I don't think your parents want you walking home in the dark," he said. He put his hand on my shoulder and led me to the edge of the park, where his patrol car was parked. He ushered me through the passenger side door, got in behind the wheel, and pulled away from the curb.

I bent down and tied my shoe. The police car reached the end of Main. The radio quietly squawked and spat.

"Left or right?"

"Right, sir." I hesitated before adding, "Please don't do the lights and siren."

He hazarded a sideways glance. "I wasn't going to."

"Thank you, sir."

When my house was still a block away, I asked him to stop. He reached across me to open the door of the car, and I stepped out.

"Anything you want to tell me, son?" the policeman asked.

"No, sir."

"Sure about that?"

"Yes."

I stood on the sidewalk as he turned around and drove slowly back toward downtown. When the car was out of sight, I hurried the last block to my house, climbed the unlit front steps, and silently opened the front door.

The house was dark, save for the cold glow coming from the kitchen. I could hear water running. The clock on the mantel said it was a quarter to ten, past my bedtime by more than an hour. I was uncertain how aware they would have been of my absence—it was possible that, in the heat of their argument, they would have assumed I had merely gone up to bed and stayed there. But then again, my mother might be worried about me, and would want to know I was home safe.

I decided that, on balance, it was best to sneak up to my room. If my mother thought I was out, she would have had the porch light on, and would have been looking for me through the front window. I crept down the hall and hurried past the archway that led to the dining room.

There, however, I stopped. It was possible to see through the archway, across the dining room, and through a second archway to the kitchen, and I had caught a glimpse of my mother in her familiar position in front of the sink. She didn't turn—the sound of the running water had obscured my footsteps. But something about the scene didn't appear right, and I leaned back for another look.

The dining room table still had not been cleared, though the candles were out, and several glasses had been knocked over, staining the tablecloth. In addition, the tablecloth was crooked, hanging almost to the ground at one corner, and some dishes and silverware had fallen, spattering the floor with food and shards of porcelain. This was unusual, of course. But it was my mother's appearance that was most strange. I was accustomed to seeing her bent over in a laborer's stance, her head hung, her shoulders rolling, arms working at the dishes. She had been, of all things, a golf prodigy in high school—in fact, had dropped out in order to join the tournament circuit, in the hope of becoming a professional—but, according to family lore, had chosen my father over the greens, and put away her clubs for good. I had always been impressed by my mother's athleticism, and her willingness to have abandoned her ambitions for the smaller accomplishments of home. But now I was given to doubt, for the first time, whether this life was what she really had wanted. She stood motionless at the sink, her head high, as though she were staring out the window. The window, however, was curtained. The honey-colored chignon into which she had arranged her hair was half-undone across one shoulder, and she was leaning slightly to one side.

I watched for a good minute, expecting her to break out of her reverie and return to work. But nothing happened. The water was running at full blast, making quite a racket in the otherwise silent house, and I began to grow nervous.

"Mother?" I said.

There was no response. I walked into the dining room and made my slow way around the table, warning her of my presence. "I'm home," I called out. "I'm sorry I'm so late."

I peered into the kitchen. Up close, her stillness seemed even stranger. I could see now that her dress hung crookedly across her shoulders, and the heel of one of her shoes was missing. That accounted for the lean.

"Mother?"

I entered the kitchen, treading heavily, so as not to shock her when I tapped her shoulder. Soon I was standing beside her, looking up.

"Mother!" Her right hand was hanging beside her, and I took it in mine. It was cold. She didn't look at me.

Her left hand was in the sink, under the water. It alarmed me at first to notice that only the hot was turned on—I thought she must be burning. A few plates and forks were stacked under the flow, and her hand lay on top, the water cascading over it. I reached out and moved the faucet over to the opposite sink. It, too, was ice cold. I turned off the water and pulled my mother's hand out.

She had begun to tremble. I ran my hands up her arms—she was freezing! "Here, Mother." I pulled the wooden stool out from under the small table the telephone sat on, and placed it behind her. I told her to sit. She didn't seem to hear me. I pushed her gently, reached up and pushed her shoulders, and she sank slowly, trembling, until she landed on the stool. "Stay there," I said. I ran to the living room, turned up the thermostat, and removed the knitted afghan from the sofa. Back in the kitchen, I wrapped it around her shoulders. Then I took the box of matches from the drawer, turned on the oven, and lit the pilot light. I left the door open—she was sitting right beside it. I heard the furnace clank on beneath us and roar to life.

She was blinking now, and seemed to have noticed me.

"Are you okay?" I asked. "You had your hand under cold water."

Her face was shaking now, too, and her shoulders. Her eyes were full of tears.

"Stay here, Mother," I said. "I'll clean up for you."

I left her there, and went into the dining room. I picked up the debris from the floor, and collected all the plates, glasses, and silverware. I removed the tablecloth and took it downstairs and put it in the washing machine. Then I came back and cleaned up the fallen food, including a bit that had somehow gotten stuck on the wall. Perhaps that had been my doing. I turned the water back on in the sink, and washed the dishes, taking periodic breaks to warm my hands over the oven door.

All the while, my mother watched me in silence. She stopped crying after a few minutes and just watched, her eyes following me around the room. I tried to smile at her every now and then. She seemed to appreciate the work I was doing, or trying to do—I was not yet fully adept at housework, as I am now—but there was something in her gaze that was unfriendly. I couldn't put my finger on it. When the dishes were finished, I went downstairs again and transferred the tablecloth to the dryer, then I returned to the kitchen and took the broom out of the closet.

"Stop it," my mother said.

She was no longer shivering. The afghan had slipped off one of her shoulders, revealing a mark I hadn't noticed before: a livid bruise on her neck, just above the clavicle.

"I'm almost finished," I said.

"Stop it, Eric, please."

I didn't understand. I waited for further instruction, but when none came, I put the broom away and turned off the oven. My mother was still watching me with that slightly hostile, perhaps fearful expression. I tried to think of what I had done to displease her, but came up with nothing. So I went to her and embraced her.

I felt her entire body wince underneath the afghan. She patted me, perfunctorily.

"Go to bed, Eric. It's very late." Her voice was terribly dry and faint.

"Did you like the way I cleaned up?" I asked, embarrassed even as the words left my mouth.

"Yes, thank you."

"I'm sorry I spit food at dinner."

Her only response was a slow nod, which trailed off into a very direct and very discomfiting stare.

"Mother?"

"You know what you are?" she said, her voice flat. "You are your father's son." She blinked. "You should go to bed now."

I paused a long moment before obeying, climbing the stairs to my room in some confusion and unease. When I arrived, I found a small, dark object inhabiting a shallow depression in my pillow. It was the toy locomotive.

The following Saturday morning, my father woke me at the break of dawn. "Get dressed," he said. "You're going to see Doctor Stiles."

FIFTEEN

I woke slowly, as if rising to the surface of a very deep lake. I could feel a pressure gradually lifting, only for it to be supplanted by nausea, faint at first, then increasingly intense. Light gathered, my head throbbed, and soon I found myself violently sick. I heard the sound of rain and could smell its tang, and I shivered. My vision was blurred. I squeezed my eyes shut, blinked, worked away the haze until I could see my surroundings.

I was inside a wooden cage—the same cage, in fact, that I had noticed on my way into the compound. Rusted iron shackles ringed my wrists and ankles, and my body was naked. And though I lay on my back on the cage's floor, my shackles were chained to its ceiling, and my limbs were suspended several inches above the ground. My fingers and toes were cold and numb, and my privates had shrunk to a tiny ball of exposed flesh. I felt terribly weak and very thirsty.

I tugged at the chains, but nothing in the resistance I felt suggested that any was liable to break. Furthermore, my movement had the effect of draining what little energy I possessed, revealing in its wake a deep soreness that pervaded every muscle. My thoughts, too, were dull and uncomprehending, and I struggled to remember what I had been doing that led me here. I recalled a fire in a darkened room, but that was all. I coughed now, as though from a memory of smoke, and my throat felt raw.

"Hello, Eric," came a voice from behind me.

I was startled, and jerked suddenly against the chains, sending another wave of pain washing through my body. I tipped my head back and saw a tall, stooped figure making its way around the cage. It was a man, very old, carrying a wooden chair. The chair was simple, spattered with many colors of paint, and roughened around the edges of the seat by irregular slots, as though someone had been using it as a sawhorse. He set the chair on the flagstones at my feet, lowered himself onto it, and stared at me, his thin, tan hands folded between his bony knees. He wore a torn but close-fitting V-neck sweater and a pair of faded and stained khaki pants. His feet were filthy and bare and his short white hair stood up on his head in all directions.

The old man was Professor Avery Stiles, of course. His face was the same, and when I saw it, I remembered the events that led to my capture, along with the grim reminiscences I indulged as I fell unconscious. I gasped for breath. Doctor Stiles smiled, a gentle, sad expression that nevertheless appeared to harbor great strength. He opened his mouth to speak.

"What do you want from me?" I demanded, and his eyebrows rose, as though with approval at my interruption.

"I might ask you the same, Eric."

"I don't understand." My voice was wet and strangled. I turned my head and spat.

He cocked his head, blinking. Then he straightened, leaned back, and crossed his arms over his chest. Through the sweater I could see his biceps, thin and stringy. His jaw moved involuntarily.

"I was sorry," he said, "to hear about your parents."

I merely stared. When ten seconds or so had passed, he appeared mildly surprised and, again incongruously, somehow pleased.

"I had thought your father was a kindred soul," he went on. "But it appears I was mistaken. A tragedy."

I tried to speak, but all that emerged was a low, spitting growl.

After a moment's thought, he leaned forward, gripping his knees. "I understood that your father possessed a great hidden well of anger. But I never imagined he might commit such an act." Almost as an afterthought, he added, "She was a lovely woman, your mother."

"Her death," I managed at last, "was an accident."

Again the eyebrows went up. "And his own?"

"He couldn't bear the guilt."

As I said this, I recalled the bruise I had seen on my mother's neck, and felt a shiver of revulsion run through me. Professor Stiles studied my movement with a clinical eye.

"Uncomfortable, Eric?"

I said nothing.

"You should be able to free yourself, you know."

Again, I offered no response.

He held out his palms, his long arms like the wings of some great, ancient bird. "I have confidence in you, Eric. You'll find a way."

I gathered my strength and tried to spit at him. But my dehydration was too advanced. Furthermore I sensed that, even had I been successful, he would barely have noticed. His imperviousness was absolute.

He studied me for some seconds, his face knotted with curiosity, and apparent, but surely false, concern. He stroked his white-bristled chin in a parody of deep thought. He leaned forward farther still, until his narrow face was framed by two of the wooden bars.

"Eric," he said, "I think you need to ask yourself what it is, exactly, you're doing here."

I began to feel myself growing tired and nauseous again. I inhaled deeply, to clear my head, but the only tangible result was dizziness. I coughed, gasped, and then failed to suppress an enormous yawn. "You came," I said. "To me. To my house."

But Professor Stiles was shaking his head. "No, Eric. You need to understand the real reason you're here. Not simply to these woods. Home. Why did you come back to Gerrysburg?"

"That's none of your concern," I managed. I could no longer lift my head to see him.

"Where did you live before this, Eric? Why did you leave the place you were before?"

"That's . . ." I muttered. "You . . ." But I could no longer speak, my exhaustion was so profound. Tears gathered in my eyes and rolled down the sides of my head.

Before I fell unconscious, I saw him get up and walk away.

I believe that my first visit to him was in his office at the college. Not the building where I encountered Professor Lydia Bulgakov—a different, older, smaller structure that, as far as I know, is no longer even standing. I recall that the room was taller than it was wide, with windows that stretched floor to ceiling and looked out upon a tree-covered hill that rose up and out of sight. It was my father, of course, who delivered me there, and I remember that he was uncharacteristically subdued, as if in awe. I had, as I've described, seen him indulge in some chummy banter with people in the past, and had known him to brood, or to explode into anger. But I had never seen this state—one of muted respect. Of course I followed suit.

Professor Stiles sat at a large wooden desk that took up a full quarter of the room, its veneer bubbled and peeling and thick with dust. He peered out at us through a canyon formed by a dozen high piles of heavy books, each appearing likely to fall at any moment. His smile when he saw us was wide and humorless and accompanied by a simple nod of acknowledgment.

"Eric," my father said quietly, "sit down." And he pointed to an arrangement of two chairs that stood in a bookcase-lined corner of the room. One was simple and wooden and appeared uncomfortable; the other was large, and thickly upholstered with worn leather. I chose the leather chair, of course, and slid onto it, tipping my head back to examine the incomprehensible titles on the spines of the Professor's books.

My father spoke quietly to Professor Stiles about when he ought to return for me, and a moment later he caught my attention at the door. He said goodbye and told me he would be back soon, and I thought I detected a momentary expression of worry on his heavy, rather tired-looking face. I nodded, he nodded, and he was gone, the heavy door falling shut behind him.

With the door closed, the silence in the room was total. In spite of the windows, it seemed entirely cut off from the outside world. I stared at the door for a moment—a curled and yellow poster on the back bore an etching of some spear-bearing warrior at the wall of a city, a dead man crumpled at his feet.

I then noticed a marked change in the air of the office.

Professor Stiles had stood up behind the desk, and he stared at me now, over the towers of books, with something that appeared to me like hatred. His hair, thin even then, stood up in mad black spikes, and his face glowed faintly with some obscure emotion. I cringed, sinking back into the leather chair.

A few scant seconds later, and with nothing but two long steps, he had crossed the room and struck me, open-handed, across the face.

I was too stunned to cry out, too frightened to move. Professor Stiles leaned over me like a great bird or dinosaur, his deep brown eyes drilling into mine, and snarled, *"What are you doing?"*

Surely there was a correct answer. I stammered. "I . . . I . . ."

"Get off that chair."

I jumped down without hesitation. My legs trembled; the floorboards creaked beneath my feet. The Professor grabbed me by the shoulders and pushed me down into the other chair, the wooden one, which was spattered with paint and squeaked and leaned under my negligible weight.

"In this office," he said with quiet and terrifying intensity, "you do precisely what you are told to do, and nothing more. Did I tell you to sit down?"

"No," I whispered.

"Then why did you sit down, Eric?"

The answer, of course, was that my father had told me to. But it was clear that my father held no sway here, not now, not ever, and that, for the foreseeable future—an hour, but an eternity to me—I would answer entirely to the authority of Professor Stiles. I said, "I . . . I don't know."

"In this room," he said, straightening, "you do everything for a reason. And that reason is that I told you to do it. Do you understand me?"

"Yes."

"Excellent." And with that word, he seemed suddenly to soften. His shoulders relaxed, the creases in his face smoothed out, and his hands found the pockets of his slacks. Beneath the fabric, his bony fingers danced and twitched. "So!" he said, with a smile. "Would you like something to eat?"

Lunch, in fact, was more than an hour away, and I was indeed quite hungry. Still cowed, I merely nodded to indicate my desire.

The Professor strode out the door, and returned a minute later carrying a small china plate. On it lay a fork and a square of frosted cake. "Our department secretary, Mrs. Choate, had a birthday today," he explained. "We celebrated with a bit of cake!" He handed the plate to me, then settled into the leather chair with a satisfied sigh. I forked off a small piece of the cake, and put it in my mouth.

I'd barely had time to taste it when the Professor leaped from his chair, lunged across the space between us, and again struck me on the face, this time knocking the cake from my mouth and the plate and fork from my hands. He had hit me harder this time, and a bloom of dull pain spread through my jaw. I was unable to restrain myself from crying.

"Did I tell you to eat the cake?" he hissed, his face up close to mine, his dank breath in my nose.

"No!" I blubbered.

"Did I not tell you to do nothing that you are not told to do?"

"N—Yes!"

He raised his hand again. I cowered. The hard wooden seat was hurting my behind, and my jaw throbbed. "Did I tell you, Eric," the Professor growled, "to cry?"

"N-no, sir."

"Did I tell you to *cringe?*"

"No, sir." I began to straighten, then abruptly stopped. The Professor smirked.

"Very good," he said. "You may sit up straight."

I obeyed, moving slowly, willing my body to stop shaking. My mind raced—just how precisely, I wondered, must this rule be observed? Would I be punished for sneezing, for twitching? For drawing breath? Would I be slapped if my eyes strayed too far to one side? If I crossed my legs, licked my lips? My face must have been a mask of terror and calculation, and the Professor studied it carefully, eventually drawing back, settling into his chair, and nodding with evident satisfaction.

"Very good," he said again. "You're attempting to determine the parameters of the rule, aren't you? You may answer."

"Yes, sir."

"Be assured, Eric, that you may continue to breathe. Should you feel ill, or need to use the toilet, you are permitted to raise your hand and inform me. You are never to speak without being asked a question. You are never to answer a question with more information than was requested. Do you understand?"

"Yes." I opened my mouth to add, "I think," but restrained myself. For having done so I was able to feel a very small amount of pride.

For some time I would despise Doctor Stiles. In fact, I took the risky step of telling my mother this, though I didn't dare tell her what had gone on at that first meeting. I realized my mistake almost immediately, as my mother leaned close—we sat at the dining room table, me doing my mathematics homework, she her mending—and whispered, with desperate intensity, "What happened, Eric?"

In retrospect, I think it is possible that she had already begun to develop the loathing for me that she would eventually come to embrace fully, and for which I have always been more than willing to forgive her. If I might venture an armchair psychologist's opinion, I believe that, for her, assigning me the role of my father's confederate, and making me complicit in his shortcomings, was less painful for her than the alternative, which was to understand that she ought to have protected me from what was to come, but was powerless to do so. Thus, even at this early date, an edge of resentment and doubt could be heard in her voice, even if I was too young and inexperienced to identify it. I knew only that the question made me uncomfortable.

"N-nothing," I replied.

"Something must have," she demanded.

"We talked."

"About what?"

"Just . . . we talked."

My mother's eyes were pink and wandering, taking in my face as if the truth could be found somewhere on it. When my father's footsteps sounded on the stairs, she pulled back and resumed her work, and I resumed mine.

My sister, however, seemed to know precisely what had transpired at my meeting, or at least understood that I had been severely disciplined. She came into my room that night after I had turned out the light, and knelt by my bedside to interrogate me. The smell of her cigarettes was heavy on her, and I found her presence somehow comforting. She said, "What'd he do to you?"

"Nothing," I answered, for the second time that day.

She shifted her body, making herself more comfortable. I could make her out, just barely, her arms wrapped around her ankles, her chin resting on her knees. "My friend Amy used to know the girl that died. His daughter. She said her mom looked like a concentration camp victim or something." She inclined her head closer to mine and lowered her voice, as though our sleeping parents might hear. "They told her she could kill the cancer by *thinking* about it. And she had to wear old-fashioned dresses and stand with a book on her head."

I didn't respond.

"That's why I split that time he was here," Jill went on. "I figured it was all going to be about making me behave."

Another moment of silence passed. Somewhere outside my cracked-open window, a dog was barking.

"Eric, did Dad hit her or something?"

"Who?" I asked.

"*Mom,*" she said, sounding somewhat exasperated. "She looked nuts the next day. Like . . . just really loony."

I pulled the covers up to my chin. "I should go to sleep now," I told her.

She waited. I heard her tongue move across her lips. "Just watch out for that guy, Eric," she said. "Seriously. You don't have to do what Dad says. You don't have to listen to anybody."

Jill stood up and, seemingly as an afterthought, patted my curled-up form through the blankets. A momentary impulse almost made me ask her to stay, but I kept my mouth shut. Seconds later, she was gone.

The second of my weekly meetings with Doctor Stiles proceeded in much the same way as the first, with the Doctor testing my adherence to his code of conduct, and punishing me with sudden vehemence when I strayed from it. The third week, he slapped me only once, and that merely when the chair beneath me creaked—a circumstance arguably beyond my control. By the fourth week, it was nearly summer, and Doctor Stiles had the windows of his office open, and a spring in his step. I sat, as he had commanded me, in the straight-backed wooden chair, and I had begun to experience what would eventually, in later years, come to be a familiar sense of anxious well-being. I was comfortably suspended in a web of interlocking strands of obligation, strength, and bureaucratic mastery. I was tense, alert, and on the verge of contentment. Doctor Stiles waited long minutes before he spoke, during which I stared straight ahead, at the curled yellow warrior poster on the back of the door. That poster—which I would later learn depicted Achilles' defeat of Hector at the siege of Troy—had become the linchpin of my inner calm, the mast that I had learned to lash myself to when the ship of my tutelage encountered stormy seas.

It was around this time, I believe, that I began to feel different from the people around me. I had never been close to any of my classmates at school, but after a few weeks in Doctor Stiles's presence, I began to take notice of their apparent lack of self-control, their irrational responses to simple problems, their disrespect for their teachers. But my feelings were more complicated than that: the teachers themselves came under my scrutiny as well, and I could not help but notice the inexpertise with which they wielded their authority. By comparison, Doctor Stiles was a master of consistency and restraint. Though I appreciated my teachers' praise of my newly adopted poise, obedience, and serenity, I had begun to realize that they were weak leaders, easily swayed by their emotions, easily manipulated by their charges. At times, when the only response they could muster to a rowdy classroom was a deep, tired sigh, I pitied them.

Now Doctor Stiles broke the silence of his office. "Eric, I have something I wish to tell you today."

I remained still, concentrating on the crumpled form of Hector at Achilles' feet.

The Professor crossed the room and stood before me. "Please stand up," he said, "and sit in the leather chair."

I did as I was told, without registering the surprise I felt. The Doctor took my place in the wooden chair, leaning back without fear of the chair's collapse, despite its unnerving creak. He threw one long leg over the other in a fluid, almost feminine motion, and one might have thought, to look at him, that he was more at ease there than in the soft and sturdy chair I now occupied. I gazed at him in silent anticipation.

"Perhaps you know that I am without wife or child," the Doctor began. "My daughter died of an illness some years ago, and my wife, by a cruel coincidence, also died soon after.

"My daughter was named Rachel," he went on, "and she was preoccupied with the notion of living in a castle. I suppose this is the case with many girls, but in Rachel's case, the desire was very intense, and I felt dutybound, as her father, to provide her with the same. In addition to my salary here at the college, I am fortunate to possess considerable family wealth, and I set out to create a home for my family that would fulfill my daughter's wishes. Based on a drawing she made of the castle she envisioned, I designed a dwelling, a small castle, and hired contractors and builders to help me make it a reality. I chose a secluded, wooded area on our property, a clearing at the base of a large rock outcropping, and began construction. That was seven years ago.

"This might be difficult for you to understand, Eric, but my wife—and yes, even my daughter—did not appreciate my plans. At first they did, of course—there is a romantic charm to the idea of building a castle, in this day and age. But the project soon came to obsess me, and I lost sight of the very people whose lives I hoped to enhance with it. I spent most of my time at the building site, particularly in the summer, when the weather was fine and the college was not in session. My daughter cried herself to sleep some nights, and my wife eventually ceased conjugal relations with me."

He paused, and frowned at me. "Do you know what that means, Eric?"

I did not speak.

"You may speak."

"Yes, sir."

"Tell me what it means."

"It means sexual intercourse?"

Doctor Stiles scowled at my interrogative tone. I knew that I was on thin ice, and might soon be struck. I knew very little about sex, my mother having sketchily explained it to me after I inadvertently caught a glimpse of her in bed with my father.

"Do you believe that it means sexual intercourse, or not, Eric?"

"It does mean sexual intercourse, sir."

"Do you know what sexual intercourse is?"

I knew that I had to be decisive. "Yes, sir."

"Eric, tell me what sexual intercourse is."

"It's a man and a woman," I said. "And they . . . they have no clothes on, and are together in bed. And it makes her pregnant. Sir."

I felt certain now that he would slap me, but instead, a small smile appeared to play at his lips. He let out a long breath that I had not noticed him drawing, and continued his story as though he had never paused.

"It is an unfortunate fact, Eric," he said, "that people's desires are irrational. My daughter wanted a castle, and my wife wanted me to please my daughter. But neither considered the incidental costs of the fulfillment of such a desire, and it was this cost—my absence from their lives—that they had failed to imagine. This did not prevent them from complaining about it, however.

"My wife and I never resolved our differences over this issue, Eric, but Rachel and I did. When she was in her sickbed, she used to gaze out the window at the rock under which her castle was being constructed. She kept her drawing of the castle taped to the wall beside the window, and she imagined what it would look like when it was finished. Unfortunately, she was never to see the completed structure. She died of her illness while I was at work upon it."

Doctor Stiles gazed at me hungrily. I remained perfectly still.

"Eric, though my family is gone, my castle is finished. Its purpose, until now, was uncertain. But you have given me the inspiration to put it to use. I want to tell you that you have shown tremendous potential in these sessions, and I would like to continue them with you, at my castle. The tests of personal control and endurance you have been given here, you have passed with flying colors. You could become a young man of tremendous strength and loyalty, and a great leader. I would like you, Eric, to spend the summer in my castle."

Though I did not, of course, reply, I felt an upwelling of pride and personal satisfaction at the Doctor's words, even as I felt a deep anxiety about what he was asking me to do, whatever it might be.

"Is there anything you would like to say, Eric?"

This was not a question he had ever asked me before. I cleared my throat.

"You may speak," he said.

I hesitated before replying, "Thank you, sir. No, sir, I have nothing to say."

He nodded once. "Good. I will speak with your father, then."

SIXTEEN

There was a fight. It seemed to me at the time that it was my mother who was being unreasonable, and who threw the first punch. Or perhaps it was a slap. In my mind's eye, I can see her strike my father, open-handed, on the face, and my father recoil in shock and surprise. In fact, I remember him stumbling backward across the living room, tripping over the ottoman, and banging his head, hard, against the mantel. I also remember seeing him with bandages around his head, and a limp.

However, I also remember coming home from school to find my mother missing and my father waiting in her place, and hearing from him that Mother wasn't feeling well, and they had had an argument while I was at school, and she had forbidden me to spend the summer at Doctor Stiles's. My father, however, had extracted a promise from her that I would be permitted to attend sessions with the Professor twice weekly for the entire summer, beginning the week school let out.

In my memory, my father was unharmed during this conversation, and I recall not being allowed to see my mother for several days due to her illness. And that, when I did see her at last, it was she who had a limp, and her face was purple and swollen, and she didn't speak for quite some time.

It is difficult to reconcile these memories, I'm afraid. Perhaps I am recalling a different injury of my father's, one he sustained at work. I vaguely remember something about a fall from a ladder. And, rationally speaking, it seems unlikely that I would have been present for this fight. Yet I am struck by the vividness of this memory—the balletic grace in my mother's slap, the studied athleticism. I see the slap being delivered with the same strength and precision I imagine her golf swing to have possessed, back before she married my father.

In any event, a fight did occur, the result of which was that I would be given over to Doctor Stiles's care twice weekly, from sunrise to sunset. Though I expressed disappointment that I wouldn't be there for the entire summer, I was privately relieved, as I had been looking forward to spending time alone as I usually did, wandering through the neighborhood and exploring the swamp and woods. I felt mildly guilty, harboring this desire, and chastised myself for my weakness.

In the final week of June, on a Friday morning, my father woke me before dawn and told me to get dressed. When I came down into the kitchen, he was waiting there with a cup of coffee. "It's time you tried it," he said.

I took the hot mug into my hands and blew on the oily black surface. I had sipped my mother's coffee once, and found it peculiar but nonetheless appealing. That coffee, however, had had cream and sugar added. I looked at my father.

As if reading my mind, he said, "No sugar and milk. That's for women."

I nodded, and sipped. The coffee scalded my mouth. I surprised myself by suppressing my cry of pain, and realized that it was because of Doctor Stiles's training that I was able to do so. The thought made me proud. I was a person who could endure pain. I wondered, idly, if any of my acquaintances at school could say the same, and I surmised that none could. There was no time to drink it all, though—my father soon led me out to the car, and we took to the road in the pink light of sunrise.

My father, true to form, did not speak as we drove. It occurs to me now to wonder what it must have felt like to him, to be so uncomfortable in the presence of his own son. Most likely his own feelings of low self-worth—his fear that he was, or was perceived as, stupid—came into play here. I know that he considered me to be intelligent, because he once wondered aloud how it was possible I was so smart, as I didn't get it from him, and I sure didn't get it from my mother, and my sister sure as hell didn't have it, either. Of course he underestimated my mother as well as himself, and perhaps even my sister, too. At any rate, I was now under the tutelage of a "famous professor," as I had heard him tell the man at the hardware store, and this fact must have both intimidated him and filled him with pride, two emotions that tended to have the effect of silencing him entirely.

Over the next twenty minutes, we wended our way out of town and out into what appeared to me at the time to be untrammeled wilderness. My family was not "outdoorsy" and rarely left the house except to run errands in town, so this trip had the flavor of the exotic and new. I gazed into the dark woods, imagining what might be in them. Soon we had crested a hill and there, in an intersection, stood a white house.

The house was two stories, clapboarded, and surrounded by what must once have been a lovely flower garden and arboretum, with curved paths running through it, and trellises and gates, and low stone walls. It was obvious to me, even at the age of ten, that the garden had not been tended to for some time; the plants were shaggy, crowding one another, and wild grapevine had begun to overwhelm the whole.

We parked on a gravel drive and were met at the door by Doctor Stiles. Here, at his home, he looked very different. He wore torn and discolored khaki pants and a khaki shirt with four pockets, two on each breast. His boots were heavy and worn, and his eyeglasses were absent. I had dressed much as I had for the office visits, in dress shoes and pants, and a plaid short-sleeved Oxford shirt, and I suffered a moment of embarrassment as he glanced pityingly at me.

"Good morning, Eric."

"Good morning, sir."

He turned to my father. "That will be all, Brian," he said.

My father's hand had been resting on my shoulder. Now it tightened, as though nervously, and slipped away.

"All right then!" my father said, drawing a deep breath. "So I should see you here at . . . ?"

"Sundown."

"Eric," my father said, "I'll see you later."

I stood very still, and did not speak.

"Son, I'm heading out."

Doctor Stiles faced me, his brow creased, his hard eyes boring into mine. I blinked and tried to look past him, at the house. I hoped my father would understand that I was not able to speak. But he persisted.

"Son, turn and say goodbye to your father." He was angry, to be sure—he grabbed me by the shoulder and spun me around to face him.

"Good*bye*, Eric," he said, in a tone that would brook no argument.

Quietly, as if there were some chance that Doctor Stiles wouldn't hear, I said, "Goodbye."

"Speak up," my father answered. "I can't hear you."

At last I gave up all pretense. I stood straight and barked out a second farewell: "Goodbye, Father." My father smiled, less at my words, I think, than at the fact of his having retained authority over me. My goodbye extracted, he shook Doctor Stiles's hand and drove away.

As soon as the car was out of sight, I heard the faint crack of Doctor Stiles's shoulder, and the whisper of his sleeve against his arm, and a moment later I found myself lying on the gravel, my right ear exploding in pain.

My instinct was to get up, but I remained on the ground. I heard the Doctor's footsteps as they climbed the front stoop, and the sound of the door being opened. A few minutes later, I heard him emerge.

"Stand up."

I did as he said, and faced the road, as I had been doing when he hit me.

"Turn around."

His face was expressionless. "You will be very uncomfortable today," he said, "and your clothes will be ruined. Next time, you will dress more appropriately." He paused to make sure I wouldn't answer. Then he nodded once, and said, "Follow me."

I followed Doctor Stiles to the treeline, where he stepped over a deadfall and into the trees. Though the sun was fully risen now, the air was cold and the light dim. The woods, though hardly impassable, were tough going, and I had difficulty keeping up. The Doctor walked with complete confidence, seeming to follow some zigzagging, almost arbitrary path, and I understood that, wherever we were headed, I would be entirely incapable of finding my way back without him.

We walked for what must have been the better part of an hour. My blood raced and my mouth was dry, perhaps from the coffee I had drunk, and to which I was unaccustomed; and I was growing very tired. In addition, I had to urinate, and Doctor Stiles, disinclined to turn around, would never see my raised hand. Branches raked my face, my good pants tore on a fallen tree limb, and my stiff dress shoes were rubbing my skin raw.

I was momentarily distracted from my discomforts, however, when the trees thinned and what I thought to be a huge gray wall came into view. It was, in fact, a giant stone, protruding from the ground as if dropped there from the sky. The wall was sheer and stretched high into the air.

But Doctor Stiles did not stop to admire it. Rather, he turned left and continued around it, at an increased pace now that the ground was clear of trees and brush.

Ironically, it was at this moment that my fatigue overwhelmed me, and my thin legs gave out. I lay in the dirt as my bladder emptied, and tears stung my hot and filthy face. I wanted to cry out, to ask the Doctor to stop and wait, but I knew how such a request would be met: with violent, dispassionate cruelty. I thought, uncharacteristically, of my sister, and longed to fall into her arms. And it was this very thought—and my growing disgust for myself, for thinking it—that eventually forced me to my feet, and the tears from my eyes. I stood panting for some seconds, trying to get my bearings. The enormous wall of rock was to my right, and we had arrived from my left—but what these directions represented, and what our goal might be, was impossible to discern. I assumed I was being led to Doctor Stiles's castle, but none was in sight. I could only continue in the last direction I had seen the Professor walk—and so, gathering up my strength, I set off along the rock wall.

In a moment, the rock began to curve, and soon it had turned a corner, running off to the right. It was less smooth here, but still rose nearly vertical into the sunny sky; I walked along it for a few minutes more.

And then, at last, I came to a man-made wall about twenty feet tall, and I knew I had arrived at the castle. The wall terminated at each end with a tower, one topped by a conical turret, the other stout and square with slotted sides. The slots seemed to penetrate deeply into stone, giving the castle an impression of tremendous strength. There was, however, no sign of my tutor.

I continued around the castle, staring up at the towers, alert for any movement. Soon my neck grew tired and I was forced to lower my head. Eventually I made it all the way around, and came to an enormous wooden door, bound together with iron straps and spikes. There was a handle, as well, but no matter how hard I pushed and pulled, I could not budge it.

It was when I stood back to reconsider my tactic that I heard the Doctor's voice, faint and distorted by echoes, bouncing off the cliffs above.

"Eric. Find your way in."

May I say that I am embarrassed to recount the relief, even joy, that I felt when I heard that voice? It was as though I was hearing the voice of God. My exhaustion, the acrid damp of my ruined pants, my aching feet: all of it fell away and I felt the full, validating force of my mentor's call.

I knew better than to reply—for that, I would be punished. I began to examine the enormous door more carefully now, searching every crack and irregularity for some hidden lever, hasp, or key that would allow me to open it. I must have spent half an hour, at one point even dragging a large branch from the woods to climb up on, in order to search the upper portion of the door. My efforts were futile, though, and I returned the way I came, feeling along the curtain wall for some handhold.

An hour's work made it clear that there was none. I tried several times to climb the wall, but the masonry was even and firm, and I slipped back down to the ground each time.

For some long minutes I sat on the forest floor, my back against the wall, and I fell asleep. When I woke, the sun was lower in the sky, my mouth was rank and dry, and I was very hungry. Yet I was determined to attain my goal.

I walked back the way I had come, toward the wooden door, then passed it, heading for the place where the wall met the rock. And it was there I found my answer—a narrow gap between the two, wide enough to admit me. I hurried down it, my eyes raking the ground for the point of entry, and within minutes I had discovered the hole in the wall, and the wooden block with the handle. I pulled it out, ducked inside, and shimmied through the tunnel and into the castle.

I would soon have ample time to take in the courtyard, but at this moment my attention was focused, fifteen or so feet from where I stood, upon a strange but welcome sight—a crude wooden table, standing on the flagstones, overlaid with a white cloth, and bearing a single dinner plate, utensils, a drinking glass, and a folded napkin. The plate was heaped with mashed potatoes, steak, and peas, and the glass full of milk. Even from here, I could see the steam rising from the food. I raced to the table, tripping and nearly falling on my way, and collapsed into the wooden chair tucked underneath the place setting. I had never been so famished, and began to shovel the food into my mouth, barely chewing before I swallowed and scooped up another load.

Because of my manic attention to the meal, I failed to notice precisely when Doctor Stiles appeared and sat down across the table from me. I only registered his presence when I heard him say, "Stop eating."

I looked up, stunned, and swallowed the bite of potatoes and meat I had been chewing. My eyes narrowed involuntarily as I awaited the blow, but it didn't come. Instead, the Doctor rewarded me with a half smile.

"I'm sorry, Eric," he said. "Please, continue."

After a moment's hesitation to make sure I wasn't being tricked, I resumed eating, this time at a more reasonable pace. I hazarded a glance at the Doctor every few seconds, alert for changes in his demeanor. He appeared strangely composed, given the unusual setting, and our having made our way here through those dense, treacherous woods.

"Have you noticed, Eric," he asked me suddenly, "anything unusual about these woods?"

I slowed my chewing as I considered, then swallowed and said, "No, sir." My voice came out hoarse, as if I'd been screaming for hours.

"What usually bothers you, Eric, when you eat outdoors?"

"Rain?" I offered, and drained the milk glass.

"Perhaps, but what I'm referring to is insects. Have you noticed any here?"

"No, sir," I admitted, shaking my head.

"What about squirrels?"

"No, sir."

"Aside from a few birds high overhead, or perched on the rock," Doctor Stiles said, "there aren't any. Not that I've seen. At first, I thought that the construction of the castle had simply disrupted their environment. But it's been several months now since it was finished, and the animals have not returned. Do you know what I think, Eric? I think this place is tainted."

The food was almost gone. I couldn't remember ever having eaten so much in a single sitting in my entire life.

"I'm sure you wonder what could taint a forest. I'll tell you my theory. I believe this is where, in the early 1800s, every single member of the Kakeneoke tribe of Indians was massacred by white settlers. I have read about this massacre in a few books of local history, and a number of historical journals. It is also mentioned in the handwritten journal of a retired Revolutionary War soldier named Ezekiel Cordwell, who homesteaded nearby. None of these sources are specific about the time and place of the massacre, and they all have spelled the tribe's name slightly differently. But I believe they are all referring to the same event, and I believe that this event happened here." He leaned forward. "Do you wonder, Eric, what evidence I have for this belief?"

"No, sir."

"I'll tell you, Eric—I have no evidence. But I can feel it, in my gut. Do you know what I mean by that?"

"No," I said, and a jolt of fear sent me bolt upright in the chair. I had left off the "sir" and expected the Professor to hit me. But he continued to speak as if he hadn't noticed.

"I mean that I have taken all available information—the peculiarity of the woods, the stories I have read, the maps I have pored over—and processed it through the unique filter of my particular intelligence, and have come up with a feeling, an almost physical sensation, that I am correct. Sometimes, Eric, it is possible to *know* you are correct. The feeling I get when I am right about something is very powerful, and infallible. The massacre happened here.

"I'll tell you something else," he went on, stretching out his legs and gazing at the sky, as though to judge the time of day. "I believe that whatever lingers here from that gruesome event, whatever force or substance or *idea* that has tainted these woods, is what sickened and killed my wife and daughter. Somehow, the essence of the massacre has remained here, in the ground, in the very trees and wind and water, and has retained the power to kill." He paused, then turned to me, his gaze frightening and direct.

"You and I, Eric, are in no danger. I can promise you that. We have something my family did not—we are strong. We are destined for greatness. Don't forget that."

He was through speaking, and he stared at me now for many minutes on end, seemingly without blinking. For my part, I did not entirely understand what he said, though I would remember his words and reflect upon them often in the years to come. I did understand, though, that I had been declared exceptional, and I believed it to be so. I *knew* it to be so.

I don't accurately recall the journey out of the woods that night, although I do remember that it was nearly dark when we emerged at the house, and that my father was there to collect me, and that he was forced to pull over to the side of the road on the way home, in order to let me vomit. I also remember my mother's stricken expression when she saw my face and clothes, and the wonderful sensation, once I had bathed and was comfortably tucked into my bed, of succumbing to absolute exhaustion. I don't think I have slept so deeply in my life, nor do I expect to ever again.

SEVENTEEN

That summer, and the next, were filled with moments of terrible isolation, loneliness and fear, hours in complete darkness, exhaustion and pain. But I also know that I experienced great joy there—with Doctor Stiles's help, I honed my strength and agility, lifting and building structures, climbing walls, hunting the Doctor and hiding from him in the woods.

It was this latter activity that has provided me with perhaps my most intense memory of those days, an event that occurred in late summer of my second year with Doctor Stiles.

For some time, the Professor had petitioned my parents to allow me to spend the night in the castle with him. This would certainly have been acceptable to my father, and to me as well, but my mother objected, and for whatever reason, her opinion was respected. It was understood that I would be returned at the end of every training day to the house at the top of the hill. Eventually this arrangement became routine, and after a while I no longer even thought about the possibility of its being otherwise.

Each morning, when the Doctor and I embarked upon our journey to the castle, we entered the forest from a different location at the edge of the yard, and struck out through the trees in a different direction; on the way back, we would do the same. Though I sometimes thought I recognized some familiar landmarks—a particular stand of trees, or marsh, or patch of moss—I never felt as though I could find my way to the castle on my own, nor find my way back out to the house or road. Initially, this disorientation caused me some unease, but I had long since grown used to Doctor Stiles's unorthodox ways, and come to expect these idiosyncratic treks. Indeed, at the time this incident occurred, I had even become rather complacent— though my days in the woods were always a challenge, I was confident that the challenge was always one I could meet.

On the morning in question—a hot, overcast, and muggy one in the middle of August—the Doctor and I set out as usual, with him nimbly hopping over bramble and deadfall, from one clear patch of ground to the next, and me following carefully about ten steps behind. By now I knew how to dress on these outings—I had acquired a pair of khaki jungle pants with zippered legs that could be removed below the thighs, to protect from abrasions or excessive heat, and wore sturdy, lightweight boots and a wide-brimmed hat. I remember feeling particularly self-assured and comfortable that day—at the age of eleven, I had achieved what I considered to be an unusual level of self-confidence and physical well-being.

About half an hour into our journey, the Doctor stopped suddenly, raised one hand in the air, and cocked his head, as though to better hear some faint noise. Needless to say, I stopped as well, and listened carefully.

We were standing on the sloping bank of a slight depression in the forest floor, with a patch of swampy ground at the bottom, bisected by a moss-covered fallen tree. I could neither see nor hear anything out of the ordinary. Ten feet ahead, Doctor Stiles lowered his hand and used it to reach into his pocket. He pulled out a small mason jar, unscrewed the lid, and removed what appeared to be a white handkerchief. Then he set the open jar down on the ground. As I looked on, he slowly turned and made his way toward me, on his face an expression of slightly amused alertness. I waited for him to address me.

Instead, he reached down and placed his free hand on the back of my head. The gesture was affectionate, even loving, and for a moment I wondered how I was expected to respond. But before I could, the Doctor brought up his other hand and pressed the handkerchief to my face.

His grip was strong, and I was unable to move. The handkerchief reeked of something acrid and antiseptic, and I gasped in spite of myself. My throat and nose burned, and I thought I could feel the burn rocket straight up through my sinuses and into my brain. I crumpled, insensible, to the ground.

When I woke, the day seemed later, the sun higher in the sky, the air more oppressive. My head ached, and sticks gouged my side where I lay. I was incredibly thirsty.

I reached down for my canteen and discovered that I was naked.

The realization motivated me to sit up straight, and I let out a yelp. I looked around me. There was no one and nothing. I had fallen somewhat farther down toward the center of the depression, and one of my heels rested in the pool of water at the bottom. Sunlight filtered through the trees, and my lungs burned as I drew breath after gasping breath.

Slowly I remembered what had happened—Doctor Stiles, I understood, must have knocked me unconscious. I began to lay out, in my mind, the possibilities. This act could indeed have been of sinister intent, but it was much more likely to be some kind of escalation in the Doctor's testing regimen. The latter explanation gave me some comfort, but I was still a child, accustomed to the supervision of an adult, and still quite modest about my body. It occurred to me that Doctor Stiles must have been the one who undressed me. He had seen me naked! The thought disgusted and excited me—I tried to put out of my mind this strange and entirely unexpected transgression.

I stood up slowly, wary that I might be sick to my stomach. But it seemed that my head had cleared, and though I remained thirsty, I felt otherwise physically sound. I looked around, taking stock of my surroundings, wondering what I was supposed to do now, and where I was supposed to go. I had no compass, no rope or knife, not even any shoes. I was not terribly uncomfortable now, but I knew that, as soon as I began walking, my feet would be cut and scraped, and would likely become infected. The tasks and challenges the Doctor typically assigned to me always seemed to have some purpose—the strengthening of a vital survival skill, or the sharpening of my wits—so I struggled to understand what the point of this one might be. But after long minutes of contemplation, I was forced to admit to myself that I had no idea.

Of course, this might be the point—perhaps Doctor Stiles intended for me to realize that there was no point. Maybe I was supposed to be learning how to act with no goal in mind, and no viable option for proceeding. If so, I was failing, because all I felt was a growing despair and boredom, and a creeping fear. I had never been naked anywhere, let alone the woods; and though Doctor Stiles insisted that there were no wild animals here, the likelihood of attack seemed high. Surely the beasts of the forest could sense the presence of an unprotected human being. Were there bears here, or mountain cats? What about hawks and vultures—did they ever attack human beings? I looked down and found my genitals covered by both my hands, in an involuntary, instinctive, and futile gesture of protection, and I'm afraid I began to cry. Was the Doctor watching? Was he off somewhere in the trees, observing, noting my transgressions against his tutelage? What punishment would be meted out for my weaknesses? I must have stood there, intermittently thinking and blubbering, for at least fifteen minutes. Then, at last, bored and disgusted with myself, I took my first tentative steps out of the depression.

It must have taken me ten minutes to reach the lip and peer around the surrounding woods. Already my feet were tender, and everything looked exactly the same in every direction. I had no compass, of course, and above the forest canopy the clouds now blocked the sun, leaving its position unclear. I tried to remember what side of the trees the moss was supposed to grow on—I thought it might be the north—but when I examined my immediate surroundings, the moss seemed to be growing arbitrarily wherever there was room for it. I had the distinct, if foolish, impression that the landscape stretched identically in all directions, forever. My eyes stung and I choked back a sob.

With nothing else to do, I chose a direction and walked in it. The going was slow and painful. As I had predicted, my feet were poked and scratched, thorny branches kept swinging into my path and scraping my legs, and I was growing thirstier—and now hungrier—with every passing moment. Because I felt compelled to keep my hands over my genitals, my balance was poor, and I nearly fell several times. And though I stumbled through the trees for what seemed like hours, the position of the sun never appeared to change.

I did, however, have one conviction that kept me from complete despair, and that was the inevitability of my return to the house at sunset. At some point, Doctor Stiles would have to find me, return my clothes to me, and lead me back to the hilltop, where my father would be waiting in his truck. All I had to do was endure the day—and though I was certain that this tactic would not meet with the Doctor's approval, I was already beyond caring. Whatever punishment he chose to administer, I would accept it. But I would not play his game.

My memory is unclear on the precise manner in which I passed the afternoon. I would imagine that I did a lot of wandering, and perhaps took a few naps. I remember very clearly one particular nap, because it was upon waking from it that I realized the hour had grown late, well past the time when Doctor Stiles and I generally began our trek out of the woods and back to the house. Indeed, judging from the filtered light of the forest, it was possible that my father was already waiting for me there.

I spoke for the first time in hours, breaking the cardinal rule of speaking only when asked to. I called out his name, first quietly, then more loudly, until I was fairly screaming it. I had not realized just how completely a dense wood could swallow up a person's voice; I had the distinct impression that, even had Doctor Stiles been standing a mere twenty-five feet away, he still might not hear me.

I stood up and began to pace, straining my eyes to look more deeply into the forest, hoping to make out a figure there, or some evidence that I was, in fact, close to the hilltop after all. But the woods appeared just as inscrutable and frightening as ever. I called out until my voice grew hoarse, then called out some more, and as the sunlight leached away, my voice became weaker, and I could no longer deny the obvious fact that night was falling, and I had been abandoned to my fate in the dark woods.

For some minutes, I simply leaned against a tree and sobbed. I felt as though I had no other option, that I would starve or freeze—for the temperature had begun to drop—or be devoured by animals, and could only stand and wait for my fate. My thirst, however, which I had temporarily managed to forget, returned with almost unbearable force, and it motivated me to start moving again.

There must have been a full moon, or close to it, because the darkness never enveloped me completely. In a sense, I could actually see better this way—my field of vision, limited by the dim, was more focused, and I was not confused by the enormity of the forest. I moved steadily, feeling from tree to tree, careful not to walk in a circle by mistake. I was thinking of the drive here and back with my father—many of the roads we traveled upon ran along creeks or ditches, and there had been rain the day before. If I walked in a straight line for as long as possible, I would eventually come to a road, and beside that road there might be water. It wasn't much of a plan, but it was the first real plan I had come up with, and it gave me the impetus to move.

I walked for hours, or what seemed like hours. And eventually, I was rewarded with a sound: the very faint gurgle of water.

I wanted to increase my pace. But the woods here were unusually thick, and I was forced to grope toward the noise. It was real, though, the distinct sound of a creek, straight ahead. It seemed like an hour or more before I reached it, and when I did, I nearly fell in—the trees ran right up to its edge, and the bank dropped off sharply, straight down into the water. The stream was perhaps four feet wide, and flowed quickly, considering it was late summer. Bracing myself against an exposed root, I stepped gingerly into the current.

My relief was profound. So good did the cool water feel on my aching, wounded feet, that I let out a mad-sounding laugh. I bent down and scooped up a double handful of water, intending to examine it in the dim moonlight, to see if it was too silty or muddy to drink. But once I had brought it to my face, I couldn't resist. I gulped it down, then fell to my knees and thrust my face into the current. I gulped in long, choking draughts until I was sated, then I sat up, grew dizzy, and collapsed on my back into the creekbed. It was only a few inches deep, and I lay there with the water running over and around me, and thanked the God that I don't think I had ever before believed in. I may even have slept there, with the water lapping against my cheeks, and the forest canopy moving above me, shifting and throbbing, a darker black against the faintly glowing black of the sky.

Indeed, I must have slept, because I remember waking to even deeper night, and cold. I was cold there, in the water, freezing in fact, and I began to shiver, so violently that I thought I might break apart. I sat up and let out a cry, and saw a smear of movement out of the corner of my eye.

It was a ghost.

Or so I thought at first. It stared at me out of round black eyes; its chest was broad, its hair white and strangely peaked above the ears. It stood on a pair of spindly legs and appeared to have no arms at all.

I stared at it, and it stared back, insensible and silent. Then I blinked, and the ghost moved, exposing its flank.

Of course it was a deer, a white deer. I had seen them before, elsewhere in the Town of Henford, while driving with my parents. It was my mother who habitually pointed them out, usually just before sunset, when we were on the way home from one of our infrequent nights out for dinner. But I had never come near one. Indeed, I had never before seen a living thing in this forest.

I stood up slowly from the water, eager not to frighten the animal. My heart thumped. I noticed that my shivering had stopped, and I stepped out of the creek.

The deer bounded off, twenty paces away, and looked at me over its shoulder. Without forethought, and feeling a new warmth race through my body, I took a step, and then another. When I was almost near enough to reach out and touch it, the deer leaped again, this time veering off to the left.

Again I followed, and again it bounded away and looked back. It would have been sensible to think that it was merely trying, though not very skillfully, to evade me—surely, at any moment, it would give up the game and dart away for good, beyond my field of vision. But I had become convinced that the deer wanted me to follow it, that it knew I could see no more than ten yards into the woods, and took care not to move beyond that distance.

The going ought to have been rough, as it had been ever since the Doctor knocked me out and left me to my own devices. But my feet fell only upon patches of moss, flat stones, and soft humus, and I was moving fast enough to break a sweat. I should have been exhausted, terrified, consumed by anger. I was not. I felt as though the woods were mine—that I knew every twig, every bramble and pebble, every handful of earth, by heart. It was as though I were dreaming.

But if it was a dream, it was the most intense, the most detailed, I had ever experienced. I believed that I possessed spectacular agility, strength, and stamina; that I could have described every footstep in aching detail, could have shown how I turned my ankle, and flexed my toes, the way I fell to earth and landed gently and firmly, and sprang up again to find the next patch of welcoming ground. I did not panic, nor did I fall, or doubt for even a moment the rightness of my direction. As I followed the deer, I became the deer. As I negotiated the woods, I became the woods. As I raced through the night, I was the night.

And then, suddenly, the deer was gone. It stepped behind a tree and never emerged on the other side. I stopped, and my foot came to ground on a sharp twig, which snapped with a deafening crack. Where had it gone? I leaned to one side, then the other, and saw no sign of it. I made my way to the tree—slowly and carefully, as the ground here was suddenly uneven and littered with obstacles—and walked all the way around it, once, then twice.

There was nothing. And for a moment, I felt despair creeping back into my heart, because I thought that I was lost once again.

Then I looked up, and saw the wall.

It was, undoubtedly, the wall of the castle. The deer had led me here, then melted away into the forest. I stepped out of the trees and across the clearing, and slipped into the now-familiar opening between the wall and the rock. In almost total blackness, I felt my way to the wooden block, and pulled it free, and wriggled through the tunnel and into the courtyard.

The clouds had parted and moonlight flooded the castle. The silence was total. I stood on the cool flagstones, panting faintly, waiting to grow calm. The cage, the balance table, all the devices I had trained upon were motionless, yet they seemed filled with grim potential in this eerie light. I was filled with a sense of well-being, a strange confidence and maturity, as if I were safe at home, in my bed, instead of naked and alone under the yawning sky. I blinked, waited another moment, and then moved.

From time to time I had seen Doctor Stiles disappear into the low compound in the corner of the yard, and it was to this doorless opening that I now crept, with as much stealth as I could muster. I stepped over the threshold, alert for signs of life; my eyes grew accustomed to this deeper gloom, and I saw that the room around me was empty. Stone steps extended into the ground before me, and faint light emanated from the stairwell, and the smell of smoke. My fingers brushed the walls as I descended, steadying my tired body. I reached the bottom and walked through the open door.

He lay, wrapped in an army blanket, on the floor beside the dying embers of a small fire. He faced the ceiling and his eyes were closed. Beside him, about three feet away, my clothes were neatly folded in a pile. The room was spacious and low-ceilinged, and contained nothing else but Doctor Avery Stiles, the fire, and my things.

I moved around the room, staying close to the wall until I could reach the clothes. I picked them up, stepped back, and lay them down again, out of the Doctor's reach. Then I approached him, knelt, and studied his sleeping face.

The Doctor was not a good-looking man. Of course I would not have understood this at the time—I was a child, and had rarely had the opportunity to look closely at anyone, let alone a grown man who wasn't my father. But his face was distinctive, severe, the cheeks and eyes sunken, the bones sturdy and ghoulishly pronounced. The muscles of his jaw were twitching in the ember-light, as if he were dreaming of something frightening. His neck was long, and rough with beard stubble, and his Adam's apple, the largest I have ever seen, moved up and down with haunted slowness, like a will-o'-the-wisp.

I became fixated on that Adam's apple, and the neck that contained it, the tendons taut and long, the throat a dark depression between them, the blood pulsing in the vein. And when my hands moved toward it, it was as though they were someone else's, and I a passive observer. They were curled like claws, these hands, and crusted over with earth, the fingernails long and filthy, the creases and pores standing out in sharp relief. They were like the hands of an old man, wizened but still strong, and I understood that they meant to murder Doctor Avery Stiles, to choke him in his sleep.

They had that power, I knew. He would struggle, but I would not let go. I would press the life from him, crush his throat, cut off the blood to his brain. (I knew about these things from comic books and films—or thought I knew, as, in retrospect, I am certain I could not possibly have killed Doctor Stiles.) My hands drew closer and closer, and then, when they were about to make contact with his rough flesh, they stopped.

His eyes were open. They were darting back and forth as though following some mad insect as it flew around the room. It took several seconds before I realized that he was still asleep.

Before I could relax, however, his head turned, and those eyes appeared to stare at me, and his face softened, and the eyes went limpid and sad, and tears ran down his cheeks.

"Rachel," he whispered.

I did not, could not, speak.

"Rachel . . ." His hands came up, out of the blanket, and found my cheeks; he stroked them, gently, as he cried.

I could stand it no longer; I backed away, disgusted with myself and with his touch. Confusion crumpled his face, and he looked as if he might sob; but instead his eyes fluttered and closed, and his breaths quieted, and lengthened.

I gathered my things and retreated up the stairs. Outside the compound, a rain barrel stood underneath a crude gutter made from a hollowed-out log; I dipped my cupped hands into it and splashed my face with water. Then I put my clothes on, found a suitable flagstone, and curled up there to sleep.

As it happened, Doctor Stiles had made prior arrangements with my parents, or at least my father, for me to stay overnight. From his questions the next day, I gathered that my father had been told I would be learning to make camp, build a fire, and cook my dinner and breakfast. In fact, I had barely slept, had made no camp, and had eaten nothing since he dropped me off the day before. He seemed to sense that there was something wrong, or at least something peculiar—he stole glances at me as he drove, and at one point seemed almost on the verge of speaking. But he didn't, and we arrived home without any understanding having been reached.

My mother, on the other hand, was more direct, and took me into her arms with desperate relief, studying me as though I had been gone a year: my face, my hands, my arms and hair.

"What happened to you?" she demanded. "What did he do to you?"

I wasn't certain how to answer. Something about her eyes, their penetrating anger and love, seemed crazy to me. Or more likely, as I was only eleven, I was merely disoriented and frightened. In any event, I had never seen her in this state. She wore her bathrobe, though it was past noon, and her hair, usually tied back into a casual, efficient ponytail or bun at this hour, was sticking out in all directions, as if from an electric charge. She smelled unclean, and her chest heaved with shallow, quick breaths.

"Nothing, Mother," I said.

"What, then!" she said. "What did you do, all night?"

"We went camping."

"Are you hurt? Are you all right?"

"I'm fine, Mother."

She embraced me tighter then, and took me by the shoulders and held me at arms' length, observing, analyzing. Slowly her desperation receded, only to be supplanted by skepticism and, soon, disappointment.

"You're not telling me the truth, are you, Eric?" she asked me.

"Yes, I am."

She frowned, releasing me from her grasp.

"All right, Eric. All right." She stood up from the chair she had fallen into to study me. "I'm glad you're home."

"I'm glad to be home, Mother."

She had begun to walk away, but now she stopped and, looking over her shoulder, leveled a pained, unhappy gaze at me. She opened her mouth to speak, but, like my father on the ride home, she never did. Instead, she tightened her robe around her waist and climbed the stairs to the bedroom. I watched until she was out of sight.

When I turned, my father was standing by the fireplace gazing at me, an expression of stern approval on his face. And for a moment, I felt great pride at my ability to lie to my mother, and a mixture of pity and condescension for her, for having accepted my lies. I felt respected, and strong. I felt like a man.

EIGHTEEN

I fell in and out of consciousness, only intermittently aware of where I was, or what was happening. My eyes were fixated on a black spot somewhere in the distance, around which something, some lesser darkness, flowed. I strained in the dim silver light to see the spot more clearly, and as I came to, it resolved itself into a knot in a broad plank, the lines of current around it no more than the grain of the wood. I blinked. My senses returned, slowly. Deep aches uncurled in my shoulders and knees, and I was cold. I remembered now where I was: suspended in a wooden cage, my limbs bound by rusted iron shackles and chains. I couldn't feel my hands or feet. The rank scent of my unwashed body was sharp in my nose, and my mouth was dry and sticky and tasted of mud.

As I endured this moment of vulnerability, the courtyard began to fill up with memories: the tests of balance and concentration I faced on the tipping board; the feats of agility and strength I was asked to perform; the marathon sessions of stillness and stealth, such as the time I was made to perch in a tree for six hours without moving, or hide in a dark room all day, or hang from a branch, or crouch in the brush. I remembered now the Doctor's strange demand that I give up my possessions, the things I valued the most: my G.I. Joe, and mushroom book, and canteen. The treasure map. The toy train he himself had given me, the day we met. A warrior, the Doctor once said, must be able to survive without the comfort of material possessions. He must require nothing but his muscles and

his wits to defeat his enemy. Everything else—home, family, love, sex—
was burden.

And now it occurred to me, at last, where the box of bones had come
from: an ongoing experiment in which I was taught to inflict pain—in this
case, upon a squirrel that the Doctor had caught and caged, and that I was
charged with torturing over a period of weeks. As I hung there, between
numbness and agony, between wakefulness and sleep, I remembered.

It was a common gray squirrel, presumably caught outside the barren
woods, fat with the bounty of summer, cowering in a corner of its cage,
its small eyes staring, its tail twitching. The Doctor set it before me on the
crude dining table in the courtyard, and explained the aim of the project:
to hurt it as much as possible, for as long as possible, without killing it.

I had, of course, no interest in harming this animal—indeed, the prospect disgusted me. As though reading my mind, Doctor Stiles nodded in
apparent sympathy and placed a bony hand on my shoulder.

"Eric," he said, "you will have to free yourself of all personal sentiment.
A day will come when misplaced empathy could lead, I'm afraid, to your
death. In what we think of as the civilized world—a world, I must inform
you, Eric, that is soon to collapse into chaos and lawlessness—it is a virtue
to do no harm. In the world to come, it will be a skill as valuable to you as
the ability to start a fire, or build a shelter. Throw away your human regard
for this animal, Eric. It is an impediment to our goals.

"Now," the Doctor went on, "if you wished to inflict pain without doing
permanent harm, how might you go about it?"

I gazed at the squirrel dolefully, my legs and arms turning to rubber. I
wanted to go home. "I . . . I don't know, sir."

The Doctor shook his head. "Think, Eric."

I understood that I would not be given another chance before I myself
became the one to experience pain. "Its . . . tail," I blurted. "Sir."

"What about its tail?"

"We could . . . cut it off, sir."

From a sheath on his belt the Doctor pulled his bowie knife, which earlier I had watched him whet against a stone to a deadly sharpness. He now
held it out to me. "*You*, Eric," he said.

I suppose I should be expected to say that I felt something awful when
I crossed this line—that this first experience of doing intentional harm to
another creature powerfully impressed me as the deep, terrible transgres-

sion that it was. But that's not what it was like. The Doctor helped me to hold the squirrel down on the table, and I raised the knife and chopped off its tail; the animal squealed and bled. We put it back into its cage, and watched as it continued to cower. Without a doubt, I was saddened by what I had done, and faintly disgusted by the results. But I overcame my disgust very quickly, and put it behind me, and moved on. And with every passing day, the torture of the squirrel became less and less offensive to my sensibilities, and I was able to do it with great efficiency and skill, and without any apparent negative psychological effects. I remember being surprised to learn what I could become accustomed to—perhaps I was, after all, a born warrior.

The squirrel endured a great number of injuries in the next few weeks, losing several limbs and its eyes and ears before at last refusing all nourishment and succumbing to starvation. At this time the animal was skinned and its carcass buried; and a few weeks later, when we dug them up, we found that the bones had been picked clean by insects and bacteria. We allowed them to bleach in the sun for several days, and then I was permitted to take them home. I kept them in my cigar box, with some birds' bones I had found, and my cicada shell, and my map. It wasn't until the following summer, when the Doctor and I began to experiment with larger game, that I was forced to give up the box. By this time, however, the sacrifice of worldly goods had become routine, and I handed the box over without the slightest hesitation. I knew that the lessons I had learned from its contents would be with me always.

It was my memory of that younger, newly emboldened version of myself that brought me back to my senses, and focused my mind on the problem of escaping from the wooden cage. The cage was, of course, made of wood, save for the shackles and chains that bound me to it—and now it occurred to me that, if it was the same cage I knew from my childhood, it could not possibly be as strong as it once was. I gathered my strength and tugged as hard as I could with my right leg. The cage emitted a promising squeak.

My ankle, however, had begun to bleed, and it was with considerable anxiety that I realized I hadn't felt the wound. The sight of the red blood, set off against pale flesh, filled me with revulsion and desperation. I set to work freeing myself.

I heaved my body up off the floor, trembling with the effort. Then, gently,

I tugged upon the chains that held my left arm and left leg. My body swayed to the left, then swung back to the right—which motion I reinforced with a tug on that side's chains. When I reached the rightmost point of my swing, I tugged on the left side again, then the right, then the left, until I was swinging as far as I could go.

Blood rushed back into my muscles, giving me the strength to continue—but the revivification of my nerves brought terrible pain to my limbs. I stifled a cry, continuing my swinging, and soon the cage itself began to groan, then squeal, then rock back and forth.

At this point, my muscles were crying out for relief. But it seemed unlikely that I could ever again achieve this momentum, and I found the inner reserves to continue. The cage was leaning now, first one way, then the other, and for a moment I wondered if perhaps I had made a grievous mistake, that I might be torn apart with it—and then, with a terrible screech and a sickening lurch, the entire thing leaned, then cracked, then folded up like a cardboard box.

Of course I was inside. The roof of the thing—a thick piece of hardwood ply, if my observations were correct—lay on top of my bruised and bleeding form, having crushed my face as it fell. I could feel blood coursing out of my nose. I managed, somehow, to roll over, my chains having broken free of their mounts, and push up the roof with my back. In a few seconds, I had managed to wriggle out from under it, and lay in the courtyard, delirious with pain. It was there that I fell unconscious.

When I woke, my clothes, pack, and quiver lay by my side, and the shackles had been removed from my wrists and ankles. In the peculiar state of mind that my incarceration had engendered, I did not stop to consider the implications of this fact—namely, that Doctor Avery Stiles had seen me lying there asleep, and had freed me completely, leaving me armed.

It was ten minutes, perhaps, before I was able to sit up. With great slowness and deliberation, I dressed and took up my quiver and pack, and when I was through I carefully got to my feet, bracing myself against the wall of the compound.

The courtyard was echoless, the night clear, the moonlight bright.

I stumbled to the compound doorway and quietly made my way down the stone staircase. The Doctor wasn't there, only the glowing remains of his fire. My childhood possessions, as well, were gone. I climbed back up and staggered toward the tunnel in the west wall, my knees quivering, my breaths quick and shallow. I crouched down before the tunnel opening and crawled through. I had escaped from the castle.

I stood outside the curtain wall, scanning the treeline with my tired eyes. My muscles throbbed, and I wanted nothing more than to lie down on the ground and go to sleep. But I could not. I had to find Doctor Stiles.

Convinced that no one was watching, I limped across the clearing and stepped over the deadfall and into the woods. Little moonlight penetrated here, so I waited as my eyes, already starved for daylight, adjusted to the gloom, and my body tingled and ached. I breathed in the humusy air and tried to imagine what the Doctor was doing out here, and where he might be. Was he waiting for me? Did he expect me to escape? Did he wish to test me, once again, in the wild?

I was not permitted to go to the castle with Doctor Stiles the week after my all-night adventure, nor the week after that. I was uncertain what had transpired between my parents, but there was a tension, and more than once I spied my mother, through the bathroom keyhole, applying makeup to a bruise. Her resistance to my father, at the time, seemed to me pig-headed and foolish—why couldn't she see that what the Doctor was teaching me was for my own good, that I was being formed into a man? I had not, of course, forgotten the terror and agony I endured that night in the woods. But already those emotions seemed like the products of a childish imagination, signs of weakness to be renounced and forgotten. I hardened my heart against my mother's best intentions.

Now, in the forest, my vision had returned, and my body was once again under my control. But I remained still for some time, alert for the presence of my quarry. There had been a breeze when I emerged from behind the castle wall; now the wind had died to nothing, and the woods were silent.

Perhaps it was a sixth sense that caused me to think of the rock. I took a step back, then another to the west, until an opening revealed itself between the boughs of the tall pines, and I was able to see up the cliffside to the northern lip of the "ankle." At first, I believed that I was seeing nothing more sinister than an unremembered outcropping. But then it moved, and I realized that it was the Doctor's form, outlined against the starry sky. He had been there, watching me, waiting for my next move.

Before he could decide to give up his wait, I retreated farther into the trees and made my way west, and then south, toward the "toe." The woods were fairly sparse for the first twenty or so feet beyond the treeline, and I stuck to this easier terrain, taking care not to strain or twist my weakened legs. It wasn't long before I had made it to the southern end of the rock, and I crept to the clearing's edge, and peered out from the cover of the woods. The moonlight sharply outlined the rock, and I searched its face for any sign of Doctor Stiles. If he still stood on the northern lip, my angle of sight made it impossible to tell.

I waited several more minutes, to be sure I was safe, then gathered my strength and sprinted across the clearing to the "toe."

It was easier, this time, to climb up over its lip, and onto the broad plateau where the lone pine grew from its soil-filled bowl. I soon found myself at the base of the "ankle," staring up into the moonlit night, and trying to remember the series of hand- and footholds that had taken me safely to the top. Time was of the essence—Doctor Stiles wouldn't stay there forever, and I did not wish to meet him on the rock face, where his doubtless superior climbing experience would put him at an advantage. I could not be burdened by my pack, so I lowered it quietly to the ground, keeping only my climbing shoes, gloves, and quiver. My helmet I had left behind at the house, never dreaming that I would need to scale the rock face again—I would see if the smug sporting goods clerk had been correct in his confidence that it was unnecessary.

With as much speed as I could muster, I began to clamber up the sheer face, pushing my weakened arms and legs to the limit. It was with some surprise that I remembered my former path of ascent—the holds came quickly and naturally, and my progress was speedy. Under normal conditions, I am certain, I would have been unable to find the strength to climb that cliff, but extreme circumstances draw out hidden powers in men, and my aching body proved more capable than I could possibly have hoped.

I paused on a ledge to catch my breath and give my fingers a break. The wind, which had died down to nothing some minutes before, now somehow seemed deader still, as if time itself had stopped, and not merely the motion of the air. I had reached the roof level of the forest canopy, and the treetops stretched out in all directions like a stubblefield. If I didn't know better, I might have thought it would be possible to walk across it, this landscape of gentle silver swells, or to sail it, navigating around those few signs of human habitation below: radio antennas, church steeples, office buildings. It was a heartening, restful sight.

But for now, my rest was over. The motionless air pressed in. Every sound was magnified—my shoes on the rock, my shallow breaths. I turned back to the wall, found my handholds, and climbed.

As I came closer to the summit, I slowed, and concentrated on keeping quiet. I hoped for a breeze, to cover the noise of my ascent, but there was nothing. Soon I could detect the cliff's edge just above me, and I knew that Doctor Avery Stiles was there—possibly at the northern lip of the "ankle," standing with his back to me, and possibly just above, waiting for my face to appear, waiting to send me to my death with a single kick.

For one brief moment, I wondered if it was all really worth it, if I should simply turn back and leave all this behind—the woods, the castle, the rock, the Doctor. I doubted the very reasoning behind my entire mission: was it absolutely necessary to have come out here in pursuit of the old man? If Doctor Stiles wanted to kill me, then why didn't he come into my house while I slept, and do away with me there? There had been ample opportunity for him to take me by surprise, to attack when my guard was down. Indeed, his capture of me was entirely attributable to my encroachment into his territory. If anything, it was I who was the aggressor.

And what would I do once I'd gained the upper hand? Would I attempt to extract some promise from him, that he would never bother me again? An admission that he was no longer my master—that I had absorbed, then exceeded, his tutelage? Or would I merely kill him?

Moreover, was this the reason I had come to Gerrysburg? To find an old man and murder him? Clinging there on the rock face, I cast my mind back to the day I decided to return to my home town. Obviously, I believed I had unfinished business here—I thought that, by revisiting the site of my tutelage, I might somehow clarify my memories of those strange years, and soothe the humiliations of the recent past. But specifically how this would work, I didn't know. In fact, I didn't believe that I'd ever known; and the details of my decision to begin this adventure seemed hazier in memory by the minute. I shifted my position incrementally, seeking a more comfortable hold, and wondered about my motives and desires. In my life, I had dedicated myself to understanding the motives of others, through careful study of their words and actions, as had Doctor Stiles before me. But could it be that neither of us had ever really known himself—indeed, that such understanding was impossible? That this mad adventure in the forest was the product of little more than blind instinct, a pathetic expression of formless paranoia and masculine pride?

I felt rather dejected at this moment, and once again considered turning back. But I shook off my doubts and began to build my resolve once more. To succumb to confusion would be to fall directly into Doctor Stiles's hands. The danger he represented, after all, had always been subtle, insidious, and difficult to pin down. He controlled others by the threat of action, not by action itself. His very existence was the threat—indeed, he was most dangerous when he was doing nothing, allowing his victims' imagination to run wild with the terrifying possibilities. My job, as I saw it, was to neutralize this danger, and to shirk that duty would represent a grave cowardice.

With these thoughts still ringing in my head, I drew a deep breath, reached up to the final handholds, and swung myself onto the roof of the rock.

He was there, right where I had imagined him, facing north and peering down at the clearing he mistakenly thought I might, at any moment, recross. The sound of my shoes scraping the rock surface spun him around. At last, I faced my nemesis.

The moonlight revealed a wry smile on that ageless face; the Doctor relaxed his stance and took two casual steps forward before he stopped suddenly and raised his hands into the air.

"Eric!" he called out. "What are you doing up here?"

"I've come to kill you, Professor."

It wasn't until I'd said it aloud that I realized it was true—the Doctor's death was indeed the real objective of my mission. I felt a long-missing piece of my life's puzzle falling at last into place. The words hung between us, awaiting a response.

He gave his head a rueful nod, still smiling, as though, in disappointing him, I had nevertheless confirmed some idea he had long harbored about me. He said, "I haven't been a professor for years, Eric—they took that away from me soon after they took you." His voice, undiminished by time, carried flawlessly through the motionless air. It was as though he were standing beside me. He took another step closer.

"Don't move," I said, reaching for my quiver. "I don't intend to listen to your explanations. The time for those is over."

But Doctor Stiles merely shook his head. "You were an excellent pupil, Eric. I had high hopes for you."

"You should not have made me your enemy, then," I replied, and I drew forth my bow and nocked an arrow—the arrow that had murdered the white deer.

The Doctor's grin widened. "Ah! I see you have a bit of my handiwork, there," he said.

"So it was you."

"Of course it was," he replied. And then, after a moment's pause, he relaxed his smile, his eyes narrowed, and he went on. "Eric, I can see your mind is made up about me, and about what you're doing here. But I want to tell you that destroying me is not the answer. In fact, you don't even know what the question is, do you?"

I drew back the arrow. My fingers ached from the climb, and my right arm trembled.

"You think that by taking my life, your own will be restored." He lowered his hands, and slipped them into the pockets of his pants. Indeed, he appeared relaxed, as if I were no danger at all. "The fact is, Eric, that you cannot restore your own life by killing me.

"Furthermore, your life doesn't need to be restored," he went on, edging away now, toward the northern lip of the rock. My aim tracked his slow movement. "It merely needs to be seized. And my life—my life was never here to be taken."

I was puzzled by his words. But if he believed that my confusion would throw me off my guard, he was sadly mistaken.

He lunged. At the same moment, I released the arrow. Belatedly I realized that he had not been attempting to evade my shot. Instead, he had thrown himself off the rock. His leap took him high into the air, and it was at the zenith of that leap that the arrow met him. It was a perfect shot, striking him in the back, low between the shoulder blades and slightly to the left. And as the arrow passed through him, he vanished from view.

I listened for his cry. But there was none. For a moment, the silence seemed to deepen, the stillness to take on weight. And then, from behind me, I heard a rumble, and the light dimmed. I turned. A cloud was moving across the face of the moon. Before I could wonder why it had brought no wind, the wind came, curling around the summit and raising, briefly, a vortex of dust and dead moss before gusting in earnest, pressing my clothes against my body and blowing leaves and pine needles against my neck.

A storm was coming, and I had to climb down before the rain began. But first I ran to the northern lip, lay on my stomach, and looked down over the edge. It was no use—with the moonlight now occluded by clouds, and the rock's blurry shadow extending to the woods, the clearing was lost in murk. I could see nothing.

I scrambled to the southern edge and began my descent, with the wind alternately pressing me to the cliffside and straining to pluck me away. How had I failed to notice the approaching storm? I was barely a third of the way down when I felt the first drops on my cheek, and then, seconds later, the sky opened up and lashed the cliffside in a fusillade of raindrops. Immediately the rock face became slick and unnavigable. One of my feet slipped, then a hand, and I nearly fell.

Instead, I managed to find a lower hold, and then one lower than that. Several times I lost my grip and slid the length of my body; once I fell entirely and only avoided serious injury or death by grabbing hold of the ledge I had rested on during my first ascent, days before. At last I arrived, bruised, scraped, and soaking wet, at the lone pine, where I grabbed my pack and made a run for the "toe," limping and bleeding as I went. The wind howled and the rain fell in sheets, and I almost slipped again as I lowered myself to the firm ground of the clearing.

I might have gone for the cover of the trees. But I had to reassure myself, first, that the Doctor was really dead. By keeping close to the western face of the rock, I was able to avoid the worst of the storm, and soon I had arrived at the northern end, beneath the cliff he had leaped from.

He was there. He lay curled in the lee of the rock, his head thrown back, one arm flung over his shoulder. His arrow was lodged deep in his back, and I had no doubt that it had pierced his heart.

This is not something I say lightly, but the first things I felt upon finding the Doctor's body were horror and revulsion. I have had the misfortune of seeing many corpses in my lifetime, and have been witness to all manner of misery and brutality, and never have I lost my sense of sadness and injustice in the face of such things. But something about Avery Stiles's lifeless form, its crumpled brokenness, its stark corporeality, filled me with disgust and fear. I trembled, and struggled to calm my rising gorge.

I had never seen my parents' bodies. Evidently, their faces had been disfigured by the violence that ended their lives, and their caskets remained closed. Gazing at what had once been my mentor, I wondered if my doubts about my parents' deaths might have been resolved, had I forced myself to look at their ruined faces. Jill, after all, had identified their corpses. She had had no doubts. Quite suddenly, I experienced a wave of guilt, for having allowed this rift to open between us. Perhaps I had been the unreasonable one all along.

I knelt beside the dead Doctor and choked back a sob. I had murdered my teacher! Of course I understood that it was his desire I should come to get him, that he had martyred himself, ultimately, for some obscure purpose that would never be known. The rain fell, and I crouched there in the dim, feeling very much as though I had lost, as though I had missed something important that the Doctor hoped to impart with his suicide.

My contemplation was shattered by a tremendous roll of thunder, which, instead of trailing off into a low rumble, grew in intensity and pitch, until the ground shook and the air was split by a deafening crack. I fell to the ground beside the body, my hands clapped over my ears. The sound seemed to go on for hours, though surely it lasted less than a minute, and when it finally stopped, the light had changed, the moon emerged from behind a cloud, and the air smelled strange—fresher, cleaner, as though a lid had been removed from the world.

I stood up and took a deep breath. My wounds throbbed, but my head felt clear. I looked down at Stiles's corpse and felt none of the revulsion I had felt mere moments before. Indeed, it was as though the lightning had broken something in me, some blockage, or wall, beyond which some hard wind was blowing. To be sure, the feeling made me uneasy. But, at the same time, I felt that I could now move forward, that I must move forward. There was nothing for me to do now but to retreat back into the woods and find my way home.

First, however, I took hold of the Doctor's body and dragged it to the castle wall. With great effort, I was able to pull it through the hidden entrance and deposit it upon the flagstones. All around me stood the castle, illuminated by moonlight that shone now from underneath the bank of black clouds. It appeared old and ruined, as it had when I saw it, for the first time in many years, only days before. The rain slowed, and thinned to a piercing mist. The chasm that the storm had seemed to open in me yawned wide, and my unease deepened. I exited the courtyard the way

I came in. At last I crossed the clearing and plunged back into the woods to find my way home.

As soon as I passed over the treeline, however, I heard an unfamiliar sound. The wind had died down, yet something was moving overhead, through the woods, in small, frenetic bursts of activity. I froze, and remained still until the sound moved out of range. Slowly then I began to creep forward, into the greater dark of the woods, and almost immediately I was alert to another motion: something in front of me, close to the ground and off to the left. Above the trees, the moon appeared, and a beam of its dully metallic light came to rest on a patch of lichen a few feet ahead; through it passed, quite suddenly, an animal, perhaps a chipmunk or small squirrel.

In spite of myself, I jumped. I hadn't noticed such a creature in days— what had happened here? It was as though the storm had awakened the sleeping life of the forest, or, quite possibly, awakened me to it. As I considered, I began to hear the chitter and whirr of insects, and the breaking of branches somewhere deep in the trees, as if some great beast were lumbering about.

And now I noticed that the air, like the air outside the woods, was different as well. It was less close, less enveloping. It smelled of ozone and pine sap. It was as if the sky had shouldered its way in, and I felt the yawning enormity of the world around me. For the first time since I entered these woods, I felt utterly exposed—to the elements, to the creatures of the trees, to chaos itself.

I shivered, against the coolness of the air and against my fear, and I hugged myself for warmth. I was hungry, and thirsty; my unease, at this moment, was profound. I turned, intending to go back to the clearing, where at least I could stand in the full light of the moon. But there was nothing behind me, no clearing, and I realized I had been walking, running even, through the trees as I held myself, and I no longer had any idea where I was. I had thought I was facing north—but surely the moon, already past its zenith, would then be on my right? And yet it was behind me, and then, moments later, in front of me, and I began to have trouble remembering in what direction my house lay.

Slowly I began to feel terror, more than I had ever felt in my life. I closed my eyes, trying to fall back onto my training—focus on the immediate danger, consider my options, take the steps necessary to deliver myself to safety.

But instead my trembling increased: first my hands, then my arms, and then my entire body shook uncontrollably, and I fell to my knees and drew long, ragged breaths.

The fact was, there was no clear danger at all. It was *everything* that I was afraid of. I managed to gather myself, to struggle back to my feet, and then I ran. I ran recklessly and without direction, my weary legs pumping maniacally, at the very limit of their capacity. I felt my bow and arrows tumbling out of my quiver, but kept on: indeed, I threw off the quiver entirely, threw off my pack, and sprinted headlong through the tangled underbrush.

That I would fall was inevitable, and in fact I anticipated it with eagerness. I wanted nothing more than to stop, for at this moment I believed that, if I continued, I might lose my mind.

My fall, however, when it came, was not the expected kind. I did not trip over a bramble or root; I did not lose my footing on a tricky rise. I was running, my feet pounding on the forest floor—and then, suddenly, I was running through the air, and falling. Before I understood what was even happening, my face and body struck dirt and I felt something crack deep in my nose. Next I knew, I was lying on the ground, sharp sticks poking into my back, my head screaming, my breath caught in my throat, my back afire with pain. I was at the bottom of a pit—perhaps, though not necessarily, the same one I had fallen into before. And this time, the sticks at the bottom *had* done their work: I was bleeding, and ribs had surely been broken. When I tried to roll over, I convulsed in agony. I looked up and saw the section of the pit wall I must have struck. I reached up and touched my face, and the pain sent me into a swoon. I passed out.

When I came to, it was daylight, and sunshine filtered down through the leaves. I heard a slow crunching in the humus above me: the sound of careful footsteps. I tried to right myself, and my body protested, and I fell back. I called out, a wordless cry that sounded like nothing that had ever come out of my mouth before. And then I managed a single word, "Help!"

A shadow fell across my face: a figure stood on the lip of the pit, peering down at me. I squinted at the silhouette, my eyes still struggling to adjust to the sun.

"Please," I said, and my voice was thick with sleep, hoarse and cracked as if by hours of screaming. "Help me."

The figure knelt, his hands braced on the edge of the pit. It was a man, I was certain of that now: a rugged man, his face strong, the eyes dark and intense and trained upon me. On his face was no expression at all.

I squeezed my eyes shut, and when they opened, I recognized the impassive face that hovered before me. It was my own.

NINETEEN

I knelt, my hands braced on the edge of the pit. The man inside was curled in a corner, his arms around his knees. The pit was ten feet deep, five by five feet in breadth, and made of cement; I had overseen its construction the year before. The floor sloped down to a central drain covered by a metal grate the size of a coffee can lid.

We had built the pit as a disposal for liquid waste; there were two more like it here in the yard of the detention center. The soldier who had come to get me was standing ten feet back, next to two others, all three of them holding the M243 squad assault rifles that three months ago I had promised would soon be replaced by more effective weapons. The men were bored, the detainee was weeping, and all of us were very hot. We had put this man out here after an outburst in his cell during a sandstorm the day before, and he hadn't been given food or water since.

I took pity on the man and threw down the canteen I had brought for him. The cap was loose and the water began to leak out onto the cement. The detainee grabbed it and greedily drank what was left.

The solider who had summoned me stood waiting. His name was Fayette, and I must confess to some sympathy for him. He was a beefy young man, a former football player who had put on weight since he was deployed here, in spite of the terrible food; he appeared to squirm inside his uniform in an agony of sweat and discomfort. I approached him purposefully, betraying no emotion. The others stepped away, turning their backs to us.

"Why did you come to me, soldier?" I asked him.

"The detainee, sir. He was freaking out."

"You said he wanted water."

"Yessir," Fayette said. "He was saying water, sir, the rest he was just talking Arabic."

Behind me, in the pit, the detainee resumed crying.

Fayette and I stared at each other until he turned away. Beyond us, over the wall to the southeast, was Balad Air Base, its control tower visible from where we stood. In the other direction was the runway, and past that lay the barracks of Logistics Support Area Anaconda. All that could be seen from the bottom of the pit, on the other hand, was a square of sky— I knew this because I had climbed down in it, some days before, while assessing it for possible repurposing as an aid to the extraction of intelligence. So far, this tactic was not working well.

"Get the canteen back from him when he's done," I said, and went back inside.

I was a chief warrant officer in the U.S. Army, a logistics expert charged with overseeing the construction of a new detention center in Iraq for the processing and temporary housing of detainees arrested in connection with terrorism, and with gathering information from those detainees. Our facility had seventy-five units, and was capable of accommodating 150 detainees, but we'd never expected to fill it—rather, it had been designed as a high-value temporary detention site for persons of great importance to U.S. intelligence. When the facility opened, it held several members of Saddam Hussein's regime, and a number of suspected al-Qaida operatives, spillover from the detention center at Camp Cropper. The facility—which came to be known as Camp Alastor—was medium-sized, with a double-fenced compound anchored by four towers surrounding an impenetrable L-shaped concrete enclosure. I had designed it.

Our corner of Anaconda was desolate, with only dirt and sand for a half mile in each direction, and no sound but that of wind, and of planes taking off and landing. And for all my pride at my work on the facility, I had expected it to remain a lonely outpost on the edge of the base. Indeed, I'd imagined that within a year's time after the site's construction, we would all be redeployed, and the facility would slowly fill up with blown dust. The war, after all, was supposed to be brief.

Instead, in the summer of 2004, we received a new influx of detainees. We were told they were terrorists, captured by the First Armored and First Cavalry divisions during sweeps of suspect neighborhoods in Baghdad, and we were assigned to keep them isolated from one another, and to begin gathering intelligence from them.

To be truthful, I was at first quite excited by this development. The initial trickle of detainees had disappointed me somewhat—the Baathists had turned out not to be remotely close to Saddam, and were eventually freed; the purported al-Qaida operatives were mostly street criminals, who had little information to offer, and resigned themselves quickly to imprisonment. I was eager to prove myself as an information specialist, having arrived at my rank through my infrastucture expertise, and I wished to demonstrate to my commanding officers that these areas of endeavor were, in fact, intimately connected—an idea that they had at first resisted. Thus far, I had failed to make much progress, owing to the dearth of subjects; now, unexpectedly, I could put my ideas to the test.

But things immediately became complicated. In three weeks, we received 280 detainees, far in excess of our capacity. Some of the detainees were very young, as young as thirteen, according to our two reliable translators, who had spoken to them. There were four women, one of them pregnant. According to her documentation, she had been found in a house containing terrorist suspects, some of whom had been killed in combat, and she was to be questioned for information pertaining to their activities. In addition, a rifle had been found in the bedroom where she slept, and so she herself was also under suspicion, in spite of her condition. It was at this time that I began to feel out of my depth, and to worry that I was in danger of losing the firm control of the facility that I had taken such great pride in maintaining.

Up to this point my military career had been a textbook success, even if my path to this success had proved unusual. As it happens, I was well prepared for army life by Doctor Stiles and his unorthodox methods of training. This training, unfortunately, had been brought to an abrupt end not long after the terrifying night I spent in the woods; it appeared that my mother had prevailed, having given my father some kind of ultimatum that he could not ignore. But I didn't forget the Doctor, and when I grew old enough to use public transportation on my own, I took a bus to the college to visit with him. These visits became a regular part of my adolescence, and we carried on long, intense conversations about politics, society, and war.

Eventually, however, the Doctor disappeared, and along with him my sense of moral direction. My parents' marriage appeared to be in shambles, and I spent most of my time away from home, taking long walks along the railroad tracks, or camping out in the woods by myself. In time, I moved out, gathering my things into a duffel bag and riding a freight train out of Gerrysburg. I didn't finish high school, and only later would I earn my equivalency degree through an army program. I wandered around the Midwest for several years, doing manual labor—mostly landscaping—and rarely keeping an address for more than a few months.

I might have continued on this path for years, for I felt as though my life had lost its direction, if it ever had one; and I spent my days in a state that today would be diagnosed as depression. Then my parents died. I was devastated—not by their absence, which I had grown accustomed to, but by the fragility of their lives, and the banality of their deaths. I feared a similar fate for myself—indeed, in the weeks after their passing, such an outcome seemed inevitable. But soon this fear gave way to frustration: at the meaninglessness of life, at the laziness of my generation, at the way we took America and its accomplishments for granted. While I was drifting along the West Coast, I witnessed a group of youths mocking an army recruiter in a public square, and I muscled through the crowd and impulsively enlisted. The rightness of this gesture invigorated me; it was the most definitive act I had ever performed, and I never looked back.

It did not take long for me to be singled out by my commanding officer, for my intelligence and my potential for advancement. Once I had my high school diploma, I was transferred into the warrant officer school at Fort Leonard Wood, Missouri; and upon completing the program there, I assisted in the organization and planning of several bases inside our borders. Later I was shipped overseas to help renovate and repurpose the army's European assets. At the time Operation Iraqi Freedom began, I was working alongside a team of architects and contractors on the design and maintenance of bases.

But something was missing in my career, and it took a curious incident to make me realize what it was. I had been visiting a base in Japan, in order to inspect an aging barracks that was under reconstruction, when I happened to overhear, through a half-open door, the sound of an officer reprimanding a soldier. I paused and took a surreptitious glance into the room, a small windowless office containing a desk, a filing cabinet, and a computer. The soldier in question was standing at attention in front of the desk; meanwhile, the officer sat behind it, part of his body blocked from the soldier's view by the large, already-obsolete computer monitor. To his credit, the soldier seemed to display the proper respect for his superior. But the officer himself appeared small, weak, and uncomfortable, hemmed in by the trappings of his position.

Over the next few weeks, I thought a great deal about the ergonomics of military life. I made a few sketches of bases, barracks, and prisons that incorporated my recent thinking, and showed them to the officer, a CWO3, under whom my division was then working. He passed them on to his superior, and soon I found myself face-to-face with a CWO5 and a brigadier general, who pointed to my prison drawing and said, "We want you to build that." He was referring to the project that would eventually become Camp Alastor.

Needless to say, I was pleased. But my reassignment to the prison project gave me pause. I had had no direct experience in this arena, and was quick to remind my superior officers of this when they informed me of my redeployment. Their response was to remind me that this assignment was to be considered an honor, and they assured me that the higher-ups had perfect confidence in my abilities.

And for some time, it appeared that this confidence was justified. I led a team that included two architects, several builders, and a consultant CWO2 from Military Intelligence, and we completed our work under budget and ahead of schedule. Rumors abounded of the disastrous exploits of civilian contractors, with their bloated budgets, corrupt middlemen, and poor skills, and we were delighted to be able to report our successes to our commanding officers and prove ourselves superior to our rivals. When, early in the spring, the prison at last opened its doors and began accepting detainees, I led their questioning, bolstered by my structural improvements to the interrogation environment. The facility's labyrinthine corridors, through which we led detainees in different directions at different times, contributed to a general sense of confusion and dependency; windows as narrow as arrow slits, drilled through overspec'd, two-foot-thick walls, reinforced the impossibility of escape. Cell floors were angled slightly down from the corridors, elevating army personnel several inches above the cells' inhabitants, making them feel helpless and overpowered. Intelligence-gathering, its limited utility notwithstanding, went smoothly, with few attempts at resistance.

The overall feel of the facility was one of calm. The dry season had not yet begun, and the interior of the building, and of our barracks, remained fairly cool, in spite of the brilliant sun. The detainees were far from cheerful, but we fielded few unreasonable complaints, and were only rarely forced to break up a fight, or settle a disagreement. Quiet Arabic conversation filled the halls; it seemed the detainees, like us, had settled in to wait, and to see what happened next. The only incongruous element during these nervous, patient days was a sound: a low, mournful whistling. Not quite tuneless, but embracing no particular melody, it sometimes had the quality of a plaintive call, as though for a beloved pet. At other times, it sounded like a small, elusive movement of some forgotten sonata; still other times it sounded like the wind. We didn't know who was doing the whistling, or why, but as the days lengthened, it became a soundtrack to life in the facility, an ever-present, if elegiac, companion to our work.

Then came the summer.

The weather was very hot and dry. There was some relief from the *shamal* winds, when they blew; but when the air was still, time seemed to stand still with it, and the temperature routinely rose above 110 degrees. The weeks dragged by, and more detainees arrived. We requisitioned temporary off-site housing for them, but none was forthcoming, as supply lines were clogged, and the detainees, we were told, were far too dangerous to be housed outside the main compound. And so, instead, I ordered construction to begin on a new wing of the facility, and soon it was under way. Through it all, the days were colored by the aimless whistling that haunted the corridors—and though it was bothersome, no one complained, as though, in some oblique way, they thought they deserved it.

It was around this time that I first took notice of the boy, the thirteen-year-old who had come in around the same time as the pregnant woman. We had housed him in the area of the L where our three female detainees were held, and they now all occupied the same cell, at the very end of the hallway, where they could at least experience some modicum of privacy. It was off of this hallway that I had decided the new wing would be built, and I found myself here quite often, supervising the demolition of the outer wall and the construction of a new passageway. The boy's name, I learned, was Sufian.

Most of the detainees would spend their time slumped against the walls of their cells in silence. Some talked in low tones. Many of them had a copy of the Qur'an, but most had nothing. Because we had never received the shipment of inmate uniforms we had been expecting, they were dressed in the clothes in which they had been captured, trousers and short-sleeved shirts, *abayahs* and dishdashas, and in this respect, Sufian was no different. He wore a filthy dishdasha, its grubby fabric torn and stained, and he sat on the floor at the front of the cell, peering through the steel mesh as we worked.

There was something slightly unnerving about the boy's gaze. His brown eyes were large and alert, possessing none of the deadness and despair evident in the eyes of many of his fellow inmates. His face was thin, his cheekbones high; combined with his lively eyes, these traits made him appear curious and highly intelligent. It was difficult to tell, however, as the boy never spoke, at least not to any of the men and women under my command.

Though it was our policy to try to keep the Sunnis and Shiites separate, we could not determine in which, if either, category the boy belonged; even the women he now resided with had evidently ceased to bother speaking to him. He merely sat in his cell, watching and listening to all the facility's goings-on with apparent fascination. As for me, I wondered about the child's parents—whether they wondered where he was, or if they were even alive. I was not unfamiliar with the solitude and alienation associated with that age, particularly if one lived at some emotional distance from one's family. And so I resolved to pay special attention to the boy while we worked nearby, and to try to make his detainment less unpleasant than it might otherwise be. Perhaps, somehow, this experience might even prove constructive for him—he could learn self-reliance, and to tell right from wrong; he would participate in this important new chapter of his country's history.

After a few casual visits to the boy's cell, however, I grew perturbed by his strange stare, and turned over supervision of the corridor reconstruction to a subordinate.

My superiors had given me clear instructions about what kind of information to seek when we interrogated detainees. We wanted to know, of course, which detainees were part of terrorist cells, which were Baathists, and which were in contact with foreign fighters, particularly Syrians and Iranians. Our political leadership was convinced that the Iranians were infiltrating the Shia, and so it became necessary to find out who was related to whom, and who knew whom; to separate them, and to play them off one another, telling them that their brothers or friends had talked, and had implicated them, and so on. The new influx of detainees was more fruitful in terms of intelligence; their social connections were many, and their various rivalries made it easier to goad them into revealing other detainees' secrets.

But there were far too many of them, and tensions among my CWOls and enlisted men and women were high. We now housed 374 detainees in a space built for 150, and our requests for matériel were taking an increasingly long time to be filled. From the tone of my communications with my superior officers, I could tell that Camp Alastor was becoming a place that people in positions of responsibility wanted to have had nothing to do with. I continued to receive effusive praise for my work, and while I relished this praise and believed it to be in earnest, I had begun to be troubled by the notion that perhaps it was motivated, in part, by a desire to keep Camp Alastor at a distance. Perhaps, among the officer class, information had begun to circulate about difficulties at prisons elsewhere in Iraq, and those who wished to be relieved of responsibility for the consequences had already started passing the buck. To be sure, I felt an increasing disgust with the poor planning and sloppy execution of our mission, and with the people who, so far, had failed to take responsibility for these errors. But it was not my place to judge—rather, it was my place to do as I was instructed, and so I tried to blind myself to the larger picture, and continued to do my job to the best of my ability.

My office was a small, windowless room at the center of the compound with cinderblock walls, a large aluminum-frame desk, and two chairs. I had spent much of the past several months here, filling out requisition forms, managing our overcrowding, and disciplining and counseling exhausted soldiers. I did not miss the irony in the fact that this room was much like the one I had spied in Japan, the one that had inspired my shift into ergonomics, and eventually intelligence: the one I had found so lacking at the time.

I had been hard at work one day drafting yet another requisition form, when a private first class named Jennifer Moss came to my office with a question about detainee interrogation. I had particular fondness for this soldier, as she was nineteen years old, and, like me, had had no idea that she would ever be serving in a prison in Iraq, expecting instead to become a tactician—still, so far as I knew, her goal in the armed forces. I had learned this by asking her, late one insomniac night when I encountered her patrolling the cell block. She was stoic about her disappointment, which she otherwise felt comfortable confessing to me; her official position was that she wished to serve her country in whatever capacity her country saw fit.

And so I was surprised to find her standing before me wearing an expression of profound unease. Even after I asked her to sit down, she slumped crookedly in the chair and declined to look me in the eye as she spoke.

"Private," I said, feigning displeasure, "state your business."

"Sir," she began, wiping her tired and dirty face with a small white hand. "Okay, sir? Me and Lukens and Geary were talking to this guy, right?" Lukens was a big man, a fellow private, and, I believed, a good friend—perhaps a lover—of Private Moss; Geary was one of our translators, a short, nervous boy just out of graduate school. "And it got all complicated, sir."

"Complicated how, Private?" I asked.

"It's like . . . the guy got hostile, sir? And he spit on Lukens? And Lukens didn't hit him or anything, but he cuffed him to the bars, sir, like on the window? And he's been there a while, and I don't know, sir, every time Lukens gets near him the guy spits. He doesn't spit on me, sir, but Lukens doesn't want me to have to do all the questioning."

"Are you certain," I asked, "that he knows something?"

She began nodding before I had even finished speaking, as though this had already been thought through.

"Uh-huh, yes sir, that is our assessment."

"What makes you think so?" I asked.

"One of the other detainees said he was al-Qaida, sir."

"I see."

"And so we ask him if he's al-Qaida, and he spits on us and calls us names, sir."

We sat in silence for a moment, and then I asked her to lead me to the detainee.

The soldiers had set up an empty cell at the back of the north wing as an interrogation room. Its interior could not be seen by the other detainees, but anything that went on there could be heard by all. As we walked down the long hallway, the detainees stared at us through the bars, their expressions angry and deflated. It occurred to me that many of them had been here for months, and I had heard nothing from anyone that indicated they would soon be transferred or freed. I was beginning to think that Camp Alastor was no longer considered temporary—that these people would be here for a long time, and I would be here with them.

The scene in the interrogation cell was grim. Lukens was next to the door, as far from the detainee as possible. He faced the hallway and his features were hard. He stood with his rifle in both hands and his lips pressed together. Geary, the translator, was seated on a metal stool in the far corner of the room, his hands dangling between his knees, his head hung low. The hair was receding on the back of his head and his bald spot gleamed faintly in the yellow electric light. The detainee was pressed to the far wall, underneath the window, with his arms in the air above him, handcuffed to the bars. One of his feet rested on top of the other, and his knees were slightly bent in a kind of plié. He was not much taller than five feet, was thin, and appeared to be around forty. You would not think to look at him that he was capable of much resistance. Yet he had spit on Lukens.

"Moss," I said. "Uncuff him."

For just a moment, Moss appeared frightened. Then she nodded, and asked Geary for the stool. Geary got up. She moved the stool over next to the detainee and climbed up on it to undo the cuffs. The detainee turned away, as though in disgust. Soon his wrists were freed. His arms fell to his sides, his legs trembled, and he slid to the ground, where he gulped down a single sob. From down the hallway came the sound of the other detainees shifting wordlessly in their cells. I heard, faintly, the distant familiar sound of whistling.

The detainee appeared to try to move his arms, but for the time being they could do nothing more than twitch. His hands somehow found his lap, where they lay useless, palms up, as though waiting for something to be put into them.

I motioned Geary over to the man, and then knelt down a few feet before him. Behind me I heard Lukens shift position.

"Ask him why he spit on Private Lukens," I said.

The translator spoke. A moment passed without any reaction from the detainee. Then he tipped his head up, regarded me with sad, empty eyes, and spat.

Without hesitation, Lukens came up behind me, stepped between me and the detainee, and rammed the butt of his rifle into the man's face.

For a moment, no one moved. The rifle butt had struck him high on the cheek, just below the right eye. The flesh opened up and blood pooled in a ragged line. The man tried to lift his hands to cover the wound, but he couldn't get his arms up all the way, and blood began to drip onto his lap. Geary and Moss stared in astonishment.

"Get the medic," I said to Geary. And to Lukens, I said, "Wait for me in my office, soldier."

Lukens nodded. There was embarrassment in his face, but not fear or remorse. He turned on his heel and walked out, throwing shut the cell door behind him.

I went to the detainee and pressed a clean handkerchief to his face. Soon the medic arrived and took over. I motioned for Moss and the translator to follow me, then ordered another soldier out of the hallway and into the cell with the medic. A few minutes later, I had the three of them, Moss, Lukens, and Geary, crowded into the office. I stood beside my desk. The two chairs were empty. I turned to Lukens.

"What on earth happened in there?" I asked him.

"He can't do that to you, sir."

I felt a small shiver of fear touch the small of my back. "He did nothing to me, soldier. He didn't even have anything to spit. When was the last time you gave him water?"

Lukens and Moss looked at each other.

"He didn't ask for water, sir," Moss said.

"The guy wouldn't even answer our questions, sir," Lukens said, his voice louder now, and angrier. "All we wanted to know was who he knows in Dora who's al-Qaida. It's obvious he knows people. We were just following orders."

"I didn't order you to hit him."

"I was just trying—"

"Private!" I shouted, and was surprised to find myself trembling. I did not know what I was doing. I could feel the operation getting away from me. Perhaps it was already gone.

"Sorry, sir."

I glared at Geary and Moss. Their faces were tired, and they were frowning. All of us wanted to be somewhere else. To the translator, I said, "What are you hearing?"

Geary shrugged. "They don't understand what they're here for. They keep asking when they're going to be released. They ask if we think they're criminals."

"They are criminals!" Lukens said suddenly.

"Private," I said, "wait outside."

Lukens opened his mouth, then shut it. He turned and marched out, slamming the door behind him. The three of us looked at it for a moment, then I turned back to Geary.

"Go on."

"There's nothing to say, sir." He rubbed his face with both of his hands. "Maybe a few of them know something—about the insurgency or something—but I'm not sure." He paused again, swallowing air. "I've never done this kind of thing before. I don't know how to put it so they'll talk. Or even if there's any way to get them to. I'm just . . . I . . ."

His voice trailed off, and he stared at the floor.

"Sir?" It was Moss. "Most of us are with Lukens, sir." She spoke quietly, as she had done the night she told me about her goals in the military. She had never seemed younger to me than she did now. "I mean, some of these people, they're obviously not al-Qaida or anything. But, I mean, it's a war, sir. They're the enemy."

Geary was shaking his head. "But they don't know they're the enemy. They don't know why they're here."

"Some of us think they're just playing dumb, sir," Moss went on.

Geary didn't respond, except to continue shaking his head. From outside, we heard Lukens's enraged voice, reverberating down the long hallway: *"Hajji, quit the fucking whistling!"*

Involuntarily, I let out a long sigh. Now I would need to discipline Lukens for losing his temper. But he had only given voice to emotions we were all feeling. The whistling—everything, in fact, the weather, the overcrowding, all of it—had come to seem like an accusation, one to which there was no reasonable response.

I sat down behind my desk and stared at the wall over Moss's shoulder. A calendar hung there, one I had brought from the States. Each month bore a different kind of weather—hurricane, tornado, snowstorm. There was a thunderstorm in San Francisco—that was the photo for April—and a foggy Boston street scene for October. December showed now, and the picture was of a row of icicles hanging from the eaves of a barn in Maine.

I had seen none of these phenomena in Iraq. There was no sandstorm on the calendar, and no drought. Soon I would need a new calendar, and the varieties of American weather would be thrown away. I began to wonder when I would next see an icicle, or a thunderstorm. I fell into a reverie of sorts then, remembering. I don't know how long it was before Moss roused me with the clearing of her throat. I looked up.

"Sir?" she said.

"Bring the detainee to the infirmary, please," I said. "You guard him, Private, until the medic says it's time to put him back into the population. Geary," I added, "go get some sleep. Let everyone get some sleep. And send in Lukens when you leave."

"Yes, sir," Moss replied. Geary nodded. And they walked out.

That was the beginning of what would prove to be a time of many problems at Camp Alastor. The problems I refer to are now well known, from the photographs taken elsewhere. I will not claim that we were entirely innocent of adopting such tactics with our detainees—we knew how to "push their buttons," how to make them feel unclean, and humiliated. We understood how to frighten them—how to convince them that death was imminent without causing them lasting physical harm. We used dogs, and even snakes. We desecrated their holy books, blasphemed their God.

But we had been assured that the work we were doing was necessary and good, and that it would save lives. And there was a sense that, if only our expansion could be completed, if only more personnel were to arrive, then everything would settle down, and our work could be streamlined, and we could learn what we needed to without so much strenuous effort. Every day I expected the supply trucks to arrive, the troop transport vehicles. Every day I thought might be the day that we turned the corner.

TWENTY

Instead, three months later, I walked away from the man in the pit, entered the building, stumbled into the latrine, and vomited into the closest toilet. Then I walked to my office, closed and locked the door, and sat down behind the desk.

I didn't move for some time. My body was slick with sweat and filth that even repeated showering had failed to remove, and the inside of my mouth was rank and gluey with sick. The calendar I had stared at during my discussion with Moss and Geary was gone now, and none had arrived to replace it.

Things had deteriorated quickly after the incident with Private Lukens. In retrospect, I see that I ought to have dealt with his actions more severely; or, ideally, I should have predicted the level of despair to which the situation would soon descend. Foremost among my failures had been my obliviousness to the anxiety faced by the men and women under my command. They, I now understood, were no better suited to the task of managing a vast and diverse prison population than I was; indeed, they were far less so. They had been trained in desert combat and, to a lesser extent, urban warfare. They knew how to identify an enemy and neutralize it. Now they had been charged with the welfare of hundreds of the very people they had learned to hate and fear—and been ordered, by me, to extract information from them.

Our mission was a failure. We had discovered close to nothing about the enemy, except how to hurt him.

And we did hurt him. The man Lukens had struck with his rifle endured further questioning, under even greater duress, and he gave us some names, which we passed on to the CW5 for intelligence in our theater. What value these names might actually have had, or if they were the names of real people, or people the man had invented to satisfy us, we never learned. But the names did represent a success of sorts, and the soldiers who extracted them were singled out for praise. And so our questioning intensified. That man, in fact, was the man in the pit, the man I threw my canteen to. We had likely gotten from him all that we could. Yet we couldn't stop interrogating him. It was as though we had become addicted to him, fixated on the moment of relief we felt when he talked. We wanted to feel that relief again. We wanted to please our superiors and bask in their implicit approval.

We forced people's heads into tubs of water and covered their faces with soaking rags. We burned them and bruised them and shocked them and bled them. We stripped them naked and paraded them in front of their countrymen. We threatened to murder their children.

It wasn't that we felt nothing for these people, whose guilt or innocence was unknown to us, and unknowable. Indeed, we felt disgust. If they were guilty, then they were disgusting for their crimes; if innocent, they were disgusting for being foolish enough to be apprehended. When they cowered in terror from our blows, we hated their cowardice; when they tried to fight back, we hated their arrogance. When they begged us to stop, we hated their weakness, and when they silently endured, we hated their imperturbability. They were less than human, these people, these idiots whose language could not be understood, whose ways of living were so foreign. The more we hurt them, the more we hated them—how could they be so weak? How could they sit there and take it? Why didn't they rise up against us? Why didn't their people come with guns and bombs and free them? There were hundreds of them and dozens of us, and still they let themselves be dominated. And they said they knew nothing and no one, and yet, in spite of everything, they named names, they named places, they named times. And we gave the information to our superiors and the information was swallowed up, never to be heard again.

Two things happened in February. The first was that we had begun to hear rumors that there were photos, not from our camp, but from elsewhere, and that these photos had made their way into the civilian world.

There was no immediate fallout from this revelation, but it cast a dark cloud over our operation, and made us all feel as if our work here was drawing to some kind of ignominious close.

The other thing was Sufian.

It was the boy, the one who was detained with the women. I had ordered him to be questioned when another detainee claimed that his father was a member of the insurgency loyal to Shiite cleric and Baghdad hero Moqtada al-Sadr.

I had told two soldiers to go and get the boy, and insisted that he be questioned in my office, not in the room where the other interrogations had been taking place. By this time I was well aware that the questioning had gone too far, but I no longer felt that I could stop it. I no longer felt that I had the authority to, and I had so come to despise the facility, my role as its commanding officer, and the detainees themselves, that I had no desire to. But I did not regard the women and the boy as part of the general population of the facility, did not regard them as dangerous or as valuable sources of information; and for the most part they had remained quiet and calm, had demanded little, and had acquiesced quickly and without complaint to all of our commands. And so the boy would be given special consideration during questioning.

The boy sat across from me, occupying the only chair other than my own. He was very thin, and slightly stooped, like a grandfather; his unlined face was dark and inscrutable, and the beginning of a mustache stained his upper lip. He was no longer wearing his dishdasha; at some point he had been given jeans and a golf shirt, and these now hung from him like pieces of mold that had grown there, and their reek filled the room. Nobody appeared to be bothered; we were all accustomed to this odor, and at times exuded it ourselves. Geary, the translator, leaned listlessly against the wall to my right; the two soldiers who had brought the boy flanked the door, their rifles at the ready. Geary looked terrible—his eyes hollow, his lips cracked, his hair lank. He was now the only translator. The other had been transferred abruptly, and his replacement never arrived.

"Ask him," I said, gazing at the boy, "his father's name."

Geary blinked and turned to the boy in slow motion. He spoke with lethargic ease, as though he were drunk.

The boy blinked as well, as if in response. Then he tilted back his head, cleared his throat, and began to whistle.

Here in the confines of my office, the mournful sound of Sufian's tune-less whistle came as a terrible shock. It was him—he was the whistler! I had not been aware of how completely this sound had infected my wak-ing hours; it seemed a permanent, obscure, and distant motif, a kind of haunting. My body tensed, and my hands found the edge of my desk and gripped it.

The two soldiers shifted their weight from one foot to the other. Geary let out a long, terrible sigh. I removed a handkerchief from my pocket and wiped my forehead. I said, "Ask him again."

"He won't say anything." Geary had long ago stopped calling me sir, and I had stopped caring.

I shrugged.

Geary asked again, and the boy merely continued to whistle.

Every one of my muscles was clenched now. The boy's cheerless passiv-ity was maddening. Didn't I deserve at least some acknowledgment of my efforts to protect him from harm? Wasn't it clear to him that he had been favored, and that this favoritism had a source? The least he could do was answer my very simple question—or even refuse to answer it. Anything but this—this whistling, which felt as though it was boring into my head like an auger. It occurred to me that the melody, if you could call it that, never seemed to repeat itself, never seemed to break into any particular theme or phrase; and yet I could have recognized it anywhere: it had an identity, a personality. For all that, it resisted understanding. It was foreign, far more foreign than this place. It was alien.

Through gritted teeth, I asked several more questions—who his father's friends were, what cafés he frequented, what mosque he worshipped at. The boy Sufian paused after each, then displayed a small, grim smile, and resumed his whistling. I don't know what purpose the whistling served—whether it meant something to him, whether it was a comfort, or a weapon, or simply a way of passing the time. I only know that I felt deeply, pain-fully tired of it.

At this point I gave up, and ordered everyone but Sufian out of the room.

The specifics of what happened next would be difficult to relate, even if I was able to remember them clearly. Much has been said about the "fog of war" that clouds our judgment in times of great stress; the term could also be applied to the tendency of memory to twist and reshape itself, especially the memory of dramatic moments. What is clear to me is that I had intended to make the boy Sufian talk, regardless of the relative unimportance of anything he might say. Indeed, with the translator gone, it was unlikely that I would have been able to understand him, even had I been successful. In any event, the fact remains that the boy's continued silence (his speechlessness, that is—I am not figuring his strange, frightening whistling into this characterization) represented a danger to the stability of the facility, the morale of the men and women under my command, and the pliability of his fellow detainees.

In addition, I am certain, and I openly admit this, that I used some degree of physical coercion in my efforts to break the boy's silence. This would have been inevitable, given his failure to respond to verbal persuasion. And the one other certainty, as far as I can tell, is that the boy must have had some physical infirmity, perhaps the result of the violence in his neighborhood before his apprehension by U.S. troops, perhaps some congenital condition, which made him particularly susceptible to the effects of rough handling.

Whatever the case, I of course regret the outcome. But the actual end result was not, in fact, my original intention; and while no one can be blamed except myself, I consider it reasonable to regard the boy as, in a larger sense, a casualty of war.

I do remember my profound exhaustion at the end of that day, and I recall taking the unusual step of returning to barracks and going to bed before it was dark. I also remember the soldiers who came to me the next day to ask me what should be done with the boy's body.

In addition, I remember, with quite painful clarity, the faces of the men and women under my command when I gathered them together in the mess and tried to initiate a conversation about where, and how, precisely, our efforts had gone awry, and what we might do to begin to rectify our situation. Their misery and confusion were manifest in their stunned staring eyes, and when I received no reasonable comments or suggestions, I understood that my authority had finally been stretched beyond its limits and snapped. I forgave them all in that moment, for it had been my own incapacity to lead that had brought us to this juncture, and it was beyond my power to bring us out.

And now, at last, I sat at my desk, having come in from the drainage pits and thrown up, and I stared at the empty chair where the boy had sat, and I wondered what had been done with his body, and whether I had been told and forgotten, or never been told, or whether it was all just a nightmare from which I could not, however desperately I struggled to lift my head, wake up. My mind, at this juncture, was far too tired to hold on to any thought for long. I barely had the strength to take my keys from my pocket, or to insert one of them into the bottom right-hand drawer, let alone to remove from that drawer the warped and cracked wooden box that contained my father's Enfield. But I did it: I set it on the desk before me, and lifted the creaking lid, and stared for seconds, minutes, maybe hours at the gun there.

I did not, of course, kill myself—in retrospect, I doubt the thing would have fired, so long had it been since I had cleaned or even inspected it; and I don't believe that suicide was even my intention. Rather, I was reminiscing about my father, about our terribly flawed life together, and his sad end, when a knock came at the door, and the knob rattled, and I heard the jingle of keys. A moment later the door fell open.

They were hard and healthy, the soldiers, in contrast with my own. They were from the general, I understood, and had come for me at last. I went willingly, leaving the Enfield behind, and I never saw the gun, the facility, or any of my men again.

I was taken care of in the days and weeks leading up to the hearings. From my Washington hotel, I gazed out upon the busy lives of civilians, who had already grown weary of the war, which they thought they'd been permitted to forget, which was supposed to fade away into a memory of triumph.

The hearings themselves were of little consequence. By and large I was questioned gently, apologetically, and what few difficult questions arose, I was evidently able to answer to the satisfaction of all. When I was asked about the boy, I told them that I didn't know how he had died. When I was asked if he had died during an interrogation, I replied that, no, he was no longer under questioning at that time. When I was asked if perhaps he had been beaten by one of his fellow prisoners—perhaps a terrorist eager to prevent his divulging vital information—I answered that such a thing was indeed a plausible explanation.

I was followed at the stand by a physician I had never seen in my life, who testified that, after examining the body of the dead detainee, he could find no evidence that he had been questioned under duress, or in any way abused by prison guards.

When it was over, I was told to choose a place to live, and I chose a small town in the Midwest where I knew no one. I was put on indefinite furlough, set up in an apartment, and given an assumed name. A bank account was established for me, and soon my back pay and previous savings were transferred to me, along with an additional large amount, the purpose of which was never clearly articulated.

I don't recall with any degree of precision what I did in those months. I was aware that my case was publicized, but by that time the election had taken place, and people were no longer engaged by the Iraq prison torture story. My own awareness of the situation in Iraq was vague, though it seemed clear that it was going no better than it had been when I was there, and perhaps had grown worse. In any event, I tried not to give it much thought. I think I spent a lot of my time walking, out to the edge of town and back, and then out to the other edge of town. I believe I read a lot of books, though I don't recall which ones, or what they were about. I did not have a television; however, I am not certain what I did with the time I would have spent watching television, if I'd had one.

I began to feel as though I had chosen the wrong place to live, and that I should leave and go somewhere else. And one day, many months after my discharge, I closed out my bank account, and loaded everything I owned—it was not much—into my car, and drove east until at last I arrived in Gerrysburg, and bought the land upon which the house and the rock and the castle stood. I suppose that, in the end, this was something that I needed to do.

With painful effort, I managed to stand and raise my arm up to my own waiting hand. I braced my feet against the pit wall and began, slowly, to scale it; my other self leaned back, counterbalancing himself against my weight. My broken ribs rang with pain, but I would not stop until I had reached the top. When I had nearly made it, a second hand appeared to pull me the rest of the way, and I grabbed it. At last I was up and out, and I released my grip, and as I collapsed to the forest floor I was surprised to discover that my other self was nowhere to be seen.

I must have passed out, for when I opened my eyes, the sun had moved, and the light was golden, and the air warmer. I got to my feet and began to walk, and the sounds of the forest were the same as those of the night before, except that now they did not terrify me; rather, they recalled the sounds I would hear in the gentler days of my early childhood, before I was sent to Doctor Stiles, when my mother was still able, from time to time, to find happiness, and I would walk to the end of Jefferson Street to the swamp and explore the woods in solitude, content with myself and my mind and my senses, and know that I could come home to a warm meal, and a warm bed, and my mother's loving arms.

I don't know how long I wandered, but I do know that when I emerged from the forest I was terribly hungry and tired, and it was morning again, though which morning I don't know. The bright sun was high over the house, which looked the worse for wear, as if a long time had passed since I renovated, or perhaps as if I had never renovated at all. But the unmown grass smelled wonderful, and I settled myself down into it, and lay on my back and let the dew soak into my clothes, and I closed my eyes and felt the sun on my face, and fell into blissful sleep.

TWENTY-ONE

When I woke, it was once again to bright light, this time from a window, divided into strips by open vertical blinds. Beside the window stood a woman in white, who smiled at me, and came to where I lay on a crisply sheeted bed. I felt her hand on my forehead, it was very heavy, and I felt myself drifting back into sleep.

I woke again. This time it was evening, the blinds were shut, and a different woman sat beside my bed, reading a paperback book under the light of a table lamp. The woman was my sister. She turned to me, and her face registered surprise. She lay the book face down on the table, beside the lamp.

"You're awake," she said, her rough voice light, cheerful. She was smiling and she smelled of cigarettes.

I tried to ask where I was, but all that came out of my throat was a croak. I became aware of my body: I hurt, everywhere. I felt simultaneously heavy and insubstantial, like a rusted thing, a length of wire. I coughed, and the cough loosed some horrible pain, beginning in my abdomen and radiating out through the rest of my body. I groaned. A tube was taped to my arm and entered the flesh through a needle; my chest was heavily bound and bandaged.

"You're in the hospital," she said. "I found you in your yard, at the edge of the woods." Her gaze hardened into a look, perhaps of concern, perhaps of curiosity. She leaned forward. "They said your rib punctured your lung, Eric. You would have bled to death!"

I let my head roll back and I stared at the ceiling. It was white and cracked and very far away. "Thank you," I whispered.

"*Eric,*" she said now, leaning closer still. "What were you *doing?*"

I shook my head.

She asked, with a tremor in her voice, "Was he *there?*"

My sister and I gazed at one another, both of us weary, both of us older than we had ever been. She reached out, slid her hand underneath my sheets, and found my fingers. They were cold—I hadn't noticed how cold until her warm hand wrapped itself around them. I needed to go back to sleep. But I answered her with a nod, and closed my eyes.

When I opened them again, she was gone. I lay still, saying nothing, trying to put together the pieces of my past few months. I saw the pieces as though they were blocks of algae on the surface of a still pond. And I was wading into the pond, trying to lift up each piece and put it with the others. But the algae just broke up in my hands, and my movement made waves in the pond, and the pieces floated away. And then I was one of the pieces, and it was my body that was breaking up and floating away, and when I opened my eyes again it was night.

Then it was day again, and my sister was there, in different clothes, and her hair was washed and still wet and tied back in a ponytail. There was someone with her, a man I'd never seen, heavyset, with a big gray beard, and he looked at me with something like sympathy. Then I was alone, and it was night, and there was a nurse holding my wrist. And I said, "What time is it?" and she told me to go back to sleep.

Then there was a time when I was fully awake, and I wanted to get up. It was daytime, and rain shook the window. Gently, slowly, I raised my head. I was starving, and my mouth was dry. I found the call button and pressed it and a nurse came, and soon I was eating again, and sitting up straight, and felt the life coming back into me. Within a few days I was walking and breathing without great effort, and a few days after that I was discharged.

Jill came for me in her pickup, with Hank at her side. He was the bearded man I had seen. He was gentle, somewhat shy, but he shook my hand firmly and said he was glad to meet me. He seemed sympathetic—whether to my convalescence or to something my sister had told him,

I didn't know. In any event, I appreciated the welcoming kindness of a stranger, and made a mental note to reward him, sometime in the future, with an overture of friendship. I was surprised and somewhat embarrassed to discover how deeply I had misjudged my sister. Whatever I might have held against her, she had helped me when I needed her help, and appeared, in the end, to have made a good life for herself. We drove to my house in silence.

"I took your car out for a spin," Hank said, as he helped me from the back seat of the pickup. His hand was large and rough in mine, and guided me with easy, sure movements onto the surface of the lot. "It's not good to leave it sit for too long."

"That's very kind of you," I said, shaking his hand.

"Little Brother," my sister cried, throwing her arms around my neck, "I'm glad you're all right."

"Me too," I mumbled, unaccustomed to this kind of demonstrative behavior. I patted her back awkwardly before she let me go.

"We'll be up tomorrow to check on you," she said. "Be careful, okay? Don't overexert yourself."

"No, of course not."

"Just relax and heal up. Call us if you need anything. We got you some groceries, they're in the fridge."

I didn't know what to say. "Thank you" was all I could manage.

"When you're ready, I'll come over and we'll talk all this through," she went on. "We'll figure it all out together, all right?"

And though I wasn't entirely sure what she meant, I said, "Yes. That would be good."

We said our goodbyes, and Jill and Hank got into the pickup and disappeared over the crest of the hill. It was late afternoon; the weather had turned warm. The sun was on my face, and in the windows of the house. I took a deep breath, the first one I'd taken in weeks, and then I went inside.

Nothing had changed, aside from the accumulation, upon the floorboards and furniture, of a thin layer of pollen from the trees outside. I picked up my meager mail—a bank statement, an advertising circular from the hardware store, a power bill—and carried it into the kitchen, where I dropped it onto the table beside the still-unopened official letter I had received some weeks before. I set a pot of coffee on to brew, and as it did so, I wiped down the counters, opened the refrigerator and examined the food and drink my sister had bought, and parted the kitchen window curtains. After a moment, I opened the window itself. Fresh air and light were now pouring into the room.

The coffee maker burbling behind me, I sat down at the table and opened the mail. My bank account appeared to be in fine shape; I set the statement aside. The hardware store, in preparation for summer, had patio furniture and charcoal grills on sale—perhaps someday I would build a patio outside the house, and put a grill on it, and enjoy the brief upstate summers in comfort and style. My power bill was low, owing to my absence from the house; I took out my checkbook, wrote out a check for the full amount, and sealed it up in the envelope provided.

All that was left was the official-looking letter. My name and address were printed in the center, and the upper-left-hand corner bore a familiar seal. I turned the letter over in my hands, slipped my finger under the flap, and considered, for a moment, opening it. Instead I stood up and tucked it in beside Jill's greeting card, underneath the magnet on the fridge. Then I went outside to attach my power bill payment to the mailbox.

Once I was back inside, I climbed, with some effort, the stairs, and reached into the back of my closet for my old green duffel. I packed it, then brought it down and set it beside the front door.

With that accomplished, I poured myself a mug of fresh coffee and carried it out to the porch to meet the day.

Two weeks later, I was working in the yard, planting an apple tree. It seemed a good, simple, American thing to do. Jill had been by an hour before, had seen the tree in the yard, its root ball wrapped in burlap, and informed me that I needed another, if I wanted any apples to grow. She told me the trees had to be pollinated by bees, and that one alone wouldn't do.

I hadn't known this. Indeed, there was a lot I didn't know about civilian life, that someday I would have to learn, if I wanted to live the way ordinary Americans did. This had been a prominent theme in my thoughts during the weeks since my discharge from the hospital—was this what I wanted, a normal American life? The kind of life that I had spent my career ostensibly fighting to protect?

The truth was, I didn't know if this was something I should want, or could achieve. For all my talents and accomplishments, I understood now that my experience was actually quite narrow—I remained unfamiliar with the customs and obligations of ordinary society. I was, in the end, a misfit—and should I want to assimilate myself to the world, I would have to undertake it as I would any project. I would gather intelligence, I would build a structure: something I could live in, something that would make me feel safe.

But these were thoughts for the future. This day had other plans for me.

I heard gravel crunch on the drive, and I looked up from my work, expecting to find Jill's familiar pickup. The vehicle I saw, however, was the twin of my own—a dark SUV, this one with deeply tinted windows and military plates. A driver was visible, outlined behind the windshield, and I raised a hand in greeting. He did not get out. Instead, he simply nodded. I nodded back, and laid my shovel on the ground. The planting was finished—the tree stood straight and true in the June sun.

Perhaps Jill could come and plant another, so that next spring, there would be fruit. In any event, I would probably not be here to enjoy it.

It is hard to convey the depth of relief I felt at this moment. For, although my experiences in Iraq would doubtless haunt me for many years to come, the army itself remained the same institution that had sustained me for more than twenty years, and once valued me for the skills I had worked so hard to perfect. There in the sunny yard, I began to experience a profound and uncharacteristic upwelling of emotion, akin to that one might feel if a former lover, still longed for, came to her senses and returned in tears to beg forgiveness.

I thought, with some regret, of the conversations Jill and I might have had, catching one another up on our lives. Now all that would have to wait. Everything would have to wait, except for the war, which continued in defiance of everyone's expectations.

I removed my gardening gloves and tossed them onto the ground beside the shovel before turning, going back indoors, and picking up my duffel bag. I took a last look around the house, pleased at the work I had done, pleased at everything I had learned since my return to Gerrysburg.

Then I stepped outside, pulled the door shut behind me, and set off on my mission.

NOTE

My thanks to Rhian Ellis, Bob Turgeon, Brian Hall, Jim Rutman, Ethan Nosowsky. The children's book Loesch reads is *The Nine Questions,* by Edward Fenton. Logistics Support Area Anaconda is a real American military base near Balad, Iraq, but Camp Alastor and its inhabitants are my invention.

J. ROBERT LENNON is the author of five previous novels, including *Mailman* and *The Light of Falling Stars,* and the story collection *Pieces for the Left Hand: 100 Anecdotes.* His stories have appeared in the *Paris Review, Granta, Harper's, Playboy,* and the *New Yorker.* He lives in Ithaca, New York, with his wife and two sons, and teaches writing at Cornell University.

The text of *Castle* is set in Adobe Garamond Pro. Book design by Rachel Holscher. Composition by BookMobile Design and Publishing Services, Minneapolis, Minnesota. Manufactured by Maple Vail on acid-free paper.